The Depths of Solitude

The Depths of Solitude

JO BANNISTER

This edition first published in Great Britain in 2005 by
Allison & Busby Limited
Bon Marche Centre
241-251 Ferndale Road
London SW9 8BJ
http://www.allisonandbusby.com

Copyright © 2005 by JO BANNISTER

The moral right of the author has been asserted.

A catalogue record for this book is available from
the British Library.

10 9 8 7 6 5 4 3 2 1

ISBN 0 7490 8318 2

Printed and bound in Great Britain by
Bookmarque Ltd, Croydon, Surrey

The author of over twenty acclaimed novels, Jo Bannister started her career as a journalist after leaving school at sixteen to work on a local weekly newspaper. Shortlisted for several prestigious awards, she was Editor of the *County Down Spectator* for some years before leaving to pursue her writing full-time. She lives in Northern Ireland and is currently working on her next novel. *The Depths of Solitude* is the fourth book in a series featuring Brodie Farrell, Daniel Hood and Jack Deacon.

Other titles in the Brodie Farrell series:

Chapter One

THERE WERE GHOSTS at the table. Jack Deacon could see them as clear as day: two little girls and a young man. Nor was it entirely his imagination. He knew from their expressions, from the way their eyes slid away from his and they kept the conversation so politely inconsequential there was no danger of saying anything meaningful, that two of his companions could see them too. Even the third, who – sharing no history with the disappeared – should have been immune to their claim, was obscurely aware that there were more people round the table than there were places set, and felt the tension they generated even if she wasn't sure where it was coming from.

Detective Superintendent Deacon felt himself getting more and more testy at how the absentees had hijacked his party. He'd been juggling his workload all week to leave himself free – a task complicated by the fact that he wanted the sergeant who would normally have covered for him to be here too. He'd booked a nice restaurant, and a taxi for afterwards so anyone who felt like getting drunk could do so with a clear conscience. He'd even ordered champagne, though he could have named half a dozen wines that would have done the job better, less pretentiously, for less money. He'd done everything he could think of to make the night a success.

In spite of which the four of them were sitting round the table like the shortlist for a promotion board, avoiding one another's gaze and making talk that was not so much small as microscopic.

And it wasn't like them. At least, he didn't know Helen Choi well enough to judge, he'd only met her a couple of times since Detective Sergeant Voss came into work with a glazed expression one morning and confessed he'd fallen in love at an exhibition of T'ang Dynasty art. But Charlie Voss and Brodie Farrell were the two people he knew best in the world and stilted conversation wasn't natural to either of them. Voss was subtle – at least for a policeman – with a quiet manner hiding an intellect Deacon occasionally suspected of being sharper than his own, but he never had difficulty expressing himself, even with officers twenty years and several ranks his senior. He didn't normally seek refuge in clichés or part with opinions as if they were teeth.

And the first thing Jack Deacon learned about Brodie, long before he became interested in her personally, was that she was incapable of being intimidated. His attempts to bully her had rebounded like a steel-tipped boomerang, making him dive for cover. She was a strikingly handsome woman, tall and lithe with a cloud of dark hair and eyes like gemstones; but even plain to the point of homely she would still have been a strong, determined, humorous, passionate woman who left her initials carved on men's souls. She wasn't the sort of woman to withdraw to the powder room when masculine subjects like politics and the stock market came up. She was the sort of woman who knew her own portfolio inside out and never put her gains down to luck. She was the most interesting woman

Deacon had ever known. When he learned that her husband had left her for someone else, his first instinct was to send the poor chap for a CAT-scan.

So what was she doing, sitting here with her eyes downcast, smiling politely at Helen's valiant attempts to inject some life into the proceedings, pretending an interest in girly things like fashion and holidays and – God help us all, thought Deacon despairingly – origami?

When he could bear it no longer he thumped his hands down on the table-top – flattening a paper napkin swan in the process – and rocked his big body back in its chair. Voss watched nervously. He did this at the office too, but now they bought him chairs sturdy enough to cope.

"Right," said Deacon grimly. "This is supposed to be a celebration. There may be police forces elsewhere in England, perhaps even elsewhere on the south coast, which can confidently expect to see their efforts rewarded with success on a regular basis. But here in dear, damp, dingy Dimmock it's always a matter of blood, sweat, toil and tears, so when we get a result we like to mark it. Right, Charlie Voss?"

"Right," agreed Voss obediently. He had ginger hair and freckles, and didn't usually wear a tie.

"Nine months we've been hacking away at this," Deacon continued. "Tonight I am happy to announce that we've got four crates of crack under lock and key, we've got five men in custody and we've shut down a pipeline that's been making a lot of weak people very ill and a lot of bad people very rich. On top of that we've got

Joe Loomis checking under his bed every night for bogies. Well – actually, for me. He knows I've got a rock-solid case against his most trusted lieutenants. He knows that with the prospect of ten years in Parkhurst one of them will want to cut a deal. He's on the ropes and sweating, and one day soon he's going down too. And if that isn't worth celebrating I don't know what is.

"So why all the gloom? Why the absence of cheery faces and chortling, and what passes for humour after two glasses of fizzy plonk? I brought you here to enjoy your-selves – will you at least bloody well try?"

It was a measure of Brodie's mood that, rather than snapping back at him, she started to apologise. "Sorry, Jack. Of course I'm glad you've cracked your case. It's just – "

Deacon took the sentence half-formed from her lips. But if he used words she would not have chosen, what he said was an accurate reflection of her thoughts. "It's just that you're still too hung up on past failure to want to celebrate new success. Well, clearly I've been wasting my time these last few weeks. I thought the best way to make up for a disaster I couldn't salvage was to turn around one I could. To fight a winnable battle. If I'd realised there was no point, that life as we knew it ended with the deaths of two mad girls, I wouldn't have bothered. I'd have spent nights in with my cat instead of hammering away at Joe Loomis and his Drugs R Us emporium. Silly old me, thinking there was still vital work to be done even if the Daws sisters are dead and you aren't talking to Daniel because of it."

A quiver like a little earthquake shook the table. There it was: what everyone had been carefully skirting round all night. But tact was never Deacon's strong point. He liked his enemies out in plain view where he could take a swing at them. Everyone here knew that Brodie Farrell and Daniel Hood had been good friends, close friends, important to one another, until Daniel found himself with a terrible choice to make. Lives depended on it: the lives of a pair of lethal children or that of their aunt who had never hurt anyone. Cut off from all help, Daniel chose the woman.

As a matter of fact Deacon thought he was right, but Brodie thought he was wrong and it was her opinion that mattered to the young man. On the whole Deacon hadn't much time for Daniel and his delicate sensibilities that were so often at odds with the detective's own, but for once he had a certain amount of sympathy for him. Maybe he did rely too much on Brodie's support, but if you knew their history – and Deacon had been there from the start, before it was clear if Daniel would even survive what Brodie, all unknowing, had brought him to – even that made a kind of sense.

He did survive, with Brodie's help; and with Daniel's help she'd come to terms with what her mistake had cost; and since then they'd helped one another through a number of difficulties. But not this one. Deacon would understand if Daniel's devotion was finally starting to irritate Brodie, but this was a bad time to push him away.

Brodie looked up, an angry spark kindling in her eye. "Don't talk about things you don't understand."

"Jesus," exclaimed Deacon disgustedly, "what does that leave? I have never understood this thing between you and Daniel: not where it came from and not what either of you gets out of it. But I know it matters to you. That's the only reason I give a damn about Daniel. I wouldn't worry if he left Dimmock and moved to Brighton or Buenos Aires, except that he and you seem to be joined by some kind of invisible thread, and you care about him and I care about you. I care that this falling-out is making you miserable. I don't understand why you don't fix it."

Brodie stared at him in astonishment. He was a big, tough, hard-working, unsentimental man, craggy of face and mien, who made enemies easier than he made friends mainly because he understood the mechanism better. His usual response to a friendship that troubled him was either to ignore it or to make pointed, sometimes nasty, little jokes. It was typical of him to finally acknowledge its importance to her only after it had ended.

She raised her chin pugnaciously. "Two children died because of Daniel. Am I the only one who thinks that matters?"

"No, I think it matters too," said Deacon. "It matters that he saved the life of Peris Daws. The girls were beyond salvation, they'd done too much already, but Peris wasn't. I'm just glad that the one man in a position to help her had the guts to do what was right rather than watch her die and wring his hands about it afterwards."

Brodie wasn't good at taking criticism. She leaned across the table, her retort already in her mouth. But

Deacon wasn't finished yet, and stopping him in mid-flow would have been like damming Niagara. Halfway up.

"Now, that's just my opinion, and you may think that twenty years as a detective doesn't qualify me to judge right from wrong. But then, I'm not sure the mere act of procreation makes you infallible, and that seems to be your argument: that no mother would have sacrificed two children – whatever they'd done, even to save innocent lives – so what he did was unforgivable.

"Well, Daniel's not a mother. As far as I know he's not a father. As far as I know, I'm not one either. I don't think that invalidates my opinion. In fact, I think you've let your hormones distort your judgement. You're comparing the Daws girls to Paddy. But they were nothing like your child. They were two deeply disturbed, dangerous young people. They'd killed and they were about to kill again. Daniel stopped them. It was the right thing to do, and it took real courage, and he didn't need his best friend snubbing him in a fit of sentimentality!"

Brodie's mouth was still open but for a moment no sound came. The vehemence of his attack silenced her. Not because his view was a surprise but because he never raised his voice to her. The man known as The Grizzly at Battle Alley Police Station – and worse than that in the Woodgreen Estate – couldn't believe his good fortune in landing a catch like Brodie Farrell and had been willing to bridle his most basic nature to avoid blowing this relationship the way he'd blown every previous one.

Until now. Which told Brodie something, in the calm inner core of herself where she was prepared to listen. Jack

Deacon wasn't threatening what they had together because of his fondness for Daniel Hood: he was doing it because of hers. Because he knew the split was hurting her and thought it worth almost any gamble to try to heal it. Even her anger did not blind her to the generosity of that.

She caught the surge of invective halfway up her throat and bit it back, breathing heavily while her resentment subsided like a snarling dog brought to heel. Then she said tartly, "You're entitled to your opinion, Jack. I'm sure a lot of people share it. But I don't believe ends justify means. I think there are some things you don't do, regardless of the consequences. It's nothing to do with hormones, it's about conscience. I realise that's a concept that might give you problems but I'd have expected Daniel to understand."

"And the funny thing about that," said Deacon with devastating accuracy, "is that he feels much the same way."

They stared at one another over the remains of the meal, Deacon's gaze unyielding, Brodie's flickering between anger and uncertainty. For the first time in the seven weeks since these events occurred she found herself wondering if she'd over-reacted. In a low voice she said, "Have you talked to him?"

"Recently? No."

"Then how –?"

Deacon rolled his eyes in exasperation. "Brodie, I know him, I know you, I know what happened. Of course I know how he's feeling. So do you."

Finally she let go the bitterness in a long, ragged sigh. "Yes."

"So?" demanded Deacon.

Brodie shook her head. "I don't know what to do about it. I never wanted to hurt him. I could have settled for disagreeing about the thing, I told him that. It wasn't enough. We couldn't talk about it, and we couldn't seem to talk about anything else. He moved back to his house as soon as it was weatherproof, five weeks ago. I haven't seen him since."

Helen Choi had known Charlie Voss for two months. For one of them she'd known what he'd known in the first half hour: that they were never going to do much better than one another. They belonged together, felt right together. They were able to talk to one another, about anything and everything. In consequence, Staff Nurse Helen Choi of Dimmock General Hospital knew more about Battle Alley and in particular the activities of CID than many people who worked there.

So an argument that might have left her bemused in fact made perfect sense to her. She knew about the Daws sisters; she knew who Daniel Hood was; she knew he'd lodged with Brodie's upstairs neighbour while his home – a netting-shed on the beach – was rebuilt after an arson attack. She said quietly, "I expect he's there now." She had a delicately inflected, musical voice and deeply perceptive brown eyes.

Brodie shrugged. "Probably. As long as I've known him Daniel's idea of a night out has been sitting on his steps with his telescope."

Helen picked up her bag. "Come on then. Let's go bum some coffee off him."

All three of them stared at her – Voss with admiration, Deacon with respect, Brodie with horror. "We can't!"

"Why not? If he's busy he'll send us packing. But it's as obvious as sin that you two need to sit down and talk, that Mr Deacon won't be happy till you do, and that while Mr Deacon's unhappy Charlie's going to be miserable. If he comes home glum and monosyllabic every night I may very well dump him and try out the talent in the doctors' common room. At least when I go to parties with medics we talk about people I've met!"

Voss knew it wasn't him she was getting at. He stood up. "That's it, then. If you don't want to blight my life you'll do as Helen says." He extended his hand: Brodie took it warily.

Deacon nodded approval and went to settle the bill.

Behind his back Brodie gave resistance one last shot. "The taxi won't be here for another hour... "

"We'll walk," said Voss. "It's a nice October evening, we'll enjoy the stroll. Then Daniel can make us some coffee and we'll have the taxi collect us there. This is something you need to do, Mrs Farrell. The longer you avoid talking to him, the harder it'll be."

That at least was true. In fact, most of what had been said in the last half hour had been true, and if a part of Brodie rebelled at having her affairs publicly debated another part was touched that there were people who cared enough to want to help. She shrugged and went with them. "Oh, all right... "

They walked along the esplanade with the Firestone Cliffs behind them. And if the winos who hung out in the decayed public rooms of the old Maritime Hotel thought it funny to see Detective Superintendent Deacon stroll hand-in-hand with a woman almost young enough, but much too pretty, to be his daughter, they had just enough sense to get back inside before laughing.

In the dark the three netting-sheds were black fingers poking out of the shingle shore. There were no lights to show that the one nearest to the pier was someone's home, and when the walkers reached the iron steps they saw why. The house was shut up, and there was a For Sale board wired to the railing.

Chapter Two

For a moment estate agent Edwin Turnbull thought the woman with the cloud of dark hair who was waiting when he opened the office on Saturday morning wanted to buy the netting-shed. He showed her quickly to a chair, ordered coffee, would have given her shoes a quick polish if she'd asked him.

He hadn't known what to expect of the property. Its seafront location might have sold it a dozen times over. As against that, it was clear to anyone with an eye in his head that some wild night Dimmock's crumbling pier would break up and then it would be sheer luck whether an oak pile swept the shed away or not. No one would give a mortgage on it, or storm insurance. You can't insure against the inevitable.

A cash buyer just might be keen enough to proceed with the purchase against wiser counsels, but the planning conditions attached to the property would weed out most eccentric millionaires. The original shed was destroyed by arson so the planners felt obliged to approve a replacement. What they would not agree to was any extension in the size of the footprint. No one would buy the shed for its location and build a mansion on the site.

Mr Turnbull was an optimist – all estate agents are, it's part of the job description – and knew there had to be an unmarried, childless eccentric millionaire out there who wanted to be lulled to sleep by the sound of waves on shingle thirty paces from his bijou beach-house and would be undeterred by its lack of a garden, yard, car-parking or any kind of privacy. But he doubted there were two, so when Brodie asked about the shed he had her in his office with his back against the door before she could explain the nature of her interest.

"I don't want to buy the place," she said for the third time, her voice taking on a steely timbre. "I want to contact the vendor."

Mr Turnbull gave a delicate little shudder. He was a slightly stooped middle-aged man with thinning hair slicked back in a way that hadn't been fashionable when he started doing it ten years before. "Oh no, Mrs Farrell, that's not at all how we do things. I will convey to the vendor all expressions of interest in his house and any offers for it. He will instruct me whether to accept, or reject, or enter into negotiations. I am his agent. It's why I'm called an estate agent."

"Try to understand," said Brodie with a patience that was starting to grate as it wore thin, like brake-pads. "I am not offering to buy the property. I am not trying to defraud you of your commission. I am trying to contact a man who was once a good friend, and is now so much a stranger that I didn't know he'd left town until I saw your board at his front door. I want you to tell me where he went. I want an address for him, and a phone-number, and I want them now."

If Mr Turnbull had fitted a panic-button under his desk he'd have been jabbing it. It was odd. She was clearly a respectable woman. Her request might have been unusual but she had said nothing he could take exception to. Yet he not only felt threatened, he knew he was meant to. As a professional visitor of other people's homes Mr Turnbull had met dogs like that. They didn't bark, they didn't growl, they didn't show their teeth – but you knew that if you handled the next few minutes wrong you were going to be picking fangs out of your leg.

He withdrew to his last defensible position. "It's a question of confidentiality... "

Brodie withdrew to hers. It had a big gun on it. "If you're not happy giving me the information, perhaps you'd entrust it to Detective Superintendent Deacon of Dimmock CID."

Mr Turnbull gave a plaintive little sigh and opened the file. "One moment... "

She saw him blink as what he read there jogged his memory. "Mrs Farrell, I don't think I can be much help either to you or Superintendent Deacon. Mr Hood couldn't give me a forwarding address. He said he was going to be moving around, visiting family. He promised to phone at intervals for a progress report."

"And has there been any?" asked Brodie.

"Progress? Not yet. Plenty of people have called but none have wanted to view. They're all put off by the planning restrictions."

"Good," said Brodie. "Listen, Mr Turnbull, you might as well understand the situation. Daniel put his home on the market in a fit of pique. When he calms down he'll take it off again. I realise that's not what you want to hear, but you probably shouldn't spend too much time trying to round up a buyer. The sale will never go ahead."

The estate agent knitted his brows in a thoughtful frown and pursed his lips. "Mrs Farrell – how do I put this? – I understood Mr Hood to be unencumbered. If you're telling me you have an interest in this property... "

Brodie laughed out loud. "No, I'm not his wife, Mr Turnbull. Or his lover, live-in or otherwise, or his business partner. I'm just a friend. But I know him well enough to know this is a mistake. I'm trying to save you time and effort."

"And Detective Superintendent Deacon...?"

"...is my toy-boy," said Brodie calmly. "Actually, Mr Turnbull, there is one thing you can do for me. When Daniel calls in, tell him to phone me. He knows the number."

The agent made a note in the file. "And in the meantime, should I show the house or not?"

Brodie shrugged. "I've told you what I think, what you do is up to you. But for heaven's sake stop calling it a house. It's a shack!"

She waited for the phone to ring. And it rang a lot, but it was never Daniel. She told herself it might take a few days. Longer than that: it could be a few days before he phoned Mr Turnbull, and a few days more while he debated whether to call her. But in the end he would. Whatever his feelings about her right now, Daniel Hood was not a man who fled his demons. All the time she'd known him, Brodie's abiding concern had been that one day he would stand in front of a charging elephant to prove he wasn't afraid to.

The phone kept ringing, and it kept being someone else.

After a week she called Turnbull again. He assured her he'd passed on her message, which meant Daniel was deliberately ignoring it. Brodie Farrell didn't like being ignored. It didn't happen very often, partly because she made sure it was never a cost-free option.

"So what are you going to do?" asked Deacon.

"Do?" she echoed coldly. "Nothing."

Deacon nodded. "That's mature."

"What do you want me to do? Mount an expedition to look for him? I wouldn't know where to start."

"Brodie," said Deacon patiently, "finding things is what you do for a living."

"That's right," she snapped, "it's something I get paid for. I don't see much profit in hunting for someone whose answer to a moral dichotomy is to throw his toys out of the pram! I made the first move. If he doesn't want to meet me halfway, fine. I wasn't wrong, Jack, I'm not fawning after him as if I was."

Deacon had to erase from his mind the image of Brodie fawning after anyone. It was right up there with Pavarotti Sings Shirley Temple in the pantheon of improbabilities. "It's not about right and wrong any more. It's about you hurting one another for no better reason than you can't seem to stop. Find him, Brodie. Tell him you hate what's happened between you as much as he does. He'll take it from there."

She looked at him sidelong over the petit fours. They were back in the same French restaurant. It was Deacon's favourite; if he wasn't working they came here every Friday night. He liked it because, however busy it got, they always managed to find him a nice quiet table. He thought they were protecting his privacy. In fact they were protecting the rest of their clients from the arguments that surrounded him the way storm clouds gather round mountains.

"You realise what you're doing?" said Brodie.

He frowned. "What do you mean?"

"You're urging me to make up a fight with another man. That's very Caring And Sharing of you."

Deacon shrugged like a buffalo dislodging ox-peckers. On a list of New Men he put himself somewhere below Mike Tyson – he didn't even stroke his cat. He didn't know what Brodie saw in him, and didn't ask. If she thought his rough, cynical exterior hid a heart of gold he wasn't about to disabuse her. "You want to make me jealous, you'll have to try harder than that. I may not know exactly what it is between you and Daniel but I know what it isn't."

"He's my best friend," Brodie said simply. Her tone hardened. "At least, he used to be."

"And I used to be a policeman," snorted Deacon. "Some things last. Some things last longer than you want them to."

Her eyes flared at him again. "This wasn't my idea, Jack. I didn't send Daniel away because of the choice he made in a frightful situation. He left because I couldn't give him my whole-hearted approval. I was willing to draw a line under it. He wasn't."

"He was the one who was hurting," murmured Deacon. "He needed your support. You could have lied."

"To Daniel?" Her voice soared. "You think that would have made things better? Daniel thinks lying is the sin against the Holy Ghost – except of course that he's an atheist. You can't make this my fault, Jack. It happened because Daniel's as stubborn as you are: there's only one right way and that's his way, and there's only one reasonable position for other people to take and that's lined up behind him. Well, other people's consciences matter too. I can live with what he did, but I'm sure as hell not going to fête him for it!"

Deacon breathed heavily. "You'd rather lose him? You'd rather have him ride off into the sunset and never know what became of him? And don't say yes because I know it isn't true. You want to talk about stubborn, let's talk about you. We both know you could find him in half a day if you wanted to. You've done it before, the only reason you're not doing it now is you think it's his turn to make a move. Well, maybe it is, but maybe he isn't able to. You're stronger than he is. And you haven't as much on the line."

Brodie snorted her derision. "You don't know what you're talking about. Daniel isn't weak – "

"He's fragile, and you know it as well as I do. How could he be anything else? He's lost the life he used to have. He's been surrounded by death for eight months. He needs your kindness, Brodie. You're offering to meet him halfway when what he needs is for you to follow him wherever he's gone, dig him out of whatever hole he's crawled into and bring him home."

Brodie was stilled by surprise. It wasn't that Deacon never expressed his feelings, just that the feelings he expressed were always anger and impatience. She knew there was another side to him, of course, or why was she here? But she was stunned by the unexpected opening of this window to his soul and the human decency it illuminated. She found herself glancing round, in case anyone had noticed. If they had Deacon would have some fences to mend.

But no. The waiters' strategy was sound. If the other diners realised they were arguing none had thought it interesting enough to let their own meals go cold.

After a moment Brodie reached across the tablecloth and put her hand over Deacon's. Even now she couldn't touch him without being aware of the power latent in every part of his body. Casual acquaintances saw a big, heavy middle-aged man of uncertain temper and, apart from keeping out of his way, looked no closer. But those who knew him better acknowledged that while Jack Deacon might have been carved out of a mountain, rock isn't dead. It's hard and strong, and it's thrown up by the boiling heart of the planet.

She said softly, "You're a good man, Jack. A good and perceptive man. You think I should bring Daniel home?"

"Yes," said Deacon.

"You don't think – "

"No," said Deacon.

She sighed and nodded. "Where do I start looking? I don't know where he'd go when he left here."

"Didn't Turnbull say something about family? Where's he from?"

"Nottingham. But I didn't know he had any family left. His grandfather raised him but he died a couple of years ago. That's when Daniel came to Dimmock."

Deacon sucked in his cheeks and eyed her levelly. "Nottingham?"

Brodie sighed. "Don't be so childish. Hood is a perfectly ordinary name."

"Of course it is," agreed Deacon. "I expect the Nottingham phone book's full of them. But if not I'll try official channels."

"Official –?"

"I'll call the Sheriff's office."

Brodie ignored that. "I'll wait till after the weekend," she decided. "If he hasn't got in touch by then I'll go look for him."

Chapter Three

The next day was Saturday.

It was rarely possible for Brodie to shut the office at six o'clock on Friday evening and stay away until nine on Monday morning, but she tried to organise weekends around her daughter. On Sunday mornings Paddy had her riding lesson, and Brodie clung to the fence round the sand school hardly daring to look as the child bounced around on top of an elderly piebald pony, her hands up under her nose, her face wreathed in smiles.

On Saturdays they did different things. Sometimes they went shopping. Sometimes Paddy visited her father and his new wife. And sometimes she kept Brodie company as she trawled antiques fairs and second-hand bookshops or travelled the south coast looking for the various items which people employed her to find. It was a precious time for both of them and Brodie saved tasks a five-year-old might enjoy for these weekend treasure hunts.

She knew Paddy would enjoy meeting Geoffrey Harcourt. She thought Geoffrey Harcourt would enjoy meeting Paddy.

It should have been a pretty cottage, sited as it was in a pretty lane in Cheyne Warren, one of the more picturesque hamlets nestled among the downs behind Dimmock. But the roses round the door were overgrown, the honeysuckle gone to seed, the paintwork peeling. Even Paddy noticed. "Doesn't Mr Harcourt like his house?"

Brodie squeezed the little girl's hand. "Mr Harcourt's not very well. He can't go outside."

"Has he got a cold?"

"Not that sort of unwell. More – Well, remember when Daniel was hurt? And after that crowds bothered him and he had to give up teaching? It's more like that. There's a big word for it – agoraphobia."

Paddy considered. "Did someone hurt him too?" She understood more of Daniel's situation than might be expected of a child – more, perhaps, than her mother would have liked. But Daniel never lied to anyone. When Paddy asked about his scars, quietly and without fuss he told her.

"Not exactly. His wife died, and for a long time he didn't want to see anyone. Then when he was ready to go out again he found he couldn't."

"What does he want to see you for?"

"He's a collector. He wants me to buy some things for him."

"What sort of things?"

"Wait and see."

Geoffrey Harcourt was taken aback when he answered the knock at his front door to a five-year-old girl in pink dungarees. "I hope you don't mind, Mr Harcourt," said Brodie, "but I hoped you'd show Paddy your models."

He looked like a man embarked too soon on middle age. His clothes had the same faded air as the house, and he hunched his shoulders and kept his gaze low. None of this mattered to a five-year-old. Most adults stooped when they talked to Paddy. Except Daniel, who wasn't very tall to start with.

"Delighted," said Harcourt solemnly. "Is Miss Farrell interested in machinery?"

"Tractors," the child said firmly. "Have you got any tractors?"

"I'm afraid not," admitted the collector. "I've got a showman's engine. Would that do?" He led them through the cottage to a room that opened before Paddy's eyes like Aladdin's cave. On tables and shelves at every level were jewel-like models, fashioned in wood and brass and steel, gleaming with oil. The smallest would have fitted in her palm; the largest would not have fitted on her bed. Struts and wheels and belts and gears wove complex patterns like filigree.

"Coo!" she whispered, tip-toeing along the bright rows, longing to touch and yet afraid, partly that she might do some damage, partly that the tiny engines might without warning leap into action and nip her finger. The aura of industry was such that they seemed merely to have paused in their labours and would clatter on, hammering out pixie spades, grinding fairy corn, spinning cotton and wool as fine as gossamer, at any moment.

At the end of the room she turned, face aglow, and raised shining eyes to the man with the stoop. "Did you make them?"

"Some of them. But some were made by engineers two hundred years ago to show how their ideas would work."

He found what he was looking for, lifted it onto the workbench where she could see. "That's a showman's engine. Steam powered, of course. They hauled travelling shows round the country, then when the fair was set up they powered the rides. That's from about 1890, pretty much the peak of steam engine technology."

Paddy Farrell liked being talked to as a fellow enthusiast. "Did you make that one?"

He shook his head. "I'm afraid not. Here." He took her small hand in his and led her down the gallery. "Here's one I'm working on. Can you guess what it does?"

She studied it intently. There was a wall. On one side was a wheel standing up, on the other a wheel lying down. A channel ran from the wall to a piece of mirror-glass. "Is that a pond?"

"It's a water-mill," nodded Harcourt. "The pond holds the water until the miller's ready to grind corn. Then he opens the sluices" – a thick finger showed her where to look – "the water turns the wheel and the wheel turns the grindstone." He saw her rapt little face and sighed. "Would you like to see it work?"

Paddy nodded, her pigtail dancing.

He filled a jug from the kitchen tap and placed a plastic bucket to receive the tail race after the water had done its work. The stream poured down the channel, turning the tiny wheel as it went. Gears meshed, the grindstone ground. The water dropped into the bucket, the pond emptied, the wheel stopped.

"Do it again!" demanded Paddy, enthralled.

Dutifully, Geoffrey Harcourt did it again.

"Do it – "

Brodie clamped a deft hand over her child's mouth.

"She means, Thank you very much, Mr Harcourt, that was lovely, and now she'll sit quietly while the grown-ups talk."

Brodie knew nothing about engineers' models, but after seeing his collection she would recognise one now. "I've got a digital camera in the car. If I see something you might be interested in I'll e-mail you a picture. If you want to bid, tell me what I can spend. It's not quite as good as being there but it's the next best thing."

"I'm more than satisfied, Mrs Farrell. Since this" – Harcourt spread a wry hand to indicate his situation – "the models have kept me sane. They occupy my hands and my time and keep my brain in working order. But it's frustrating. I know the stuff is out there, I know the interest in it is limited. I know that important models are lost because no one seems to want them. Well, I want them. I have the time and skill to restore them. But I can't get out there and find them!"

"Well, that's the bit I can do," said Brodie. "I know nothing about the subject, but doing it this way I don't have to. I'm just your eyes in the marketplace."

He looked at her sidelong, chewing his lip. "Can we give it a trial run?"

She felt herself quicken like an unhooded hawk. "You've heard of something."

"A Nasmyth's steam hammer. In the Woodgreen estate."

She was pretty sure she didn't let anything you could call an expression cross her face. "Yes? Fine."

Geoffrey Harcourt didn't go out. But lots of people

who did go out, who went out all the time with every sign of enjoyment, didn't go to the Woodgreen estate. It wasn't just the youth gangs that congregated on street corners, it wasn't just the drug culture. It wasn't even the risk of domestic appliances coming at you from upstairs windows. It was the difficulty of finding anywhere to leave a car where it would still have wheels on when you came back.

It would have been easy for Brodie to say that she didn't go to Woodgreen. But that would be as good as telling a client that she could only do some parts of her job – the easy, safe, convenient bits – because she was a woman. He wouldn't get that admission out of her with red-hot pokers.

So she would do it. She would find the address and photograph the model, and negotiate a price with the owner, and with luck most of her car would still be there when she returned to it. She had one thing going for her. Half of Woodgreen knew she was at it like knives with Dimmock's senior detective.

But she wouldn't go there with Paddy in the car. "I'm free this evening. Will you...?"

She managed to stop short of voicing the stupid question, but not soon enough that Harcourt didn't hear it anyway. If he was offended he didn't let it show. He gave a gentle, solemn smile that reminded her of Daniel's. "Yes, Mrs Farrell, I'll be in all evening."

She went early, hoping to be in and out of Woodgreen while the residents were still sharpening their flick-knives.

By eleven these streets would be unsafe for anyone but drug-pushers. The police, when they had no option but to enter the estate, went in threes.

But at seven on a November evening you could drive through Woodgreen and wonder what the problem was. Yes, there was some graffiti, and a certain amount of rubbish, and a number of empty houses people should have been keen to rent. Dimmock was, after all, a pleasant little town on the south coast of England, and this estate was less than two miles from the sea. Boarded-up property was unexpected.

But still the place didn't look like a wild-west town. If her life was in imminent danger the old lady walking a cocker spaniel seemed unaware of the fact. A group of under-tens were playing on bicycles, undeterred by the fact that they outnumbered their transport by two to one – and that was being generous to the bike with one wheel. Someone was washing his car by the light from his porch. It was all curiously normal. For sure, a lot of troublesome people congregated in the Woodgreen estate; but so did a lot of people who wanted nothing more than to get on with their lives in peace. The only thing they'd ever done wrong was not make enough money to move somewhere smarter. Brodie regretted now her knee-jerk reaction when Harcourt asked her to come here.

Right up to the moment when, driving under a walkway between two tower blocks, she got a split-second impression of something hurtling at her and the windscreen exploded.

* * *

Deacon was there in five minutes. He found her sitting on a doorstep, a bloody handkerchief pressed to her lip and the mandatory cup of hot sweet tea in her other hand, while a middle-aged woman fussed over her and a fat man stood guard over her car. A small crowd had gathered.

Deacon left the two constables he'd brought to organise the recovery of the car and went immediately to Brodie's side. "What happened?"

She shook her head dazedly. Blood leaked from a deep cut to her lip. "I think someone threw something."

"Dropped, more like," said the woman plying her with tea. "Off that walkway. We keep telling the council to shut it before somebody gets killed. But it's a short cut and people in the tower blocks don't want it shut. But they won't stop their kids using people for target-practice either."

Constable Batty appeared with half a brick in his hand. "That's what did the damage, sir."

Deacon stared at it. "Jesus! What kind of people do that?" He glared around him. "Did anyone see who it was?"

Like adding drain-cleaner, suddenly the knot of people thinned and dissipated. Ten seconds later there were only the policemen, Brodie and the couple from the house. Deacon sighed. "Take that as a no, should I?"

"I was in the house," said the woman apologetically.

Her husband shrugged. "I was washing my car. But I didn't see anything."

There was no way of knowing if it was the truth. And it would have been poor reward for their kindness to subject them to the third degree when answering his questions could put them in danger. "Batty, will it drive?" The constable nodded. "Then take it to Battle Alley. I'll take Mrs Farrell to the hospital."

Brodie waved a dismissive hand. "There's no need... "

"You haven't seen your face," said Deacon, with more honesty than tact. "I'll have you home for supper."

Brodie rescued her handbag from the car. "Will you make a call for me? A man called Harcourt – I was doing a job for him, he's waiting to hear from me." She scribbled down his mobile number and Deacon told him what had happened while she was having her lip stitched. He rang off while the man was still apologising. Then he took her home.

Paddy exclaimed in awe over the damage to her mother's face. Brodie knew the child would bring any number of friends home for tea during the week ahead, and by next Saturday have a new toy tractor.

"I'll let you have the crime report number," said Deacon. "For your insurance claim."

Brodie nodded cautiously. "I'm sorry to add to your workload."

"It won't take a minute. Batty'll fill in the forms."

"I don't mean that. I mean hunting the sod who did it. It's not like I can give you a description – I didn't see him."

Deacon said, "Um."

His tone made her look up. "What?"

He shrugged broad shoulders. "I'll be honest with you, Brodie – we haven't a cat in hell's chance of getting someone for this. We won't get a print off half a brick and there won't be any witnesses. Fill in your insurance claim and put it down to experience."

Her eye nailed him to the sofa. "You mean, you aren't going to investigate? Someone dropped half a brick through my windscreen. He could have killed me. He could have sent me off the road to kill someone else. And you aren't going to investigate."

"There's no point. I can tell you now, with absolute certainty, we'd learn nothing. All we'd do is stoke up ill feeling in the estate. I'm not rattling a lot of cages when I know it won't do any good. Most of the time Woodgreen is a slumbering giant. If you wake him up you'd better have the manpower to deal with him, and you'd better have a good reason. Before the month's out I may have to go in there. I may have a murder to investigate, or an armed robbery, or an abused child. For that I'll get together all the people I need and we'll put our necks on the line to do what needs doing. But not for a broken windscreen and a split lip.

"You're right, it was a crime. He could have killed you and I should be investigating. But I'm not going to light the blue touch-paper when I know there's nothing to be gained. I think, when you calm down, you won't want me to."

"I'm perfectly calm," Brodie said icily. "Just a little surprised. You always tell me there aren't any no-go areas on your manor."

"I'm still telling you that," said Deacon sharply. "It's a question of cost-effectiveness. Doing the right thing will cost a lot of time and energy, put good people at risk and provoke disorder. Doing the wrong thing will avoid all of the above, and the bottom line will be the same – we won't find the culprit. You need to understand – "

"Oh, I do," said Brodie. "I understand that someone attacked me and Dimmock CID doesn't think it's worth the trouble of doing anything about it."

"That's not what I said," growled Deacon.

"That's what I heard."

Deacon gave up. "Think what you want. I'll see you tomorrow. I'll get the car fixed, you should have it mid-morning on Monday."

"Good. I'll be busy on Monday. Guess where."

Deacon's eyes narrowed. It might have been an empty threat, but he didn't trust her to make empty threats. "Brodie, let it go. The damage was minimal. Don't put yourself in danger trying to make someone pay for it."

"What's it to you?" she demanded, reckless with anger. "Oh, that's right – if somebody murders me you might have to go in there after all."

"I'm going home now," Deacon said stiffly. "I'd like to think that by tomorrow you'll have come to your senses."

"And I'd like to think that by tomorrow you'll be talking to someone who thinks it's funny to drop masonry on passing vehicles. How fortunate we've both learned to handle disappointment!"

Chapter Four

Without her car Brodie couldn't take Paddy riding. The child's father collected her. "Are you coming with us?"

Brodie tried to see past his shoulder without making it obvious. Julia was waiting in the car. "I'd better catch up on some work."

John Farrell nodded, not offended but also not surprised. In the last few months his relations with his ex-wife had been easier but he didn't expect to be forgiven any time soon. He knew he'd hurt Brodie terribly, and regretted that. When they married he'd meant the words he said, couldn't imagine meeting someone he cared for more. He wasn't the kind of man who went around letting people down.

"Julia says, if you're stuck she can do without the Peugeot for a few days."

It was a kind offer and Brodie was genuinely touched. "Thank her for me. But I should get mine back tomorrow. Jack's pulling strings, and he doesn't take no for an answer."

John smiled pensively, wondering whether to say what was in his mind. "I'm glad. About you and Jack."

Nine months ago she'd have slapped him down, credited the sentiment to guilty conscience. Now she just nodded. "He's a good man. I don't know if we'll ever take it any further – but if we did, would you have any objections? On Paddy's behalf, I mean."

"Of course not. I'd be happy to see you settled."

Brodie smiled thinly. "Well, don't hold your breath – we're pretty settled as we are."

When the tiny equestrienne had galloped down the drive and jumped into the back of the car Brodie went back to her phone and the list of numbers she'd compiled, and began dialling.

People called Hood who live in Nottingham are used to getting funny phone-calls. When she said she was trying to trace a friend, their voices took on a weary note that only lifted when his name turned out, in defiance of experience and expectation, not to be Robin. But the first four didn't know a Daniel either.

The fifth had a brother called Daniel.

Taken by surprise, Brodie blinked at the phone for a moment. "I don't think it can be the same one. My friend doesn't have any brothers. At least" – she stumbled, trying to remember how much she actually knew and how much she had assumed – "he's never mentioned any."

"How old is he?" asked Simon Hood.

"Twenty-seven. He's a teacher. Well, he was. He lives in Dimmock."

"On the south coast? Yes, that's my brother," said the man on the phone. Suddenly he sounded wary. "What's happened?"

"Nothing," she said quickly. "Nothing to worry about. I'm just trying to speak to him. Someone said he was visiting family."

"He was here a couple of days ago," confirmed Simon. "Then he left. I thought he was going home, but maybe not."

A puzzled little frown wrinkled Brodie's forehead. There was something just a little odd about this conversation and she couldn't put her finger on what it was. Nothing he'd said; nothing he hadn't said. So it was how he'd said something. As if they were talking about a casual acquaintance, someone met on holiday who'd dropped in for a drink one evening then gone on his way. There was no note of kinship in Simon's voice, no suggestion of concern.

Brodie framed her response cautiously. "You've rather taken me off-guard, Mr Hood. I'm a good friend of Daniel's but I didn't know he had any immediate family left. I was looking for a cousin or something. I know he used to live with his grandfather."

"That's right," said Simon guardedly.

"So – who else do I not know about?"

In the pause that followed she knew he was asking himself if it was any of her business. He only had her word for this friendship: she might have been a creditor, a jilted lover, anything. But then he thought, Daniel? – and dismissed the idea. "He has three brothers. Daniel's the youngest. And there's our mother."

"Mother?" It came out as more of an exclamation than she intended. Probably Simon was beginning to think she was a very rude person, but Brodie was used to that. "I'm sorry. I just can't believe he hasn't mentioned any of you."

The voice at the other end of the phone was growing cool. "Mrs Farrell, if you want to know about Daniel's background you should ask him. If you were hoping to find him here, I'm afraid he's gone. If he hasn't gone home I don't know where you should look."

"Could you give me your mother's number?" asked Brodie. "Maybe he told her."

"That's not likely," said Simon firmly. "I'm sorry, Mrs Farrell, there's nothing more I can tell you. I suggest you keep trying his house until you get him."

"He's selling the house. Didn't he tell you?"

"No. Obviously you know more about his plans than I do."

After her lesson, Paddy's father and stepmother took her home for Sunday lunch. Brodie thought she'd go into town and check the netting-shed on the off chance that Daniel was home, just not answering his phone. She was groping in the dresser drawer for her car-keys before she remembered she had no transport. So she'd walk. It was about a mile: how hard could it be? Daniel did it all the time.

Daniel didn't do it in women's shoes with stupid pointy toes and stupid narrow heels. She felt the first blister burning before she was halfway.

But she'd reached the top end of Dimmock, within hobbling-range of a pub, a café and a taxi-office. She didn't like drinking alone and was too embarrassed to have a taxi take her half a mile, which left The Korner Kaff. Only sheer discomfort persuaded her to go through the door. She didn't generally patronise people who couldn't spell.

She kicked her shoes off and ordered coffee and waffles; and when those were gone she ordered more coffee and croissants. When those too were gone she reluctantly inched her feet back into her shoes and reached for her handbag.

It wasn't there.

Something's there or it isn't: you wouldn't think the mind would have difficulty distinguishing between the two. But the mind believes what it thinks it knows ahead of what the eyes can see. Brodie knew she'd put her bag on the seat beside her and hadn't touched it since, so it had to be there. Like rebooting an AWOL computer she went through the sequence again from the beginning. Food eaten, time to go, feet in shoes, reach for handbag...

It still wasn't there. Not on the seat, not under it, not kicked under another table by passing feet. There was only one explanation.

"I've been robbed," she told the waitress; and though the girl had heard a lot of excuses from people trying to avoid paying she was convinced by the mix of astonishment, anger and embarrassment in the tall woman's voice. Also, she remembered Brodie had a bag when she came in. Unless the waffles and the croissants and the coffee had left enough room for her to eat a big black leather organiser as well, she was telling the truth.

"Do you want me to call the police?"

"I suppose," said Brodie, still floundering. "Tell them it's Mrs Farrell."

The waitress made a note. "Why, are you" – she didn't know how to put this delicately – "known to them?"

"One of them knows me pretty well," admitted Brodie.

* * *

Constable Batty took the details. The duty sergeant had asked if she wanted Detective Superintendent Deacon informed but Brodie saw no point. It was petty crime to everyone but her.

"And you didn't notice anyone hovering round you?" asked Batty.

"I didn't," said Brodie helplessly. "There were a number of people in here over the forty minutes, but nobody seemed to be paying me any attention and I didn't pay them any. Of course people brush past you on their way in and out, but I didn't suspect a thing until I went to pay and couldn't."

"OK. Well, the first thing you need to do is get home so nobody's emptying the flat while it's empty. I'll take you there now, make sure they haven't beaten us to it. Then I'll check your office. Then you need to get your locks changed – I've got the out-of-hours number of a locksmith – and to notify your bank that your credit cards have been lifted. After that there's a limit to how much damage he can do. Was there much cash in your purse?"

Brodie shrugged. "Some, not a lot. There was other stuff that'll be harder to replace. My driving licence. Medical cards for me and Paddy. Some photographs, personal things – all of it irreplaceable, none of it worth tuppence to anyone else!"

"You might get some of it back," said Batty, more in hope than confidence. "He'll take the valuables and dump the rest. Someone may hand it in."

Brodie was jotting her name and address on the café bill. "I'll get back to you with this tomorrow."

The waitress shook her head. "The least we can do – "

"I'll settle it tomorrow," Brodie repeated.

As Batty drove her back up the hill towards Chiffney Road it occurred to Brodie that she never had got as far as the seafront and the netting-sheds. Daniel might have been there all along. The way her luck was running, though, she doubted it.

The locksmith was there when John brought Paddy home. Brodie explained. His long face between greying sideburns was sympathetic. "You're not having much luck just now, are you?"

Brodie had to concede that, forty this year, he was still a handsome man. A better looking man than Jack Deacon was or ever had been. Once that might have mattered to her. She was pleased to note that it didn't now.

She gave a grim chuckle. "As long as that's all it is. It's beginning to feel personal."

His eyes were wary. "You're joking, right?"

"Of course I am."

And it was only a joke when she said it. Given voice, though, it took on a kind of reality. The car, the bag – they might be no more than random misfortune but they could be connected. Behind her eyes she was considering the possibility that someone was doing this to her. Someone with a grudge, too cowardly to face her, content to snipe from deep cover. The idea was a nasty taste in her mouth and she made a face.

"What?" asked John.

She shrugged. "Nothing. I'm just in a foul mood."

"No change there, then," he said with a careful grin.

Nine months ago she'd have had his head for a remark like that. Now she only wrinkled her nose and shooed him away.

It wasn't even true. She'd been a good wife to him. She'd been a much nicer person then than she was now. But that was all right too because being a bit of a cow was more rewarding. She liked people handling her with caution.

She gave Julia a wave. "Thanks for taking Paddy." If it was true that John was a better-looking man than Jack Deacon, she thought complacently, shutting the door, she never had to worry about comparisons with the second Mrs Farrell. Nice woman, kind; a librarian. Dull as ditch-water, comfortable – and the same basic shape – as a pillow.

When she collected the car at ten o'clock on Monday, instead of returning to the office she headed for the Woodgreen estate. She had no excuse. She called Geoffrey Harcourt looking for one but he didn't answer the phone. She drove out to Woodgreen anyway.

She was very aware of the walkway as she passed under it. If there'd been a way to avoid it she might have done, although she might not. She didn't like feeling scared, but on the whole she'd rather be scared than scared off. In any event there was no one on the walkway. She parked at the foot of the eastern tower block and went looking for someone to chat to.

Once upon a time, old people and young mothers would have been the only ones about during the day, the men at work from before eight until after six. But things change. Unemployment in Woodgreen affected one in three, many of them young men who'd never had a job. Young mothers, on the other hand, left their babies with relatives in order to work, while the old people had mostly been shuffled off into residential care.

Drifts of purposeless men and teenagers imparted an air of casual menace to the places where they congregated. Even the locals were careful where they parked their cars, noticed who was walking behind them, and often thought better of using the lifts even when they were working.

Brodie set her jaw, gripped her second-best handbag tight under her elbow and kept her keys in her hand for use as a weapon if the need arose. Noticing a group of youths watching from a balcony, she headed their way. She began by telling them lies. "I'm looking for an address but I can't seem to find it. This is Senlac House? Then where's number 258?"

They traded downcast glances and giggled: not because they meant her harm but because they had no idea how to behave around someone of a different age, sex and socio-economic group to themselves, and were embarrassed.

Finally one found his tongue. "There isn't one."

"There must be. Mrs Taplock, 258 Senlac House. See?" Brodie showed him the piece of paper she'd readied on the way up.

The youth shrugged. "Somebody told you wrong. You're on the right landing but the numbers stop at 30."

"Damn!" she said with well-feigned astonishment. "Well, thanks for saving me some time. I've obviously taken the address down wrong. I'll have to wait for her to call again." As she turned away she seemed to notice the walkway for the first time. "Is that...?"

"What?"

"Some poor woman got stoned here over the weekend, didn't she? I heard someone dropped a boulder on her."

"It was half a brick," volunteered one of the boys.

Brodie shuddered. "It's a hell of a height to drop it on someone's head. Was she all right?"

The boy shrugged. "Never heard that she wasn't."

"The filf was here." If he'd had better teeth she'd probably have guessed his meaning before the second youth added, "That big bastard in the mac. But they didn't stay. They'd have been back if she croaked."

"Who'd do a thing like that?" Brodie asked them. "Why? Was someone angry with her, or was she just in the wrong place at the wrong time? Was it a joke and they were too dim to see what the consequences could be?"

More shrugs and blank stares. Brodie thought the idea of foreseeing consequences was an alien concept to them too.

"Dunno who did it," said the first boy. "Could have been kids. Could have been anyone. But I know why. Boredom."

"Boredom? They stoned someone because they were bored?"

Brodie was growing too vehement, making them wonder at her interest. The swelling of her lip had subsided in the last twenty-four hours but the first boy had noticed the stitches. "Looks like you've been nutting bricks yourself, missus." There was a suspicion in his voice that hadn't been there before.

Brodie touched a delicate fingertip to her lip. "Ah yes. My husband. But you should see what he did to Mr Taplock." While they were puzzling over that she beat a retreat.

Unless the boys were better liars than she thought, it wasn't common knowledge in Woodgreen who smashed her windscreen. Maybe it wasn't disaffected local youth after all. So maybe it wasn't a random attack – maybe it was personal. And now he had her handbag as well. Private things: her diary, photographs of Paddy, the names and addresses of friends, letters she meant to reply to. It was an uncomfortable feeling that someone was picking over the details of her life.

She emerged from the stairwell into a cloud of smoke. It was dense, it was oily, it stank and she couldn't see through it. She edged along the wall into the clearer air where a crowd was gathering. Across the estate she could hear the distant wail of a fire engine.

It would take ten minutes for the firemen to put the blaze out and longer than that to establish what had caused it. They should have asked Brodie, because she knew right away. It was her car, and it had been started by someone wadding a burning rag into her petrol-tank.

Chapter Five

Deacon was trying very hard not to say "I told you so." Unfortunately, he wasn't trying hard not to think it, or to keep what he was thinking from showing in his face.

Brodie shrugged his coat around her shoulders. She'd been shaking when he arrived. "I know." The odd flatness of her voice was disturbed by the slightest of tremors. "You told me to stay away."

"I did," nodded Deacon quietly. He'd have been angrier if she'd been less shocked. "I said, as I recall, that making a big deal of a comparatively minor incident could result in someone getting hurt."

"They burned my car." She looked up at him, a little life creeping back into her eyes. "The sods burned my car!"

"I'm glad that's all they burned. They could have hurt you, Brodie. I could be here investigating an attack on you. Or worse. What in God's name were you thinking of?"

It was a good question. Of all the places she might have gone after taking Paddy to school, the Woodgreen estate should have been the last. Brodie Farrell would have had trouble naming a single soul who wished her harm, but someone here had damn near killed her forty hours before. Even if it was a random attack, her car just the one that was under the walkway at the critical moment, whoever dropped the brick would not take kindly to seeing her back so soon. Her behaviour was reckless and provocative, and Brodie knew it as well as Deacon did.

But there was another consideration, and when he gave it some quiet thought Deacon would know as well as Brodie did. As much as he and his officers, she had to be able to move freely in order to do her job. She would never have to face down riots and petrol-bombs because she could do what Deacon could not: turn tail at the first sign of trouble. But she couldn't afford to get selective about where she would go on the basis of perceived risk. Once she started asking herself if she was safe going alone into this estate or up that street, or knocking on unfamiliar doors, she might as well put up the shutters at Looking For Something? because she'd be unable to do the work that running a finding agency entailed. It was all about going places other people hadn't thought to, or hadn't wanted to.

Going back to Woodgreen might not have been sensible but it had been necessary. She'd been getting back on the horse that threw her. She hadn't expected it to throw her again, and then to jump up and down on top of her. She said in a low, stubborn voice, "Someone's having a go at me."

Deacon frowned. "You think these incidents are connected?" The idea hadn't occurred to him.

One perfectly shaped eyebrow canted in the familiar, faintly disparaging fashion that reassured him she was essentially unharmed. "Don't you? I'm not rich or famous – even cranks have better things to do than threaten me. But three times in as many days I've been a victim of crime. Twice could be bad luck. After three times it would take real arrogance not to think it's because somebody hates me."

Deacon flicked her a little grin. Humour was another good sign. People who are being genuinely ground down don't see the funny side.

Which didn't necessarily mean she was right. In his expert opinion they were three quite different types of incident. "All right," he allowed, "this and what happened on Saturday are linked, at least to this extent – if you had-n't lost your windscreen on Saturday you wouldn't have come back here to lose your car today. And OK, that may not be the extent of the connection, but it could be. This isn't one of the more law-abiding parts of Dimmock. People do throw stones at cars here, and do set them on fire. It might have been the same people, it might not.

"Either way, I don't think the theft of your handbag is part of it. You were in the middle of town, you were off the street, and if whoever torched your car wandered into The Korner Kaff he'd have stood out a mile even before he tried leaving with a woman's handbag. It doesn't add up. This" – he indicated the smoking wreckage behind him – "may be a warning not to start a war over your windscreen. But the bag was just bad luck."

A certain amount of paranoia is a survival trait. If there's no one out to get you it's no handicap, if there is it gives you an edge. Brodie accepted that Deacon, a police-man for quarter of a century, a senior detective for twelve years, probably had some idea what he was talking about. She hoped she was reading too much into this: it wasn't something she wanted to be right about. If she was wrong, probably her problems were over.

She nodded slowly. "Maybe. Yes, I can see that. So what do we do about the car?"

"We," he said pointedly, "do nothing. I'll have someone take you home. Make yourself a cup of tea and then call your insurers. Again. Meanwhile I'll start asking questions, all the while hoping that no one will give me a name I'll have to follow up. Because if they do I'll have to arrest him, and that could be like chucking a hand-grenade into an arsenal."

"Yes." Brodie sucked in a deep breath. "I'm sorry, Jack. Coming back wasn't clever. I may have made a lot of trouble for you. I was angry and worried, and – well, you know what I'm like, I hit back first and size up the other guy afterwards."

Deacon chuckled. She was not only the best-looking woman he'd been out with, she was also the most surprising. She constantly wrong-footed him. She looked like a geisha, thought like a samurai and talked like a sumo wrestler. Even now she confounded his expectations at every turn, smart and sharp and perceptive, with a sure intuition for how people behaved and a lion-like courage when nothing else would serve. She drove him mad and scared him witless, and he wouldn't have changed a thing about her.

"No harm done. Except to your car, of course, but that's what insurance is for. Go home, have a hot bath and get your breath back. It's no wonder you're feeling shell-shocked, but it's over now. Stay away from Woodgreen for a few days while the dust settles. After that, if you need to come back, I don't suppose anyone'll remember your face."

Actually, he thought to himself, that's probably not true. It wasn't the sort of face that blended into crowds, that well-meaning eyewitnesses had trouble describing. But he still didn't buy her conspiracy theory. He thought she'd been unlucky, and was in no more danger than anyone else in Dimmock.

Marta Szarabeijka disagreed. Of course, Marta disagreed with most people – particularly policemen – on principle. She believed in global conspiracies: a trashed car and a stolen handbag presented her with no difficulties. The angular Polish woman lived in the flat above Brodie's, gave piano and violin lessons, and acted as a kind of surrogate granny to Paddy. The child adored her and had learned from her an extensive repertoire of middle European folk songs and swearwords.

"You got to be careful," she told Brodie over tea in her flat. Though she'd been in England for thirty years she still pronounced her Ys as Js. "Somebody's mad at you. Give them time to calm down."

"Jack thinks it was a coincidence," said Brodie, keeping her voice low. Paddy was playing in the next room. While Brodie wasn't keeping the day's disaster from her – much dimmer five-year-olds than Paddy Farrell would have noticed the sudden disappearance of the family car – she didn't want the child to think it was anything more than a nuisance. "He reckons the car was a bit of mindless thuggery by local kids while the handbag was the work of a professional thief."

Marta could invest a simple shrug with a lifetime of scorn. "Jack thinks –! Jack Deacon's a policeman, what does he know?"

Cheered as always by the older woman's subversive pessimism, Brodie forbore to answer.

After a moment Marta saw the flaw in her argument. "OK, maybe I rephrase that. What I mean is, this stuff he sees every day. It's not personal to him. Maybe he's right. But suppose he's wrong? I'm telling you, be careful for a while. Don't take no chances. Stay in town, work in the office."

"Until I can get myself some new wheels I haven't much choice." Brodie nodded. "I know what you mean. It won't do any harm if it was a fluke, and if it was more than that, well, maybe he'll settle for scaring me off."

Marta regarded her frankly across the table. "Are you scared?"

"No!" Then, more honestly, "Well, maybe a bit. Uneasy, anyway. I'll be glad to get a quiet week behind me."

"You got any idea who it is?"

Brodie gave a helpless shrug. "No. If it is deliberate someone's gone to a fair bit of trouble. It's not like a rude message on the answering machine – he's been watching me, following me, waiting to catch me off guard. You don't do that on a whim. I can't think of anyone I've annoyed that much."

"Ex-lovers? Dissatisfied clients?" It's hard enough to be

accurate when you're speaking a foreign language, almost impossible to be subtle. At least, that was Marta's excuse.

Brodie was taken aback, but she gave it some thought before answering. "Ex-lovers, no. You know better than anyone, before Jack I had neither the time nor the inclination. As for dissatisfied clients – sure, there's always the guy who quibbles about the bill. There's always the guy who pays me to find something only to see the same thing cheaper the day after he signs the cheque. But it's a far cry from being miffed to persecution. I don't recall causing anyone that much grief." Or rather, she did, but not someone who would react that way. There was a pause while she followed the train of thought. "I wish…"

She didn't finish the sentence, but then she didn't have to. "Me too," said Marta quietly. "He's still not answering the phone?"

Brodie shook her head. "He isn't there. I don't know where he is. I don't know if he's all right."

"His brother said – "

"His brother didn't know and didn't care! I told him Daniel was missing – he wasn't concerned. It was as if the milkman hadn't turned up: a bit odd but he'll probably come next week and if he doesn't someone else will take over the round. They're family, Marta, and nobody cares what happens to him. And I didn't even know he had a family."

Marta said knowingly, "There's been a falling-out."

It hardly seemed an adequate reason. "Daniel wouldn't cut his mother and three brothers out of his life just because they pissed him off!"

"Maybe he didn't. Maybe they cut him."

Brodie stared at her in disbelief. "Don't be absurd! You think in his whole life Daniel's done anything to make someone disown him?"

Marta couldn't see it either. But then, they clearly didn't know everything about Daniel Hood. They'd become important to one another in a short space of time, but the fact remained that twelve months ago they hadn't known he existed. "He lived with his grandfather, yes?"

"Until he died a couple of years ago. So?"

"So it's not normal, is it? If he had a mother and three brothers, what for is he living with his grandfather?"

Brodie had no answer. Nothing Daniel had said to her, directly or in an unguarded moment, made sense of it. "Something's gone wrong, hasn't it? Someone's done something someone else couldn't forgive. But Marta, this is Daniel we're talking about! There are amoeba that give more offence than Daniel."

It was true in a way, but it was also an over-simplification and both women knew it. You only had to know Daniel for ten minutes to know he was a kind, gentle, decent man. But when you'd known him a little longer you began to see that he was also a very determined man, as stubborn in his own way as Jack Deacon, as Brodie herself. He believed in right and wrong, and if he thought he was in the right he would stick to his guns even if it meant dying in the last ditch.

Brodie didn't want – didn't dare – to think any more about that. She retreated to safer ground. "A dissatisfied client? Someone I've let down? Someone who holds me responsible for something – either a financial loss or a personal one. I'll punch up the records, Marta, see what I can find."

Chapter Six

As good as her word, Brodie spent Tuesday in her office.
First she caught up on her paperwork, sending out invoices
and a couple of mildly threatening letters where earlier
invoices had been ignored, then she turned the scanning
electrons of her mind to a new project. Solicitors say that
the man who represents himself has a fool for a client and
a rogue for a lawyer but Brodie didn't see it that way. She
thought that a professional finder who couldn't discover
who was terrorising her should find another job.

At six o'clock she shut the door but kept working. She
had reviewed every file she'd opened since starting
Looking For Something? and copied the name of anyone
who might have been left with a grudge to a spread-sheet.
Now she was arranging them in order of probability. At
the bottom of the list were those who were least likely to
be behind her recent difficulties, at the top a handful who
were credible suspects, if only just.

A little after seven the doorbell rang. Knowing the
sound of Deacon's thumb the way morse operators once
knew one another's fists, she got up and opened the
door.

By way of greeting he said shortly, "You weren't at
home. I was worried."

"I got involved in something. Marta has Paddy, I
thought I'd finish while I had some peace and quiet."

"A job?"

"In a way. I'm trying to figure out who's yanking my

chain. Dissatisfied customers. People I've crossed in the process of satisfying my customers."

He leaned over her shoulder, peering at the screen. Brodie knew he had a pair of reading glasses: sheer vanity prevented him from using them. "Who are they? What happened?"

Brodie realised she was about to incur his wrath. "Jack, I can't tell you anything except that I doubt if any of them are involved. Yes, there were harsh words. But none of them threatened me, and none of them made me feel threatened without actually saying the words."

Deacon nodded. "Do me a print-out, I'll see if we've got anything on them."

Brodie reached for the keyboard and the screen went blank. "I can't. Whatever the circumstances, I can't open my files to the police. Not without consulting the clients first – which would rather defeat the object, wouldn't it? You know as well as I do that some of them come to me because it would be difficult to go to you. They pay me rather than take your help for free because I promise confidentiality. I'm not going to break that promise."

Deacon couldn't have looked more surprised if she'd slapped him in the face with a kipper. "Brodie, this isn't a game! You've had property damaged and stolen, and you could have been seriously hurt. Last time we talked you thought someone was stalking you. That's a serious crime, and if I didn't know you from Eve I'd still expect you to co-operate in finding the criminal."

"Well, no," she corrected him mildly, "that's what you'd want but not necessarily what you'd expect. You'd expect that a professional with a duty of confidentiality towards her clients would require you to produce a search warrant before she'd surrender her files. I can't put my own interests ahead of the paying customers' without one."

Airships could have hangared in his mouth. His eyes were incredulous. "Someone is terrorising you," he said, very distinctly. "He knows where you live, where you work, what kind of a car you drive – drove – and when you stop for coffee. Since he started by dropping a brick on you from an overpass it's safe to assume he's prepared to inflict serious injury. So you've gone through your records and put together a shortlist of people who could be doing this – but you won't show it to me unless I get a search warrant?"

"No, I won't." The ethics of the situation seemed clear enough to Brodie. So did the financial implications. "If I did I'd be doing his job for him. If he's trying to put me out of business, making me turn my files over to the police would do it. Try to understand, Jack. My clients are mostly decent people because I try not to work for those who aren't. But some are people who need an alternative to the police, not because they're involved in something illegal but because their situation is sensitive. I can't put their private business into the public domain simply because someone's leaning on me. I owe them better."

"One of them torched your car!"

"I'm not convinced. In all my files I've found about a handful of cases that could have left someone nursing a grudge against me. But not on this scale! If someone had painted rude words on my window, maybe. But attempted murder? Honestly, Jack, I can't see it."

"So give me the names and let me see what I've got on them. People who behave like this don't do it just once. If one of them's done something like it before, I bet you'd find that pretty convincing. Those who check out need never know."

Brodie breathed heavily. These days – unmarried, self-employed, head of her household with her only child just five – she didn't often have to justify her decisions. "Jack, I know you mean well. I know you're looking out for me. I'd do as you ask if I could. Maybe no harm would come of it. Maybe one of these names would ring a bell with you, and you'd pull him off the street before he was able to do any more harm, and I'd be eternally grateful and no one else would know.

"But you might not be able to keep it secret. If you couldn't find a prime suspect you'd want to interview them all, and you'd have to tell them why. The innocent ones might think I was justified in talking to the police about their private business, but I wouldn't count on it. If they disliked me to start with, can you imagine how they'd feel then? They could make a lot of trouble for me."

"Trouble?" echoed Deacon. "More trouble than fire-bombing your car, you mean?"

"Oh yes," said Brodie with conviction.

The policeman had had to make victims accept his help before now but he hadn't anticipated having a problem with Brodie. He regarded her in disbelief. "So you're going to sit on a list of suspects until one of them burns your house down?"

"No," she said evenly. "I'm going to speak to them myself. If one of them's involved, I'll tell you."

"If he lets you!" shouted Deacon.

Brodie squinted along her nose at him. "Don't take me for a fool, Jack. I won't meet them on the beach at midnight. I'll see them in public places with people all around, and I'll be perfectly safe with most of them because they never meant me any harm, and with the guilty party – if there is a guilty party – because this time I'll be expecting him and he won't be expecting me. He'll be flustered and angry, and I'll know. And you'll know soon afterwards."

Deacon still thought she was risking her safety for a quixotic principle. A man with powerful principles of his own, he was never able to see why other people felt as strongly about theirs. He was like a zealot who thought his beliefs were religion and all others superstition. But he was marginally reassured that she wasn't going to put her head on the block in order to satisfy her curiosity as to who was swinging the axe.

Still, he couldn't resist one more try. "You need someone to watch your back. I'll come with you. I'll stay in the background – unless you need help no one will know I'm there."

Brodie laughed out loud. "Jack, the background hasn't been invented against which you'd disappear! You go into a room, you fill it; you go into a city and the seams start creaking. You were cut out for undercover work the way octopuses were made to roller-skate!"

She had a point. "How about Charlie Voss? He wouldn't look like a policeman if you put him back in uniform and made him direct the traffic. Take him with you. For my peace of mind?"

It wouldn't have been a huge concession. Voss was good at blending. He could sit in the corner of a bar and the barmaid would take him for a regular; he could sit on a park bench and only the pigeons would notice. If she asked him to stay out of sight, none of those she met would see him.

But she'd still be breaking a confidence, and Brodie would know if no one else did. It felt wrong. She didn't think that being scared was a good enough reason to default on the contract she had with all her clients, past and present.

She shook her head. "I don't want anyone there. I don't need anyone there. I'm going to cause enough offence as it is, approaching five men who hoped they'd seen the back of me. I'm not going to risk them spotting Charlie, or you, or anyone else. I'm not going to get hurt, Jack, I'm not going to give them the chance. But I'm not going in mob-handed either. I can do my job without police protection."

Deacon knew he wasn't going to persuade her. But it was hard for him to watch her make a bad decision. He headed for the door, his boots all outraged dignity.

Brodie let him go. In this mood he couldn't be talked to: when he calmed down he'd come back.

With his hand on the door ready to slam it he delivered his parting shot. "I know one thing about your precious list. There should be six names on it."

Brodie was confused. "You don't know who's on it."

"No. But I know who isn't."

Six names. It was so absurd she wasn't going to dignify it with consideration. The five she'd listed were improbable enough: the sixth was downright ludicrous. She'd have dismissed the whole idea, only Deacon's reaction made it impossible. Now she had to open the clattery cupboard and let the skeletons out because the alternative was to have him shoulder the door in.

This list was a record of the things that had gone awry since Looking For Something? opened for business. The jobs she'd got wrong, or taken when she shouldn't have done, or gone on with after she should have stopped. The ones where people got hurt.

She looked at the first name on it: Trevor Parker, who lost a good job because of information Brodie provided to his employers. The information was correct: Parker was diverting company funds into another firm's account. But after he was sacked it emerged the beneficiary was a key supplier: when it folded due to cash-flow problems, Parker's successor had to spend even more money finding a new source of parts. The arrangement was unauthorised and improper, but Parker had been acting in the best interests of his company. It was a gamble, and he should have come clean instead of trying to lie his way out of trouble, but perhaps he had a right to feel aggrieved that it had cost him his job.

Was that reason enough to want to hurt her? To destroy her property, endanger her life? For some people –

for some people Brodie had known – perhaps it was. If
Trevor Parker had been the man she initially believed, it
might have been enough for him. But he wasn't that man.
He was a tolerably respectable businessman, and if he
sailed close to the ethical wind at times, and took risks at
times, and sometimes took short-cuts, he knew and ulti-
mately respected the boundaries of legality. If he'd had a
case he might have dropped his lawyers on her from a
great height, but not half a brick.

Then what about the second name? David Ibbotsen.
Ah, yes. Ibbotsen just might have resorted to physical
attacks on her. His grudge was personal, and if he decided
to repay it a brick off a bridge was just the sort of way he'd
choose. But that was the problem with Ibbotsen as a suspect: he was too much of a coward to risk being caught and
punished. Cowardice had got him into the difficulties
Brodie had caught him cheating his way out of. On
Saturday nights in a Rio bar he might dream – he might
even talk – of killing her for wrecking his plans. But the
lead would go out of his pencil long before he caught a
plane home. Not so much from fear of her, or even
Deacon, but because Dimmock was where his father
lived, and what scared David Ibbotsen more than anything else was the old pirate who fathered him.

And third on the list was...actually, even less credible.
This was getting her nowhere. She wasn't going to confr-
ont any of these men. The ones who had cause to resent
her were too decent to drop bricks on her, the ones who'd
like to were too scared. She'd annoyed a lot of people in
her time, but this was too much: a malice born of fury

and frustration. Whoever was doing it couldn't find any other way to relieve his feelings, and she hadn't caused that kind of hurt, either deliberately or unintentionally, to any of the men on her list.

Except that Deacon was saying the list wasn't long enough. And while it might be ridiculous, she knew what he meant. It wasn't the first time he'd said it. She knew he was a man who bore grudges himself. He was full of flaws, she just liked him anyway. It had seemed in recent months that the enmity the detective bore the other man she cared for had begun to fade. But no; it was still there to be resurrected when he had a use for it. It wasn't even Daniel he was angry with this time, it was her. Because when he'd said Jump she hadn't asked, How high?

It was too laughable to be offensive. Daniel didn't hurt people. Not her, not anyone; not ever. Daniel took punishment himself rather than see other people hurt. With Gandhi dead, no one on the planet made a less credible thug.

Which was perhaps as well, thought Brodie slowly, because she'd never given anyone as much reason to hate her as she'd given Daniel Hood.

She shook her head to dislodge the memory of the first time she saw him, his abused body clinging to life in ICU at Dimmock General. But it kept coming back, along with the knowledge that she had put him there. Not deliberately or maliciously, but carelessly and for money. She'd believed a woman who professed a good reason to want him found. But she was lying, and Brodie's success almost cost Daniel his life.

Which was an abiding grief to her, but didn't alter the fact that he'd suffer torture again before he'd hurt her.

Something dripped onto the desk causing a perfectly round translucent spot. After a moment another joined it. Brodie drew a ragged breath and pressed a tissue to her eyes as if staunching blood.

She didn't believe for a moment that Deacon suspected Daniel. She'd annoyed him and this was what he'd hit back with. And Brodie would accuse every man on her list, jointly and severally, in public and on their own doorsteps, before she'd give it serious consideration. It was hard to say exactly what the relationship between them was – or had been, until it foundered – but she knew Daniel too well to think he'd ever want to frighten her. He was a gentle, peaceable man, a kind man; a maths teacher and amateur astronomer; unremarkable by every standard.

Until she sold him to his enemies. In a very real sense his life had ended there, before Brodie even met him. What survived was changed in every way. Things that had mattered to him, that he'd been good at, were now impossible. He was a man with no future, not much of a present, and a past he didn't dare look back on.

Oh yes. She'd given him reason enough to hate her.

But hatred was alien to Daniel. He hadn't managed it when they met in the hospital and she confessed her role in his nightmare. He forgave her long before she forgave herself.

But forgiving was one thing, forgetting another. He'd never forget – how could he? – one moment of what was done to him. It was there in his head, inescapable. He kept it confined, harming no one but himself, mainly for her sake. Now the relationship between them had changed, might that alter how he felt about what she'd done?

But if he wanted to cause her pain he must know that all he had to do was go out of her life and never tell her where. He didn't have to risk the wrath of the law, not to mention the fury of Jack Deacon. He just had to vanish.

His house was for sale. He'd visited his brother, then disappeared. Brodie's messages went unanswered. If he wasn't trying to hurt her, it felt as if he was.

But Daniel in his right mind would never –

And that went to the heart of it. In his right mind Daniel would rather die than hurt her. But he'd been through so much, and when he needed her most she wasn't there for him. Had her delicate conscience proved the wheel that broke him? Was Deacon right, and in the end the pain had proved too much and Daniel had to start giving some of it back?

All her senses argued with it. That wasn't the man she knew. But a weasel voice inside her said that that was the point – that Daniel had held himself together so long thanks to Brodie's support. Without it he'd torn himself apart like one of Geoffrey Harcourt's models with a head of steam and the brake off. If her friend survived at all he was locked deep in a prison of pain and rage and inexpressible grief, screaming himself hoarse where no one could hear.

Brodie straightened herself, squaring her shoulders,

dropping the damp tissue contemptuously in the bin. Deacon was right about one thing: Daniel should be on her list. He should be top of her list. Until she'd found him, until she'd tried to make things right between them, and found someone to help him if it was too late for her to, she had no business even wondering about these other men.

But if one of them was her stalker, she'd make him work for his fun. Tomorrow he was taking an away day to Nottingham.

Chapter Seven

She took the train. There were a lot of faces she recognised on Dimmock station, and several she could put names to, but nobody seemed to be taking an abnormal interest in her and by degrees her level of alertness fell. She looked again as they boarded the train to see if anyone followed her, but there was no unseemly shuffling in her wake. Brodie found a seat facing back down the carriage where she could expect to see any unusual activity after the train moved off, and there was none.

Until, two stations up the line, Trevor Parker got on the train, cast around for an empty seat and picked one across the aisle and two rows down from her.

Brodie had the bizarre sensation that, even though the train was picking up speed, time inside the carriage was standing still. Her insides clenched with something that wasn't exactly fear but wasn't exactly not. Until last night, combing the old files for someone who might want to hurt her, she hadn't given this man a moment's thought since she reported his creative accounting to his employers. And this morning he was on her train. She stared at him, daring him to look up, and at length he did.

Her first thought was that dismissal suited him. His clothes might have been bought in his general manager days and recently dry-cleaned, but they looked both new and expensive. He'd gained a little weight since she saw him last, and that suited him too. He had a briefcase open on his knee and was riffling through the papers when he felt her gaze. She watched expressions chase across his face: curiosity (does someone want me?), puzzlement (I've seen her before somewhere), shock (I know where I've seen her before!) and finally anger. It was exactly the sequence you'd expect, and far from making her doubtful only convinced Brodie he'd been practising in the mirror.

She quit her seat and was at his side in a couple of swift strides, looming over him as only a tall woman can. "Why, Mr Parker," she said tightly, "fancy seeing you here."

"Mrs Farrell," he gritted. "Well, these days I'm a commuter. I used to work in Dimmock until someone told my firm I was defrauding them – but of course you know that."

The people in the seats around him had picked up the combative tones and were looking uneasy. When Brodie offered to swap with one of them, all three vied for the privilege. She sat facing Parker and the other men subsided nervously.

"You mean you're on this train every morning?"

"Yes," he said. "I haven't seen you on it before."

"This train? At this time?"

"Yes. Why?" He snorted a bitter little chuckle. "Unearthed another non-existent crime to accuse me of?"

There was no mistaking the rancour in his manner. Of course, he was entitled to be bitter. What he wasn't entitled to do was take out his frustrations on her. "Are you following me, Mr Parker?"

"That's right," he nodded immediately. "It's a particularly cunning form of following. You buy a season ticket for a train, ride it at the same time every day and wait for

the person you're following to get on. It might take a couple of years but sooner or later she will. Then, in case she
doesn't notice, you find a seat close to hers. Anybody can
follow someone. Making this much of a dog's dinner of it
takes real genius!"

She breathed heavily at him, unsure what to think.
"Are you saying you're not following me?"

"No," said Trevor Parker. "I'm not saying anything to
you, Mrs Farrell. I don't want to talk to you, Mrs Farrell.
If you continue to harass me I'll have you arrested by the
British Transport Police."

"Fine," she snapped back. "Perhaps they'd like to hear
about my interesting week as well."

They glared at one another like two dogs on leashes,
pulling and pulling and hoping like hell that nobody lets
go.

One of the other men said diffidently, "If it's any help,
I see this gentleman on this train most mornings."

Brodie turned on him so quickly he recoiled. Belatedly
she adjusted her expression. "Really? Then perhaps I'm
mistaken. Thank you for your help."

"You were mistaken before, too," said Parker shortly.

Brodie regarded him without speaking for a moment.
Then she nodded. "Yes, I know."

"I wasn't defrauding anyone. I was giving a key supplier time to get back on his feet. He'd have repaid the loan.
It would have been best for everyone."

"I know. But it wasn't your call."

"If I'd gone through the channels he'd have folded and
we'd have taken damage."

"He did fold, and everyone took damage," Brodie reminded him. "I'm sorry if your motives were misinterpreted. But your actions were exactly as I reported them to the people who hired me. You've no one to blame for your situation but yourself."

"You reckon?" He thought about it, then sniffed. "I want you to know I'm making more money today than I ever did in Dimmock. Perhaps I should thank you. I just can't quite bring myself to."

Which explained the new suit. The man undoubtedly had talents: if he'd found someone to appreciate them better than his previous employers Brodie could be happy for him. Assuming, of course, that he hadn't tried to kill her. "Mr Parker, I'm going to give you the benefit of the doubt. This time. But if I bump into you again any time soon I could get really suspicious really quickly."

"Yes? And you're usually such a good judge of character," sneered Trevor Parker.

Brodie got up, curled her lip at him and moved to another carriage. The way her luck was running, it came as no surprise that she had to stand most of the way to London.

Parker left the train before she did. He didn't look back at her, which proved nothing.

She was still fretting over the encounter as she caught the Nottingham train, but then she made a deliberate decision to put it out of her mind and concentrate on what she was making this journey for. She would need all her wits about her to get what she wanted out of it.

From Nottingham station she phoned Simon Hood's home. A woman answered. Lying fluently, Brodie said she was updating pension records and asked for his office number. That was almost a mistake: it transpired Hood worked for an insurance company. But unsuspecting, his wife gave Brodie the number and the useful information that he'd be in his office all day.

When Brodie dialled his number, though, she didn't ask for Hood: she told the switchboard she had a delivery to make and needed directions. She didn't want to give Simon the chance to avoid her. Once there, while his secretary was checking if Mr Hood could see someone about a family reunion, Brodie sailed through his door quicker than anyone could stop her.

"Sorry," she said, "but this is too important for you to fob me off again."

She'd been expecting someone of the same general appearance as Daniel. But Simon was taller, broader, darker and perhaps fifteen years older. "You're Mrs Farrell." His tone was devoid of expression.

"Yes. And I have to tell you, I'm worried sick."

Simon frowned. "What's happened?"

"I don't know that anything's happened," said Brodie impatiently. "But I can't find Daniel. You said he left here a week ago. But he hasn't come home, and I can't think where else he could be."

"He could be anywhere," said Simon reasonably. "He may have taken a few days' holiday."

"All right," nodded Brodie, "maybe he did. Where would he go?"

The man gave a surprised laugh. "I don't know! He didn't say anything to me."

"Well, where has he been before?"

Simon shrugged. "He's never been a big one for holidays. A couple of school trips when he was teaching, and he went down to Cornwall for the solar eclipse a few years ago. That's about all, as far as I know. He's never had many friends and I suppose it's something you tend not to do on your own."

"Well, he has friends now," Brodie said tartly, "and we're worried about him. What he's been through this last year, God knows what's going on in his mind. But he shouldn't be dealing with it alone."

Simon looked unsure. "Losing his job?"

Brodie felt her jaw drop and was powerless to stop it. "You don't know!"

"Know what?"

She was having trouble stringing the words together. "He didn't lose his job, he left it. And you don't know why."

Simon Hood was becoming irritated. "All right then – why?"

She could explain in a few words or half a day but nothing in between. Or she could not explain at all. If Daniel had wanted his family to know he'd have told them. But Brodie itched to shake Simon Hood's complacency. "He almost died. Someone thought he was involved in something he wasn't and brutalised him because of it. His body's a mass of scars, and I think his mind must be too. Mr Hood – what kind of a family are you that you didn't know this?"

She'd succeeded in shocking him. He shook his head, little side to side movements she thought he was unaware of. His eyes were appalled. "I didn't know. He never said."

"Did you ask why he wasn't teaching any more?"

"I assumed...cutbacks... "

"He gets panic attacks. Post-traumatic stress disorder. It may pass in time. But whenever he tries to take his life back, something happens to slap him down. Now his house is for sale, and I can't get hold of him, and he may be fine but I don't think so. I think he's in trouble, and if I can't find him I can't help him. I met him in a hospital – I don't want to say goodbye in a morgue!"

Simon passed a hand across his face. His voice was hollow. "What are you saying? That he's suicidal?"

"I never thought so, before now. But then, he never tried to disappear before. If he doesn't want to see me, that's his privilege – but only once I'm satisfied it's a rational decision. I have to find him. You've talked to him recently: did he tell you he was moving? Did he tell you where?"

In an unconscious echo of his brother, Simon thought so hard it twisted up his face. Before, he'd dismissed Brodie's concerns as trivial. Now he was worried too. But it didn't help if there was nothing to remember. He ran his hand distractedly through his hair. "No."

"So what did you talk about?"

"He just said it had been a while, he wanted to know how everyone was. He asked after my children, and James's children, and Ben's job, and our mother. I told him. We had lunch. We said we shouldn't leave it so long next time and I dropped him at the station. That's about it."

Brodie was watching him carefully. "So long as what?"

"Sorry?"

"When did you see him last?"

"A couple of years ago."

"A couple of years?" The gears of her mind meshed. "At your grandfather's funeral."

"Yes."

Her breath hissed through tight lips. "And how long since you went to any trouble to see him?"

Simon might have been unsettled by her visit, but not enough to let that pass. His tone hardened. "Mrs Farrell, I'm not sure what gives you the right to criticise my family. No, we're not close. But it's none of your business."

"It's my business," she snapped back, "because if I didn't make it my business Daniel would have no one in the world to confide in, to look out for him, to know or care if he's facing meltdown. I was amazed when I found he had family he'd never mentioned, but I'm not now. Now I wonder why he thought it was worth the train-fare to come and see you at all."

Startled by her anger, Simon struggled to defend himself. "You don't understand. There are reasons – "

"I don't care about your reasons!" yelled Brodie. "I don't care who got the best trainers and who got the new bike. I don't care if your mother never came to your sports day because she always went to his. Do you understand? I don't care! While you're raking over old scores, I'm scared my friend is so tired battling his demons alone that he's dug a hole, crawled in and pulled the earth back on top of him.

"Don't you see why he came here? To say goodbye. Except for your grandfather's funeral he hadn't seen any of you in years. Whatever caused that rift, he wanted one last chance to heal it. And you took him for lunch. And hey, you gave him a lift back to the station, so that's your conscience clear! Simon, if the reason I can't find your brother is that he's slit his wrists in a cheap hotel somewhere, because he tried to tell you how desperate he was and you weren't listening, however little he meant to you you're going to find that hard to live with."

She snatched her bag and headed for the door. Her trip had told her nothing, except perhaps why. Perhaps she had no right to be angry. Families do drift apart: she had no way of knowing who was to blame, or if Daniel could have resolved matters if he'd tried harder or sooner. In any event, it wasn't his family who let him down because he had no reason to think he could rely on them. That was her job, and her fault.

She was halfway through the door, drawing startled glances from the front office, when Simon Hood stood up behind his desk and said, just loud enough to reach her: "You're right, Mrs Farrell. My family has treated Daniel badly. You want to know why? Because it would have been better all round if he'd never been born."

Chapter Eight

"She wanted a daughter," said Brodie. Her voice was dull and empty. "She had three sons and was desperate for a little girl. She gambled everything she had, and she lost."

Marta refilled the coffee-mugs but said nothing. She was almost as anxious about Brodie as Brodie was about Daniel.

She'd got back home in the middle of the evening. The moment Marta saw her face she evicted the pupil from her piano with the promise of a free lesson next week, sat her down and put on the kettle. "Tell me."

"It's Daniel."

"Of course Daniel. What about him?"

"I know why he lived with his grandfather."

Brodie's face was the grey of old concrete. Of course she was tired, it had been a long and trying day, but it was more than that. Marta had seen her go all day, all through the night and all the next day without losing the spring in her step or the glow from her cheek. This wasn't weariness, it was shock.

"Yes?"

Brodie drew a deep, unsteady breath. She hoped that telling the story would help her to understand it in a way that thinking about it non-stop for the last six hours hadn't. "They were married at twenty. Mr and Mrs Gerry Hood: they grew up in the same street, they were childhood sweethearts. They got married, got a little house, Elaine got pregnant. She wanted a boy first and she got one – that was Simon. Next she wanted a little girl but she got James. Then she got Ben. Gerry reckoned three healthy sons were enough but Elaine had her heart set on a daughter, couldn't accept that her family was complete without one. She threatened to leave Gerry and try with someone else – she blamed him for giving her sons. He agreed to one more try.

"By now Elaine was in her thirties and didn't conceive as easily as she had in her twenties. More time passed. She got all the medical advice then available – spent money they really didn't have getting it – to no avail. Her mental condition began to deteriorate. When it seemed she'd begun an early menopause there were fears for her sanity.

"But she wasn't menopausal – she was pregnant. Twins this time: one of each."

Marta searched her eyes without finding any sign of a happy ending. "Daniel has a sister?"

"No. It was a difficult pregnancy. In the eighth month, with the babies struggling, it was decided to induce them. Both were born alive, but Samantha died after ten days in an incubator."

Marta sighed. "So Elaine had another son after all."

"Yes," said Brodie levelly, "and no. She blamed Daniel for the loss of her daughter. She believed Samantha would have gone to term and lived if Daniel hadn't been in there too. She refused to have him home. Gerry's parents took him, so Gerry could see his baby and Elaine didn't have to. Six months on she wanted to try again. Gerry refused and she cut her wrists.

"She recovered physically but her mental condition

went steadily downhill. She's been in and out of psychiatric units for twenty years. She was never reconciled to Daniel. If his name's mentioned she goes into fits of rage that last days.

"Gerry died in his mid-forties. Simon reckons it was the stress that killed him. Two years later Daniel's grandmother died, leaving an old man to raise a little boy whose mother never acknowledged him. And I," said Brodie, drained of emotion, "had the temerity to be offended that Daniel didn't tell us about his family. How the hell do you tell someone all that?"

Marta was staring into her mug. She had no idea if it was full or empty; there could have been a mouse in there and she wouldn't have known. She'd never had children, didn't envy those who had. Her life had been full enough in other ways. But the idea of rejecting a child made her blood run cold. Now she understood Brodie's mood.

"You know the saddest thing about all this?" she murmured. "A woman who wanted a daughter would have loved having Daniel."

Brodie barked a little brittle laugh. Simon's revelations had done nothing to ease her sense of impending disaster. They cast no light on the real and immediate issue, which was where Daniel was and whether he was safe. Unless they did.

"He hadn't been back for years," she gritted. "Then he turned up without warning, for no apparent reason, and caught up on everyone's news, and then he got back on the train. But not to come home. He never meant to come home, Marta – that's why he put the shed up for sale. He never meant to call me. The estate agent gave him my message but he has nothing left to say to me. I think he's tying up loose ends. Saying goodbye to his family, disposing of his property, packing his traps. He's... leaving." Her voice was reedy with loss.

"Leaving Dimmock?" said Marta, who wasn't sure she understood.

"Oh dear God, Marta," moaned Brodie, "I hope that's all."

The Polish woman followed that well enough. "Daniel? Nonsense," she snorted indignantly. "Never. That's a coward thing, and you say what you like about Daniel but he's never coward." As always when her emotions were involved her command of the English language slipped a notch. Her Ys came out as Js, her Ws as Vs, and she dealt with grammar by the simple expedient of slinging some at a sentence and seeing where it stuck.

"But he's hurting and it's my fault! I let him down, and there is no one else. He has nothing left. Nothing to go on for."

Marta shook her head. She wore her greying hair in a tight bun that made her look like a dyspeptic stork. "You know him better than that. He's stronger than he looks. And stubborn – oh yes. If Daniel was going to kill himself he'd have done it months ago, when his nights were full of horrors and his days were full of fear. He didn't get through that only to slit his throat because you say harsh things to him. Your opinion means a lot to him, Brodie, but I think not that much."

Brodie so wanted to believe her. Uncertainty sank its

claws in her. "What Simon told me alters things. We didn't know Daniel before he was hurt, we assumed he was fine. But he wasn't – he couldn't have been. His childhood was a nightmare. His mother rejected him, his father died, so did his grandmother. Everyone he needed to trust abandoned him. Anybody would be damaged by that.

"So he came to Dimmock and made a new life for himself as a teacher. Now that's gone. But there was me. I owed him, and I promised I'd always be there for him. But I let him down. He's alone again. And I know he has guts to spare, but if he doesn't want to go on that may be what gets him from making the decision to carrying it out. Suicide takes courage too. Most people who wish they were dead never do anything about it."

"Daniel Hood is not going to kill himself," said Marta firmly. "You got my word. If you ever believe anything I say, believe that. So he's acting crazy – but not that crazy. Maybe he wants a fresh start. There's not much keeping him in Dimmock now. Maybe he's thought of something else to do with his life."

"And he won't tell me about it? Even though he knows how worried I am?"

Marta gave a bony, expressive shrug. "Brodie – you don't think, when you called him a murderer, you lost the right to be consulted about his plans?"

Brodie's cheek flamed as if her friend had slapped it. "I didn't –!" And she hadn't, not in so many words. But she as good as did. She'd reached in and ripped the heart out of him. She could have lied. She did it often enough when it hardly mattered, but not to salve the battered soul of a man she cared for. Deacon was right and so was Marta. What Daniel did was justified; what she did was not. She fought back tears.

Marta's long arm went consolingly about her shoulders. Brodie shook it off more roughly than she meant. "I'm sorry. I know you're right. About me, anyway – I just hope you're right about Daniel. But if you are... "

"What?"

Brodie's long-fingered hands were prayer folded before her mouth as she thought it through. "Tell me I'm stupid. Tell me I'm wrong about this too. That it's a coincidence, that nobody goes to that much trouble, that there are simpler, quicker and more satisfying ways of hurting someone."

The older woman frowned and shrugged. "No. Maybe if you said it in Polish, but... "

Brodie knew she wasn't making much sense. She hoped it was because the whole idea made no sense. But there was some logic to it that she couldn't quite dismiss. "Suppose you're right, Marta. If you are, maybe when Daniel left Nottingham he came back here. There was nowhere else for him to go, and no reason. He'd decided to leave Dimmock but not like a thief doing a moonlight flit. He had the estate agents to deal with. Maybe he meant to deal with me too. He came back a week ago. But somebody got to him before he came to us."

Marta's forehead was like corrugated paper. "What are you saying, Brodie? That he's been kidnapped? Again?"

Brodie gave a desperate snort though it was no

laughing matter. "It doesn't seem entirely fair, does it? Lots of people go their whole lives and never get kidnapped once."

But it wasn't a joke and Marta knew it. "Spit it out, Brodie. You think someone's hurt him? Who? Why?"

"The same person who's doing the rest of it. If someone wants to hurt me, harming my friends would be a good way."

Now she understood Marta's thin brows rocketed. "The stalker? You think he's got at Daniel?"

Brodie felt sick with fear. "It's a week since anyone saw him. Simon thought he was coming home. Maybe he did, or at least tried to. Maybe he's lying dead in a ditch somewhere, and not because of anything he's done but because of something I've done. And I don't even know what!"

For long seconds Marta just breathed in and out through the O of her lips. But behind the stunned mask she was thinking. There had been times in Marta Szarabeijka's past when her life depended on being able to think fast and get the right answer, and she'd never lost the knack.

"What's the point?" she asked. "If someone killed Daniel to hurt you, he'd need you to know. To see what he'd done. Why hide the body when he needs you to see it?"

"You think he's safe?" Brodie's voice was as small as a child's begging for comfort. "Really?"

"I got no reason to think he's not," said Marta flatly. "I don't know where he is or what he's doing, but I think he does. I think it makes sense to him. You just have to wait till he's ready to talk to you."

It was the least-worst option, and Brodie wanted to believe it. "Yes. This is his way of punishing me. For what I did and didn't do. He's had enough of my moralising. He's turned his back and walked away, and he doesn't care that I may never know whether he's dead or alive." Brodie looked up, hollow-eyed. "It's over."

Since leaving Nottingham she'd weighed every possibility she could think of. She'd thought Daniel might kill himself, and been afraid that someone might kill him. She'd even wondered if her cruelty had driven a damaged, vulnerable young man to strike back at her.

Twenty-four hours ago she wouldn't have wasted thought on it. But twenty-four hours ago she hadn't known of his mother's descent into obsession that had laid the pattern for his life from before it began. Half his genes were hers: if Elaine's madness was Daniel's inheritance, the conditions were there for it to prosper. With his world trembling to its foundations he'd found something to cling to only to be rebuffed once again. Had she left him nothing to believe in? Had her pious treachery stripped him back to where he was nothing but his mother's son, raw and angry, wanting payment for his pain in hers? It was possible.

And the other possibility was that their friendship had simply run its course. Logically, it should never have been. They should have been unable to surmount the circumstances that brought them together. Somehow they'd met one another's needs for a time; and if occasionally they added to one another's burdens, still not until now had Brodie thought the friendship could end. They'd had arguments before and mended them; there'd been misunderstandings that they'd resolved. Not this time. This time it was over. She'd hurt him too much and he'd gone.

"I don't want to lose him," she whispered brokenly. "Marta, I'd do anything to make him stay."

Marta tried again with the arm and this time it wasn't rejected. She stroked the dark curls of Brodie's bowed head. But she was no good at meaningless platitudes. And sometimes when her emotions were involved her command of the English language was devastatingly accurate.

"Brodie, darling," she murmured. The G came out as a K. "I think you had the chance, and you blew it."

Chapter Nine

She got no sleep. She rose at six, quietly to avoid disturbing Paddy, and made coffee and toast, and let them go cold unaddressed. She sat at the kitchen table, turning in her mind the steps she could take to re-establish contact with Daniel. She would not accept that a friendship which had been important to both of them could be ended by a simple disagreement. Of course, she was being disingenuous. What had come between them was too big to ignore, to gloss over or pretend it never happened. Brodie was trying to believe this was possible only because the alternative was unbearable.

By eight she had exhausted all the options. There were no steps she could take. She had found his family, that a week ago she hadn't known about, and they did-n't know where he was either. He had no job, no car, no mobile phone to leave a trail she could follow. He had, so far as she knew, no friends beside her and Marta – and Deacon, if you wanted to stretch the definition – to whom he might turn in a crisis. He passed through the world alone, leaving no wake and few ripples, and if he'd chosen to move on she might never know to where.

There was nothing she could do. If she heard from him again it would be his decision.

Finally she was able to accept that it was the end of some-thing but not the world. Life would continue, so would the need to make money. Brodie turned her attention to other things that needed finding, that grateful clients would pay her to find.

Clients like Geoffrey Harcourt. She could do a trawl of the south coast curio trade, see if she could spot something to interest him. There was also Mrs Pangbourn's collection of nineteenth century linens, which would dovetail nicely. The antiques trade, at least at the lower end, is much more eclectic than people suppose. For every Sheraton sideboard there are a dozen Victorian chamberpots (one careful owner), tippling sticks (one careful toper), unattractive Staffordshire fairings, late copies of unattractive Staffordshire fairings, sepia prints of The View From Beachy Head, watercolours of sheep in meadows by artists who should never have been allowed to pick up a brush, tin trays advertising Guinness, tin-plate automata with the key missing, cut-glass decanters with the stopper missing, collections of Famous Footballer cigarette cards with Stanley Matthews missing, and Whitby jet necklaces that turn out to be Bakelite.

For Brodie, the satisfaction was in sifting the dross to find a small gem. Not a big gem – even junk-shop owners knew too much to display a Fabergé egg with sundry Easter commemoratives or sell off a Modigliani cheap because the artist forgot to paint the eyes. But with her books now full of commissions she didn't often leave a shop empty-handed and everything she bought paid her a profit.

But first she was going to have to buy a car. A true replacement would have to wait until the insurance came through, but there was enough in the emergencies fund –

all right, her building society account – to buy a tolerable second-hand car to keep her mobile in the meantime. After she'd taken Paddy to school she headed for a likely dealer.

All she wanted was something safe and reliable that would run for a few months with no trouble. She settled for a six-year-old hatchback with seventy thousand on the clock and a three-month warranty. The salesman, who thought it was Christmas when a well-dressed woman with no male companion walked into his yard, mopped his brow and settled for clearing fifteen percent on his outlay, which was about half what he'd been hoping for even without the warranty. It would be a while before he saw a good-looking woman in the same light again.

Before she set off for Brighton, Brodie called at her office to collect her messages. There was one from Daniel.

It was a long time starting, as if he couldn't decide whether to speak or not. Finally he stumbled a few words. "It's … kind of awkward. Can you meet me? We need to talk. The library? I'll wait for you. Thanks."

For a couple of minutes, which is a long time when nothing is happening, Brodie just leaned against the office door, staring at the machine. Only when her eyes started to smart did she remember to blink. So he was safe, and back, and he wanted to see her. But not here, nor at her home or his. The library was a neutral venue, and he may have hoped the signs would discourage her from shouting at him. Which suggested he had something to say that she wouldn't want to hear.

Another time she might have worried about that. After

yesterday she was so relieved he was all right she could have burst into tears.

All thoughts of the flea markets dissolved instantly. The message was an hour old: he could have been waiting for her most of that time already. He could have got tired of waiting and left. But he'd said he wouldn't do that, and his word was good. He'd wait if he had to wait all day.

Brodie wiped the machine, slammed the office door and ran out to her new car.

Dimmock's public library was on the top floor of a new building overlooking the park. For years there had been arguments over how this desirable site should be used, with competing causes lobbying the council. Finally someone came up with the obvious solution: build it tall enough to meet everyone's requirements. The social services department had its offices on the first two floors, with the Citizens' Advice Bureau, Help The Aged and Women's Aid above. But the library on the fourth floor had the best view: across the park and the lower town to the Channel.

There were flowers in the vestibule and two lifts. One had an Out of Order sign hanging from the button. Brodie thumbed for the other. At ten-fifteen on a Thursday morning she had both vestibule and lift to herself.

The first indication of something amiss was when the lift failed to stop at the fourth floor, the bulb marked Library flashing briefly on and off as the car continued up into the roof-space where it stopped.

The doors remained shut. Brodie blinked at them, perplexed. Of course the attics would be used for something, if only storage, and it would be inconvenient to carry everything up a last flight of steps. And if the lift had a button marked Attics then every sub-teen in Dimmock and quite a few of their grannies would disappear into the roof-space for hours at a time. A staff key would give access to the restricted levels. All that had happened was that the last person to use it had disengaged too quickly. She pressed the Library button again.

The lift whined into action and descended. It did not, however, stop at the floor below but continued down through the building to the basement. Eyeing it severely, Brodie pressed the Library button once more. After this, she thought, I'm getting out and using the stairs.

This time it stopped between floors. She tried the Library button again, then each of the others in turn. Nothing happened. She tried the Open Doors button: still nothing.

Fortunately, Brodie had no particular phobias. She didn't like spiders, and she'd never learned to swim, but neither bugs nor water caused her unreasonable alarm. Being stuck in a broken lift only worried her because, when she failed to arrive, Daniel might decide she'd declined his invitation and leave.

Of course, if he tried to take the lift he'd find her. Or she could hit the Emergency Assistance button. She hit the Emergency Assistance button.

After that, nothing she did had any effect on the lift. It accelerated up through the building before slamming to a halt moments before (so it felt) it would have shot out through the roof. It descended in a series of spasms, the elevator equivalent of a learner driver. It froze, ignoring all instructions, for up to a minute at a time, then took off like an electric hare with every greyhound in the White City on its tail.

And actually, it wasn't at all funny. She was locked in a steel box, the thing was clearly out of control, and no one knew she was there. She hammered on the walls though she had no idea if she could be heard. Now the box fell abruptly: when it stopped she lost her footing and sprawled on the floor. The doors opened. She was, thank God, back in the vestibule. She climbed to her feet and headed for safety – but the doors snapped shut like jaws and the lift shot upwards again. Brodie let out a cry of frustration and, now, fear.

Twice more she rode the roller-coaster through the building. The next time she hit the floor she stayed there, limbs splayed, eyes wide as if there was something other than polished steel to see. All she knew about lifts was that they were safe. If they failed, they failed safe. She had no idea how this one had managed to override its programming, or how long it could continue throwing itself around like this before crashing to its destruction. And hers.

Bizarrely enough, she found herself doing sums. Four storeys – six including the attic and basement. Four metres per storey? A free-falling object accelerates at thirty-two feet per second ... Daniel would have been proud of her, but actually she was less interested in the math than the bottom line. Could she survive if the lift tore itself free and dropped from the top of the building into its foundations?

She didn't know. The building was no skyscraper, even by Dimmock standards. But people died falling off chairs. If this thing piled into the ground she doubted she would dust herself down and walk out of the wreckage with just a broken heel to show for it. Legs, hips, pelvis, spine, rib-cage – the impact would crush her like a runaway truck. A horror of dying like that, perhaps even more of living like that, ripped from her a wail that joined the scream of machinery gone mad in a manic crescendo.

Between one moment and the next the sound changed. The lift stopped hurling itself around like a tod-dler in a tantrum, straightened its clothing and went back to doing what it was meant to: travelling at a sensible pace, halting smoothly, opening its doors where it should for its passengers to disembark.

Except that its passenger was still on the floor, her hands pressed flat against the steel walls, her eyes vast with fear. Two men, one in a suit, one in overalls, hurried to help her up. "Are you all right? Are you hurt?"

Brodie was shaking too much to stand. She took the proffered hands and let them guide her out. Someone brought a chair and sat her down. The man in the suit brought her a glass of water. "Are you hurt? Should I call an ambulance? Maybe I should anyway ... "

Brodie shook her head, spilling water over the lip of her glass. "Not hurt. Just...shaken."

The man in overalls was bemused. "I have no idea

what that was all about," he said flatly. "It not only isn't supposed to do that, it isn't supposed to be able to do that."

He was the caretaker, responsible for maintaining the building's services. The man in the suit was the social services manager. When passers-by heard the lift reverberate like a drum they alerted both men. The caretaker accessed the panel on the ground floor to get the thing under control. It didn't resist. He could see no reason for it to go ape in the first place.

Though Brodie was still trembling in every muscle, at least her mind was clearing. "It didn't just happen. It was sabotaged. Will someone call Detective Superintendent Deacon?" She gave the manager his mobile number.

For a moment, understandably, the man hesitated. "Will a Detective Superintendent be interested in a rogue lift?"

"Trust me on this," said Brodie.

Deacon was there in eight minutes, which wasn't quick enough to stop someone who didn't want to be seen leaving the building. But while she was still too shocked to stand, Brodie knew what to do. She had the social services manager shut the main doors, making what explanations he could to those inconvenienced within and without, and the caretaker secure all exits at the rear of the building. But though the task was completed before the police arrived, it wasn't soon enough. When he got there the caretaker found one of the fire-exits swinging open.

The look he gave Brodie carried a new respect. "How did you know someone did this?"

"You knew," she pointed out. "You said, lifts don't behave like that."

"But they don't behave like that if you try really hard to make them, either."

Deacon hurried across the vestibule and hunched down in front of her, peering into Brodie's face. She was pale, a little dusty from the floor, and tomorrow there would be bruises on her knees, but she'd escaped essentially unscathed. Perhaps she had been meant to. Or perhaps she'd been lucky.

"This is getting out of hand," gritted Deacon. "It has to stop before you get seriously hurt. Have you thought any more about that list of suspects?"

"I don't have to," she said in a small, tight voice. "I know who did this."

He stared at her incredulously. Then, as the name passed from her brain to his by a process akin to osmosis, he shook his head. "I don't believe it."

Brodie didn't want to either. She saw no alternative. "You told me to add his name to the list."

"I was winding you up," said Deacon dismissively.

"Maybe, but you were right. Jack, he phoned me. He asked me to meet him here. There was an out-of-order sign on the other lift" – she looked across the vestibule but the sign was now gone – "so I took this one. No one else knew I'd be here this morning. I didn't know myself an hour ago."

Still Deacon was unconvinced. "You talked to Daniel?"

"No, he left a message on the machine at work."

"What did he say?"

She remembered word for word, inflection for inflection.

Deacon nodded slowly. He straightened and walked into the lift and looked around. He came back. "Why did you think it was Daniel?"

Until then she hadn't even asked herself. She started to say "He said so" – but actually he hadn't. She started to say "I recognised his voice" – but now she thought about it she wasn't sure of that either. She'd been aching to hear from him, wanted to believe he'd called. She had noticed that he was ill-at-ease and mumbling, and rationalised it. In fact, as she now recognised, it could have been anyone.

"This is pretty technical stuff. He's tapped into the electronics and effectively operated the lift on remote control. I couldn't do that." Deacon turned to the caretaker. "Could you?"

The man shook his head. "I can change a fuse, I can grease a bearing, I can switch it on and off. Anything more complicated than that, I phone the service engineer."

"All right," said Deacon. He was looking at Brodie again. "You know him better than I do. Is Daniel the sort of kid who played with Meccano? Who built robots and crystal radio sets? Could he tap into an electronic circuit and make it do something it wasn't programmed to?"

Brodie said weakly, "He's a mathematician... "

"Yes. A theorist. What's he like with electrical equipment?"

Brodie bit her lip. "He keeps thinking his video's broken when he's activated the child lock."

Deacon rolled his eyes. "Why am I not surprised? So he knows what's going on in the hearts of stars on the far side of the galaxy but the video remote remains uncharted territory. This wasn't him, Brodie. It was a mechanic, an electrician, maybe a model plane enthusiast, but not Daniel."

A flush was creeping up Brodie's cheeks, and some of it was embarrassment but a lot of it was relief. "I'm the answer to a stalker's prayer, aren't I? He doesn't even need to follow me, he just tells me where to go."

Deacon chuckled, proud of her resilience. "If it wasn't Daniel on the answering machine, was it someone else you know?"

She tried out different voices in her mind. She tried Trevor Parker's. But all she could hear was Daniel's. "I don't know."

The policeman knew the answer before he asked the question. "And the recording ...?"

"Yes," nodded Brodie ruefully, "I wiped it."

"Come on, let's get you home. Not yours," Deacon added as he helped her, still wobbly, into his car, "mine. I don't want you on your own till we've sorted this out."

It was a kind offer but it wasn't practical. "What about Paddy?"

"Paddy's five years old," he said with heavy patience, "she can't be expected to act as your bodyguard."

Brodie gave a shaky laugh. "I mean, where are we all going to sleep? I like your house, Jack, but it's not very big."

He didn't understand the problem. "She can have the spare room."

Brodie pursed her lips. "Jack – I'm not sharing your bed with Paddy in the next room."

"Oh." He didn't know whether he should be offended or not. "Er – "

"I'll call John, ask him to have her for a few days. He'll jump at the chance."

Deacon finally decided he was rather offended. "And while she's there, I suppose John'll banish Julia to the living-room sofa."

"Of course he won't," said Brodie. "It's different. They're married."

"When did you get to be so old-fashioned?"

She shook her head. "There are some things you don't need to explain to a little girl. Not when you know that, every Monday, she gives the class a brief discourse on interesting things that happened over the weekend."

Deacon considered. "Call John," he said, "by all means."

Chapter Ten

No sooner had Brodie made arrangements for Paddy than she started worrying about Marta. If the house in Chiffney Road was unsafe for her and her daughter, how could she leave her friend there alone?

Deacon was about to insist that if they couldn't share a bed with Paddy in the next room they certainly couldn't with Marta there when the Polish woman resolved the dilemma herself. "I got a Standing Invitation," she announced with a lewd wink. "I'll have me a dirty week-end in Littlehampton."

All right, it was only Thursday; and Littlehampton didn't have the same cachet in the dirty weekend stakes as Brighton or even Bognor Regis; but if it meant Marta wouldn't be alone in a house where someone might go with malicious intent, Brodie was prepared not to enquire too deeply. Certainly Marta seemed to think that having a Standing Invitation to Littlehampton put her right up there in the front rank of fifty-five-year-old swingers.

Julia offered to collect Paddy's bag when she picked her up from school. But Deacon said he'd be passing and would deliver both the child and a week's clothing packed into a tiny pink suitcase. It didn't occur to Brodie until later that it was impossible to pass both Paddy's school and John's house on the way from anywhere to anywhere else.

So he wanted a word with John. Lunchtime was a good chance to find him at home, even on court days.

Magistrates like their meat-and-two-veg as much as anyone, which means that solicitors are mostly free between one and two-fifteen.

When Paddy bounced off upstairs with Julia to unpack, Farrell took Deacon into his study. "What's going on, Jack?"

Deacon told him. There seemed no point not doing, especially when he wanted his help. "Can you think of anything from when Brodie worked for you that might have left someone feeling this bitter towards her?"

If the answer had been yes, Farrell would have had a problem. Solicitors owe their clients a duty of confidentiality more rigorous than any other profession's. Many of their clients are criminals who wouldn't dare claim the legal representation they're entitled to if the police could access what passed between counsel and defendant. Even to protect the mother of his child he would have no right to breach that trust.

In the event, though, Farrell had no difficulty answering. "No. I doubt if there's anyone who feels that bitter towards me. And if they did, why would they attack my ex-wife when they could as easily attack my present one?"

Deacon hadn't expected to wrap up his case that simply, it was just a line of inquiry he had to exhaust before looking elsewhere. "OK." But he made no move to leave.

"There was something else?"

"Actually, yes." Deacon pursed his lips thoughtfully, unaware this made him look like a hopeful troll loitering under the mistletoe. "Until we find out what this is about and put a stop to it I don't want Brodie on her own. Even in public places. I'm going to leave a woodentop" – he meant a Police Constable – "at my house when I'm not there during the day, in case the security measures aren't enough." There had always been security measures at Deacon's house: it was the old Dimmock Jail. "She can work there instead of her office. Evenings, if I have to go out I'll try to get someone else in. But if I can't, would you keep her company for a couple of hours?"

John Farrell hadn't done many things he was ashamed of in his life; which for a solicitor is a major achievement. But he was ashamed of how Brodie had ended up paying for his happiness with Julia. He hadn't wanted to hurt her, had tried hard not to, but he knew he had. He still felt it a debt against him. He nodded immediately. "Call when you need me."

Deacon wasn't surprised at the man's willingness to co-operate; but then, nothing Farrell did would ever surprise him. John Farrell was the stupidest man he knew. He'd been married to Brodie and fallen for someone else. "If I need you. I'll wrap this up as quickly as I can. But until then, it would be a weight off my mind even if Brodie thinks I'm fussing."

Farrell nodded again. He knew the policeman would throw all the resources he could at the mystery. "Have you told Brodie you've booked a baby-sitter?"

Deacon cast him a look that, on anyone else, you'd describe as hunted. "I thought I'd phone from the office."

In fact he was more cowardly than that. He left it to

Constable Vickers to explain when he turned up at the house under the Firestone Cliffs half an hour later.

Vickers knew where the Detective Superintendent lived but he'd never been past the front door. He was intrigued, in that faintly prurient way that attends unexpected insights into other people's lives.

It was, as he discovered when Brodie let him in, almost an exaggeration to call the place a jail. It was a lock-up, consisting of two cells and two rooms where the jailer had lived with his family. Stone-built before 1800, it was also the Georgian town's pound for stray livestock with a byre at the back. Deacon got the lot for £50,000 four years ago. He'd spent as much again making it habitable. Now it consisted of a large, low-ceilinged living-room, one big bedroom and one small one, a galley kitchen and a bathroom with bars at the small high window, the whole linked by a dark, rough-plastered corridor with unpleasant penal hardware on the wall. This was Deacon's idea of decor.

When Brodie saw Vickers on the doorstep she guessed why he was here. Irritated, touched and amused in equal measure, she showed him through to the living room and listened politely to what he'd been told to say. Halfway through, a banshee scream sent Vickers leaping from the sofa, but it was only Dempsey marking his disapproval at yet another strange human in his house. Dempsey was Deacon's idea of a cat.

"You know this isn't necessary, don't you?" said Brodie. She and Vickers knew one another well enough not to have to be discreet.

Vickers shrugged. "If it was my girlfriend, I'd want to know she was safe."

"There's safe," said Brodie, "and there's being under twenty-four hour guard. Well, I can humour him for a day or two, but he needn't think I'm spending the rest of my life like this. No offence, Reg, but I'm not looking for a Siamese twin."

"None taken," said Vickers amiably. "Like you say, a few days may do it. The Super isn't pulling any punches: the station was humming like there'd been a murder when I left."

Which might have been a degree of overkill, but Brodie was secretly pleased that the campaign of terror against her – because that's what it was now, it may have started as mere harassment but now she was afraid – was being given priority. Even if it meant acceding to Deacon's arrangements for her safety.

But the afternoon hung heavy. With her paperwork up to date, all that was left was the phone. She began calling all the little shops along the coast, which first thing this morning she'd planned to visit. She negotiated a price on an embroidered Victorian nightdress for Mrs Pangbourn – sight unseen, but the shop-keeper did too much business with her to palm her off with rubbish – and persuaded another dealer to put a working model of what he insisted was called a Nodding Donkey under the counter until she could take a picture of it for Geoffrey Harcourt.

Then there was the matter of Miss Minniver's dog.

For seventeen years the constant companion of this unmarried lady of a certain age was a Jack Russell terrier called Maud. There was an album of photographs of the pair walking in the Lake District or cycling through the Yorkshire Dales, Miss Minniver in the saddle and Maud up front in the wicker basket. As they got older they took less strenuous holidays, painting and playing croquet. Finally there were snaps of them side by side in deck chairs or celebrating one another's birthdays with a cake.

Thirty-four cakes down the line, which is as much love as most human beings ever know, Maud died. Miss Minniver grieved, but in due course she saw that the greatest compliment she could pay her old friend was to find another dog to love.

This should not have been a difficult task. Miss Minniver could have gone into any rescue centre and changed the world for some unvalued scrap of canine misery. She could have approached a breeder and bought a dog whose pedigree was longer than her own. But Miss Minniver wanted another Maud – another little bitch who looked at you as if she knew what you were thinking, and didn't entirely approve but was willing to give you the benefit of the doubt because her Christian upbringing taught her that no soul is irredeemable.

Miss Minniver was not the crackpot that many people believed. She wanted help picking her next dog because she knew herself too well. If she started visiting kennels, the first dog that told her a hard-luck story would come home with her, whether it was a good choice or not. In her sixties now, Miss Minniver couldn't give a young dog the exercise it needed. She would be better with a mature animal that would settle on the sofa and watch TV with her. But she didn't want to be seduced into taking an old or ailing dog: this was likely to be her last pet, she didn't want to lose it in the next couple of years and have to tackle the whole business again.

So she'd spent an hour describing her ideal dog to Brodie, then left her to find it. Brodie was confident that when she turned up on the doorstep with a little bitch in her arms Miss Minniver would take it and look after it and love it until one of them died. With the power to make two people (using the term loosely) happy, Brodie took the brief as seriously as any other, even if Deacon thought the old duck was certifiable and Marta reckoned she should have had Maud stuffed.

Brodie liked Miss Minniver. Of course she was eccentric but she was a kind woman, and on the scale of human ambitions a little dog she could love as much as the last was little enough to ask. Brodie was happy to help. She compiled a list of rescue organisations along the south coast and phoned every few days, as she phoned about Mrs Pangbourn's linens and Mr Harcourt's models, in case anything suitable had come in.

Today she got lucky. Pet Rescue in Peyton Parvo, a small village nestling in the folds of Chain Down, had been asked to re-home a Jack Russell (probably) bitch whose owner had gone into care. He'd put it off as long as he could for the sake of the dog, but when he fell and broke his wrist his children put their collective foot down. Unfortunately, none of them was able to offer Dorothy a home.

"Dorothy?" echoed Brodie faintly. Dorothy Minniver – it had a certain ring...

"Dorothy," said the kennel-maid with a note of apology. "Not Dotty or Dolly. He was most insistent."

"How old is she?"

"Four. We've had the vet look at her – he says she's in lovely order."

Brodie wondered how to phrase the next question. "Don't put the phone down, I'm really not a dangerous lunatic, I'm just looking for a dog for someone who had a very special relationship with her last one. So tell me: how does Dorothy look at you?"

The girl at the other end giggled. "As if she's seen your end-of-term report and it was really rather disappointing."

"I'm on my way," said Brodie.

No one had said anything to Constable Vickers about jaunts in the country. He was fairly sure Detective Superintendent Deacon wanted Mrs Farrell to stay indoors. On the other hand, making someone stay indoors when they don't want to is false imprisonment. Brodie was happy for him to accompany her to Peyton Parvo. He could hold the dog on the way back.

Dorothy was everything Brodie had hoped: a little dog with a sweet but reserved nature and a face to soften hearts much tougher than Miss Minniver's. She phoned from the refuge to make sure that her client hadn't changed her mind, then the girl signed Dorothy over.

"We usually do the home inspection first," she said. "But if you're sure everything will be all right, we could call in a day or two."

"If Miss Minniver's home isn't good enough for Dorothy," said Brodie, "I shall move in with her myself."

The pleasure in Miss Minniver's face made Brodie forget the trials of the last week. That's a lucky little dog, she thought. And by God, next time someone makes fun of old ladies and their pets, I'm going to deck him.

It was early evening before they were back in Dimmock. "I'll drop you at the police station," Brodie told Vickers. "There's no point you walking back."

"Are you sure? I don't mind."

Brodie shook her head. "Jack'll be home when I get in. Listen: thanks. Will I see you tomorrow?"

"Me or someone."

"Try to make it you. We could go to look at a Nodding Donkey."

Vickers looked wary. "I'm not having that on my knee all the way home."

It was later than she'd expected, the last of the light fading from the western sky. She thought she'd find Deacon sitting at his kitchen table, drumming his fingers and pointedly checking his watch. But the house was empty. Even for the look of the thing Brodie couldn't pretend much surprise. He was never on time for anything. He'd not only be late for his own funeral, he'd probably try to fit in a couple of calls on the way.

She let herself in, nodded a greeting to the cat and went to check the fridge for the makings of supper.

The phone rang.

Chapter Eleven

Deacon was where he'd been for the last hour, mulling over the day's events with DS Voss and a mug of ale. In fact he'd kept his word and got away from the office at six o'clock. He just hadn't got any further than the public bar of The Belted Galloway.

In any town there are two kinds of pubs: those where the local villains hang out and those where the police drink. It's embarrassing to have to share. The Rose in Rye Lane was the preferred watering hole for Dimmock's criminal classes, and The Belted Galloway on Edgehill Road was where officers from the police station round the corner congregated. It was run by a farmer who'd sold his land for housing; hence the name. It used to be simply The Bull.

As soon as he'd seen Brodie settled in his house and despatched Vickers to join her, Deacon began putting together a task force. He half-expected having to fight Superintendent Fuller over this, to justify using police resources on what might have seemed like personal business, but the station's senior officer saw nothing personal about it. If a woman was being terrorised, her relationship with his head of CID was no reason to deny her help.

Anyway, it wasn't a fifty-strong murder squad Deacon wanted. In Dimmock, even murders didn't get a fifty-strong murder squad. It consisted of Constables Vickers and Batty, WPC Jill Meadows, Detective Constable David Winston, Sergeant Mills when he wasn't needed as

Scenes of Crime Officer elsewhere, and as much of his own and Voss's time as could be spared.

The advantage of a dedicated force, even a small one, is that its members aren't constantly being distracted by other matters. Also, because they can't ease their frustrations by wrapping up simpler cases, they try harder to carry this one forward. There are times when nothing seems to be happening except bored men and women glaring at one another across untidy desks. But that's when brains start firing in unexpected ways: when they're sufficiently desperate with the lack of progress along the usual avenues to break out and start forging new paths of their own.

It was too soon to expect a breakthrough. But Meadows was on the computer, cross-referencing, Deacon had largely dismissed a connection with Brodie's time in a solicitor's office, and Sergeant Mills had spent the afternoon at the library, inspecting every aspect of the lift mechanism and talking by phone to the manufacturer's chief engineer.

Between them they worked out more or less what had been done. The stalker had been in the roof-space. He'd wired in an ancillary panel to over-ride the on-board controls. When Brodie's plight was finally discovered he pulled out, tucked his equipment under his coat and left unnoticed via an emergency exit.

Sergeant Mills didn't think he'd got any useful fingerprints. He'd got prints – God knows he'd got prints, on every surface, vertical and horizontal, some so thickly caked in dust he didn't need to use powder. What he needed was a fresh set on the rear exit that matched a fresh set in the attic. He couldn't see someone who'd planned this so meticulously forgetting to put on his gloves, but Mills went through the motions anyway because you never know. If there was information to be had anywhere in the building he wanted to be sure he'd got it.

Forensics was a tool which Deacon used as he used anything that would serve him. It was not, so far as he was concerned, the core of detection. He liked having a suspect in front of him, and shouting until he got answers to his questions, and shouting some more if he didn't like those answers. Right now, though, he had no suspect. It made him even shorter-tempered than usual.

"She must know," he swore thickly into his ale. He'd been swearing at it more than drinking it. "She must."

"You think she's covering for someone?" Voss wasn't convinced. He'd seen Brodie this morning and had no doubt she was genuinely afraid.

Deacon shook his head. "I don't mean that. I think if she knew who was doing this she'd tell me." He went to take a gulp of his drink, changed his mind. It was as flat as cold washing-up water. "I mean, it has to be about something she was involved in. Maybe she's forgotten, maybe she never took it that seriously, but she has to know whoever's behind it."

"I'm sure she's tried to remember," said Voss reasonably.

Deacon scowled. "Well, yes and no. She thought of a handful of people it could be. Then she decided it couldn't be any of them. She wouldn't tell me who they were or why she suspected them because she considers that unprofessional. Then she thought of Daniel. Because if it's someone she gave grief to, he's the one with the best reason."

The best reason, perhaps; but a reason isn't the same as a motive. Voss considered a moment before answering. "Daniel wouldn't hurt Brodie if she'd nailed him to a barn."

"Of course it isn't Daniel," growled Deacon. "Daniel has enough trouble operating lifts from the inside. This is someone clever and vicious, and Daniel's clever enough but not that way. Plus, there isn't a mean streak in him."

Voss nodded pensively. "And this is mean – it's personal, and it's nasty. But I doubt we're dealing with a headcase. Brodie would know if she'd managed to upset a psychopath. You do – you always remember them. You know they're dangerous before they've done anything to make you think so."

"So he isn't mad, just very angry," mused Deacon. "Very bitter. You don't think upsetting someone that much would have made an impression on her too?"

"It may have been a long time ago," said Voss. "He may have been waiting for a chance."

"Maybe it was a while back," agreed Deacon. "But you anger someone enough that they really want to hurt you, you've got to remember doing it. It's not like she goes through life making vicious enemies – not the way I do."

Voss grinned. "This mightn't be any easier if it was you getting death threats but it would be more understandable."

Their eyes came together with an almost audible click, like billiard balls. For a moment neither man moved nor spoke. Each was turning the possibility in the privacy of his own brain, where he wouldn't make a fool of himself if he was wrong. But as the moments stacked up into minutes, they knew they were right.

Voss said carefully, "Maybe the reason she doesn't remember is that it wasn't her who upset him."

There was nothing particularly impressive about Charlie Voss, except his eyes which were more intelligent than you were ever quite ready for. Deacon stared into them as if he'd found the Holy Grail.

When he got his voice back he said thickly, "She was afraid someone had hurt Daniel to get at her. Charlie – what if someone's trying to hurt her to get at me?"

It was Paddy on the phone. She'd been crying. "I can't find Howard."

Brodie's heart swelled. Five is an ambivalent age. Sometimes she looked at her daughter and wondered at the changes that were shaping her, already a quarter of the way on her journey from dependent infant to woman. And sometimes she couldn't sleep unless she had a moth-eaten dragon to hug.

"I put him in your suitcase," said Brodie. "I remember. Have another look."

"I took him out," wailed Paddy. "I was checking he was there. And he was. So I sat him on the windowsill and checked everything else. Only, when I finished… "

"You forgot to put him back."

"Daddy says he'll go and get him," the child said hopefully, "if Marta will let him in."

"Marta isn't there," said Brodie. "Ask Daddy to pick the key up from me. He knows where I am."

"OK." Just before she rang off the child added, with the least possible note of censure: "I know where you are too."

When Deacon's doorbell rang ten minutes later Brodie checked the viewer. It was John. She joined him on the pavement, locking the door behind her. "I'll come with you. There are things I forgot as well."

It was strange to turn into the gravel drive of her own house and see no lights shining. On those rare occasions when neither she nor Marta was at home they always left a light to welcome them in. But the shrubbery by the gate drank up the glow of the street-lights and the house was only a blackness against the stars until the lights of John's car, turning in, made it familiar again.

Brodie opened the front door. "Are you coming in? I shan't be a minute."

John stayed in the car. "I'll get turned. Unless you want a hand?"

"No, I know what I'm looking for." She opened the door to her flat and switched on the lights.

First things first: she went into Paddy's room and found Howard where he'd been left, sitting disconsolately on the windowsill. "A proper dragon," she observed with gentle reproof, "would have flown across town in order to find his mistress." Howard's eyes were downcast and he mumbled something about pulling a flight muscle when he fell off the wardrobe. "Yeah, right," said Brodie, bundling him into a carrier-bag.

She went to her own room then and picked through the cosmetics for things she hadn't thought she'd need and then remembered what she looked like without. And another nightdress, and more underwear – so Deacon wouldn't have to shave in a mirror with her rinsed-through smalls dangling from it. And maybe –

The lights went out.

For a moment she thought it was just a bulb, tried to remember if she had a spare in the kitchen cupboard. But none of the lights she'd turned on was burning now. A power-cut? She made her way to the window. The houses opposite still had electricity: their lights twinkled through the trees between.

Which left a blown fuse. The fuse-box was in the hall, under the stairs which led to Marta's flat. She'd need the torch from the kitchen. And if it wasn't just a tripped switch she'd need a fuse. Well, she had some of those too, somewhere. And then she'd need –

Sometimes it's just plain stupid to keep making do with what you've got rather than fetch what you need. What she really needed was a man. She went out to the front steps. "John, can you give me a hand here?"

He made no reply. Nor had he turned the car, though he had turned off the headlights.

"John?"

The knowledge of something wrong – much more wrong than just a blown fuse – surged up the gravel drive and up the steps at her like a tidal bore. The sudden fear froze her from the spine out. "John?" she whispered – too softly if he was there, too loudly if someone else was.

Her eyes adjusting to the dark, Brodie started to see something beside the car, a dark shape on the pale gravel. It might have been a dropped coat. It might have been someone crouching there.

Though she did not consider herself courageous she faced most problems with that substitute for courage, self-respect: she knew she'd despise herself if she didn't. Occasionally, though, it wasn't enough. The survival instinct insisted it was better to look stupid and feel stupid and have to make abject apologies than to walk into a lions' den when you could hear them shaking out their napkins and rattling their cutlery.

This was one of those occasions. Not breathing, one step at a time, eyes all round her, she reversed until she was back in the black hall. Then she dived for her own front door, slamming it behind her, hearing the lock snap with profound relief.

She needed help, right now. Her phone was in her hand-bag, and her bag was – in the car. There was a land-line in the living-room. She groped for it in the crowding darkness.

She couldn't find it. It should have been on the dresser. It was always on the dresser, the dresser was beside the phone-point, it never got moved because if she wanted to call from somewhere else she used her mobile. Nonetheless, she couldn't find it.

The fuse could have been a fuse. The shadow on the

drive could have been a dropped coat. But if her phone had been moved, someone had been inside her house. And he could still be here.

Chapter Twelve

"Me." Deacon's voice was low. A taut thread of anger ran through it like a steel bar. "Somebody's after Brodie because of something I've done."

Voss was waiting for the explosion when the full meaning of that sank in. "It makes sense. If somebody wanted to hurt you – really wanted to hurt you, a black eye wouldn't do it – this would. Losing Brodie would be about the worst thing that could happen to you right now."

For a moment the big man stared at him as if it were Voss who was threatening him. Then he blinked, and passed a broad hand across his face, and lowered himself carefully onto his stool again. "So it was me who upset the psychopath."

"You've probably upset dozens," Voss said honestly. "Any copper who's been doing his job properly for a few years will have done. It's much more likely it was you who rattled his cage than Brodie."

"But – " Deacon was still trying to get his mind round it, tripping over the words. "If it's me he wants, why isn't it my head he's messing with? My car in a puddle of melted tarmac, me bouncing around in a runaway lift? If he hates me that much, why isn't he trying to kill me?"

"You're too big," said Voss, "he thought it would be easier to intimidate a woman. Which suggests he doesn't know Brodie very well at all, doesn't it? Look, he wants to make the most of this. He could run you down in his car but it would be over too soon. He wants you afraid – he wants to see you afraid. Threatening you wouldn't achieve that: you'd get mad before you got scared. And when you worked it out you'd take him apart.

"If he goes after Brodie, he has the pleasure of seeing you suffer without the risk that you'll put the pieces together quick enough to stop him. This isn't someone who hates her, chief, it's someone who hates you. With a passion, and for a long time."

"A long time?" echoed Deacon weakly.

"It isn't about something recent. It's too organised – a lot of thought's gone into it. He's been waiting, and he's spent the time planning." Voss's gaze dipped, and then came up again bravely. "I think what he's been waiting for is for you to have something to lose."

Deacon was too stunned to follow him. "Huh?"

"He couldn't have done this twelve months ago. Well, he could, but there's a limit to how much you can hurt a grown man by threatening his cat. He wanted to see you suffer. He was willing to wait, for years if necessary, until you had someone you felt that strongly about. Someone whose life mattered to you more than your own."

The gears of Deacon's brain were turning now, the engine coming into train. It was a slower process than Voss's mental gymnastics but when it got going there was no power on earth capable of halting it. "He's going to kill her."

"Yes," said Voss simply. "First he frightens her, then he frightens you. He gets you worried enough to put yourself on the line – physically, professionally, emotionally – in order to protect her. And then he kills her. He doesn't need to lay a finger on you, and risk you ripping him limb from limb. He just keeps sidestepping you until he can get at Brodie, because killing her when she trusts you to protect her is the worst pain he could inflict on you."

Deacon's features usually looked as if they were carved from granite. Right now, Voss thought with pity, he looked to be made of pumice, grey and crumbling. His eyes were hollows that went all the way down to his heart.

"Brodie?" Deacon's voice stumbled as if he had not until that moment believed in the threat facing her. "Charlie – I can't lose her!"

Voss nodded, preserving his own calm because Deacon needed him to, needed an anchor to lie to while his own warps pinged and parted under the strain. "We won't let that happen. Knowing is all the edge we need to prevent it."

"Yes." Deacon nodded too, rapidly, almost like a tic. "We'll stop him. We have to stop him. Who?"

"We'll find him," promised Voss. "Now we know how to look, we'll find him." Compassion tied a knot in his throat. Most of Deacon's colleagues, including men who'd known him for longer, would have been astonished at the transformation wrought in him by this turn of events. They thought him a hard and heartless man. Voss wasn't astonished, but he was desperately sorry for Deacon. Whoever purposed his destruction had known exactly where his heart was and how to break it. "Chief – we'll find him."

Shock held Deacon in its rigid embrace for another

minute. Then a sense of urgency overtook him. He pushed himself to his feet – clumsily, as if he couldn't feel the floor – and stumbled towards the door. "I've got to get home," he muttered thickly.

The Belted Galloway was Dimmock's coppers' pub: as he pushed out through the door Reg Vickers was pushing in. Their eyes met, glanced apart, then came back with the force of mutual alarm like elastic. They said the same words on the same beat, like choral speakers.

"What are you doing here?"

It's a long time since human beings have featured prominently on anyone's menu. Millennia. So it's racial memory that ensures that not only little furry things whose destiny is to end as a brief, shrill cry in the night, but also people with the mental capacity to harness the speed of sound and the power of the atom know how to stay alive when they're being hunted. You freeze so neither sound nor movement betrays your position. You breathe through your mouth, which is quieter than breathing through your nose and doesn't interfere with your own hearing. You put something solid at your back.

All these things Brodie did on purest instinct. It was coded into her DNA that, when your very life is at stake, you do anything that might improve the odds however slightly. So she flattened her body against the wall, and breathed through her mouth, and listened until a dropped pin would have echoed in her brain like timpani. Until she'd have heard a soft step on carpet on the other side of a closed door.

And she did.

He was in her bedroom. All right, that was not nice but not the worst. He wasn't between her and the way out. If she could do it quietly she could let herself into the hall and then outside, and if he heard her footsteps on the gravel it really wouldn't matter because she'd be going like stink by then. Any of the neighbours would take her and John in until help arrived. If she could just get out of the house.

The risk was that she would make enough noise opening her own front door to alert him. When she'd seen that shapeless shadow on the gravel she'd retreated in here too quickly to shut the outside door, let alone lock it: once in the hall there would be nothing to impede her. But if she could shut both doors behind her as she went she could slow his pursuit significantly. She opened and shut those doors several times each day, she could do it in her sleep, but could she do it when she was being hunted? If she fumbled or made too much noise he'd be on her. She needed to be ready: to plan every move so nothing would delay her from the moment she began her run until she was out on Chiffney Road screaming for help.

Another soft footfall on the bedroom carpet. Closer: he was at the door. Making his own move, coming for her. No more time to plan: if she wasn't foot-perfect now she'd have to wing it. One good breath to free up her locked limbs and push oxygen out to her muscles, then –

She was on her way. Heedless of the noise now she tore open the door of her flat and slammed it behind her, hearing the latch snap shut. She crossed the tiled hall in a couple of long-legged strides and reached the massive Victorian door, groping as she went for the big brass knocker. She couldn't find it. She handled the thing every day, how could she not find it? She was blind, not stupid!

An instant before she decided to leave it and run, her shaking fingers stubbed against the lion's mask, fastened on the ring through his mouth. She tugged the door on its heavy hinges and heard it shut and lock behind her, gaining her valuable seconds. Ahead, with nothing between, lay the safety of the road. The glow of the street-lamps fell on her light-starved eyes like searchlights, dazzling.

Searchlights mounted on a watchtower, five metre walls topped with razor-wire and a shout of "Halt or I release the alligator" wouldn't have stopped her then. She flew the steps two at a time, touched down on gravel, and dropping into a protective crouch put every ounce of fear and determination into increasing the distance between her and her pursuer.

She'd have done it, too. With a head start and a gen-uine terror of what was behind her, a whippet on steroids wouldn't have caught her. But when she swung round the bonnet of the car with one hand on the wing-mirror and the other ready to snatch John out of his seat, she saw what the shadow on the gravel was. It was a man's body, and there was really only one man it could be.

Time divided. The same seconds both raced, because of the urgency of her situation, the certainty that delay meant disaster, and stretched – dilated – opened like an iris to make room for some oddly coherent thoughts. One was that John might be dead but he might not: there wasn't enough light or leisure to make sure. One was that he was only here because of the danger to her, and though he'd proved an inept bodyguard, just trying earned him better than to be abandoned in his own need. One was that help was only fifty or sixty metres away, she could rouse the street in a minute and have four or five strong men here in the next. And the last was that two minutes was too long to leave a defenceless man at the mercy of a maniac.

She pulled up beside the car, scattering gravel like hail-stones, and spun back to face the house. She crouched over the inert body of the man who had once meant more to her than anything in the world and prepared to face whatever was coming in order to save him further harm. She thought she just might die here. She didn't feel to have any choice.

The front door opened – not with a bang, not even with much haste, just swung quietly inward on its heavy Victorian hinges – and a man was standing at the top of the steps. She couldn't see his face. She couldn't see if he was armed. All she could see was an outline that moved as a man moves, that stood at the top of the steps looking down at her. She couldn't see the eyes and so could not guess what motive burned in them.

For what seemed an interminable time they remained connected by line-of-sight, as if it had a physical existence, like six metres of fishing-line. Brodie had the oddest conviction that if she moved towards the man on the steps he'd back away to keep the tension on the rod.

Finally he said, "Brodie? Are you all right?"

And she said, "Daniel?"

Chapter Thirteen

John's car was comparatively new, Brodie had never driven it. She fumbled along the dashboard. When the lights came on they pinned him to the front of the house like a butterfly on a board. Or something less exotic than a butterfly: a moth perhaps. There was nothing flamboyant about Daniel Hood, unless it was his bright hair. He had a nice smile. Brodie had always thought he had a kind face. But then, she'd always thought he was her friend.

He put a hand up to shield his eyes from the glare. They were pale grey and not strong: Boy Scouts using his glasses to concentrate the sun's rays could have devastated whole forests. "Brodie? Is that you? What's going on?"

Spot-lit on top of the steps he loomed bigger than she remembered. As he came forward, still shading his face, he diminished step by step. He was smaller than her, and unless it was the stubborn strength of intellectual pride that occasionally kindled within him there was nothing dangerous about him. Nothing alarming; nothing she had ever felt afraid of. Until now.

Now there was light she risked a fast look down at the man at her feet. He wasn't moving and there was a wetness in his hair. She looked back at Daniel. Her taut body was bent like a bow over the injured man and her voice throbbed with anger. "You bastard! What have you done?"

Only then did Daniel seem to notice the body on the gravel. He took another step forward, staring. His light eyes quartered Brodie's face with every appearance of concern. "Who is that? John? Brodie, what's happened – what's going on?"

They had known one another for almost a year. She'd seen him in pain, in terror, in tears. He'd seen her tender, abject, joyful, and angry enough to spill blood in defence of those she cared for. He had never seen her afraid of him.

She wasn't sure what she was expecting. But when he didn't produce a blunt instrument and set about finishing what he'd started, slowly she straightened up. "I'm going to call an ambulance. And Jack. If you want to leave, now's a good time."

He flinched as if she'd clawed his face. He looked at John again and back, disbelieving. "You think I did this?"

She barked a bitter little laugh. "I know I hurt you, Daniel. I always knew there was no way to make amends. But this is...unforgivable. When Jack gets his hands on you..."

She shuddered. It had pained her that the two men she cared about could find no common ground. She'd defended each to the other until she was tired doing it. She'd lost sleep worrying what would happen when they finally clashed over something neither was prepared to yield on. Now she was worried again. But not about what Deacon's big fists would do to Daniel's slight frame, only how they might damage his own career.

"Brodie!" Daniel's voice cracked like a heart breaking.

She made the calls without taking her eyes off him. Then she squared her shoulders. There was no mildness in her eyes or her manner, no dilution of the acid in her tone. "All right, if you've got an explanation let's hear it. Why you were missing all the time someone was terrorising me. Why you didn't return my messages, let me think you were lying dead in a ditch somewhere. Now I've been put out of my home, and when I come back for a few things someone hits John, follows me inside and kills the lights. And when I beat him to the front door, who should come down the steps behind me but you? Only it wasn't you doing any of that, was it? You're going to tell me it was all a coincidence."

"Terrorising you?" His eyes were full of concern. "Are you hurt?"

"No. But I could have been. And John ... " She looked at him, tears pricking her eyes.

"Let me see." Daniel dropped on one knee beside the injured man.

Brodie's breast swelled and her fists knotted at her sides. "Don't you lay a finger on him, do you hear?"

He didn't look at her. Carefully he eased the unconscious man into the recovery position, half on his side. He parted John's hair with cautious fingers, revealing a gash above his right ear. He wadded his handkerchief firmly against the wound. Finally he looked up. "Or what?"

In that moment Brodie knew she'd got it wrong. Regardless of how it looked, or how the facts stacked up against him, or the things she could hardly explain any other way. Now he was in front of her, and his eyes were his own, not a stranger's twisted by hurt and history,

Brodie knew that if coincidence was the only explanation he could offer she would believe him.

She let go her pent-up breath in a long unsteady sigh. "I'm sorry. But you can't imagine what it's been like this last week. I've had my car torched, I've had my handbag stolen, and this morning I went to meet ... someone ... at the library and the lift turned into a cut-price version of Alton Towers. Now this. But I'm sorry. I didn't want to think it was you. It was only as I got really scared that I started to wonder."

Daniel's cheek was chalky in the headlights' glare. "You've moved out? Where are you living? Where's Marta?" She told him. "Did anyone know you were coming back here?"

"John." She looked down at him. "But that doesn't look like a self-inflicted injury."

"Plus, John would never harm you."

"I know."

"Neither would I."

"Daniel, I know that too." She reached out a tentative hand to his narrow wrist. It was, she realised with a shock, the first time she'd touched him in two months. "I've been so scared I'm not making sense any more. I thought I must have hurt someone terribly to provoke this, and the only one I could think of was you. And I couldn't find you. If we'd only been able to talk! Then you turn up here. I'm not making excuses. It's just, my head's a mess, nothing sensible's coming out of it. But I'm sorry I hurt you again."

A tiny smile flickered across his unremarkable face.

"We'll sort it out. Brodie, who did you go to meet at the library?"

"You," she said simply.

"Ah." He thought for a moment. "I don't know who you were talking to, but it wasn't me."

"I know," said Brodie. "It was a message on my machine. I thought it was you because I wanted it to be."

Help arrived in a chorus of sirens. Deacon's car beat the ambulance by so narrow a margin he must have been racing it. In an instant the drive was full of people. The paramedics took care of John, who was trying to sit up by now. Not wanting Brodie in the open, Deacon took her back into the house. Daniel followed.

Brodie recounted the sequence of events. Voss went to the fuse-box. The main switch had been tripped: when he thumbed it down again the lights came back on.

Deacon turned to Daniel. "So what are you doing here?"

"Looking for Brodie. I didn't know she'd moved out."

"But it wasn't you tripped the power?"

"Of course not."

"Was it on or off when you arrived?"

"Off. I tried the light in the hall but nothing happened."

"The front door was open?" asked Deacon.

"I left it open," admitted Brodie. "I was only going to be a moment, and John was outside, and both flats have their own doors anyway ... " It still sounded pretty stupid.

Deacon scowled at her but forbore to comment. To Daniel he said, "Go on."

"I knew there was someone home – there was a car outside. But not Brodie's, so I assumed she was out and Marta had a pupil. I was heading upstairs to ask when Brodie would be back when all hell broke loose. Doors were banging, people were running – I'd no idea what was going on. I came back downstairs – I think I called out – and someone passed me in the hall. I couldn't see who."

"Me," suggested Brodie. "High-tailing it for the front door."

Daniel shook his head. "Whoever it was went the other way."

"Other way?" frowned Deacon.

"The back door," Brodie guessed. "Through the scullery. We don't really use it. It's not in either of the flats, and I have a back door off my kitchen."

"Did you lock it when you shut up the house?"

"I checked that it was locked," said Brodie. "But it always is."

"Was the key in it?"

She nodded.

Charlie Voss reappeared from behind the stairs. "Well, it's open now."

"So that's how he got out." Deacon looked at Daniel. "Can you describe him?"

Daniel gave an apologetic shrug. "It was dark. I wasn't sure it was a man."

Brodie listened attentively as Deacon put it together. "Probably he was watching my place when John picked you up. He followed you here and waited till you went into your flat, then he decked John and followed you into the house. He found the fuse-box and tripped the switch. He knew you'd come out to check it – when you did he slipped past you into the flat.

"At which point Daniel turned up. He walked up the drive – on the other side of the car so he never saw John – and through the open door into the hall. By then both you and the man were in your flat, and you were planning your escape. Daniel headed upstairs, you made a break for it, the man followed. But when Daniel called out he thought he couldn't deal with both of you and turned the other way, making for the back door."

"He knew about the back door?" asked Brodie faintly.

"Probably. I think he was here before, at least close enough to peer through the windows. He knew where the fuse-box is and where you keep your phone. He found the back door, and everybody knows the back door key is always kept in the lock."

"Who?" demanded Daniel. "Who are you talking about?"

"I told you," said Brodie, subdued. "Someone who hates me."

"Actually, no," said Deacon. He sat heavily on the stairs. "Someone who hates me."

She stared at him until he winced. "What?"

For a week Brodie had believed she was in danger because of something stupid or unkind or just unfortunate that she'd done in the past. Now Deacon was telling her it was because of something he'd done. She went on staring at him, unable to decide if that made it better or worse.

Daniel regarded Deacon through the top edge of his glasses. "Two thoughts. Are we safe discussing it here? I mean, if he came here to hurt Brodie, shouldn't somebody check the house? For" – he shrugged – "explosives, gas leaks, booby-traps – I don't know?"

"Jesus!" Deacon shot to his feet, herding them towards the door. "He's right. Charlie, get them out of here – take them back to my place. I'll have a look round."

Voss didn't often contradict his superintendent directly, but there wasn't time to be tactful. "Better still, you take them and I'll have a look round. We know he was here ten minutes ago – we don't know how far he ran. You shouldn't stay here on your own. Offer him too tempting a target and he might take a crack at it."

Deacon opened his mouth to refuse, then thought about it. "All right. But be careful. If there's a gas leak, don't light a match to see how bad."

Voss grinned.

On the way to the car Daniel voiced his second thought. "And shouldn't we do something about John? Follow him to the hospital maybe? Tell his wife?"

Brodie rolled her eyes. "Of course we should. Jack, take us to John's house. Daniel and I will stay with Paddy, you take Julia to the hospital."

It was surreal to return to a house where she had been a young wife, where she'd lived for five years, where for the last two her ex-husband had lived with someone else. It felt both familiar and very strange.

Paddy was asleep upstairs. Brodie didn't wake her. She

went into the kitchen to put the kettle on and was surprised when it wasn't her kettle.

Daniel stood in the doorway. "If I'd known about any of this ... "

"I know," she said. But actually it wasn't enough. She turned to face him. "Why didn't you call me? You got my message days ago. You must have known I'd be worried."

"I guessed. I had some thinking to do. I didn't want you changing my mind before I could even make it up."

"You put your house up for sale," said Brodie, her voice low and accusing.

"Yes. I thought I had to get away."

"Do you still think that?"

He didn't answer directly. "I'm going nowhere until you're all right."

Brodie appreciated that. Not because she felt safer with Daniel around – as a bodyguard he was about as much use as Dorothy Minniver – but because she felt better. Stronger and calmer. At least she didn't have to worry about him any more.

She frowned. "What do you mean, you didn't want me changing your mind?"

His eyes dipped. "Well – you do, don't you? Your idea of a discussion is convincing everyone else that you're right. I envy you – I wish I was more decisive. I'm always afraid I may have overlooked something."

"That's because you're nice," said Brodie dismissively, "and worry how your actions will affect other people. I have no trouble making decisions because I'm selfish and don't worry much beyond pleasing myself."

It was an over-simplification. That's not to say she was wrong.

She said, "I saw Simon."

Daniel's face went still. But as she watched Brodie saw the shadows of expressions flitting through his eyes. Finally he said, "I didn't know you knew about Simon."

"I didn't until I found him. Don't look so shocked," she said tartly, "this is what I do for a living."

"What did you talk about?"

"You, of course!" she snapped, exasperated. Then, more circumspectly, "You ought to call him. I was worried sick when we spoke, I may have left him with the impression that...well, that you were putting your affairs in order."

He just went on looking at her for a minute. Then, without a word, he got up and went looking for the phone.

"All right," he said when he came back to the kitchen. "Now you know that the Hood family history is half Greek tragedy, half Whitehall farce. Where does it get you?"

She sat facing him, the coffee on the table between them. "I didn't mean to pry. I was afraid something had happened to you. I kept digging because I couldn't understand your brother's attitude."

Daniel shrugged tiredly. "You were expecting normal behaviour from a Hood: of course you were disappointed. We're emotional cripples, the lot of us."

But she wouldn't have that. "Daniel, you're the kindest man I know. I'm sorry about...about your mother, but somehow all that managed to produce a son most women would kill for. A man with the strength to be gentle and the courage to do what's right rather than what's easy. Don't underestimate yourself, Daniel, you're a class act. Why do you suppose I was combing the country for you?"

"And in spite of that," he said, very softly, "you thought I meant to hurt you."

She couldn't apologise for that, could only try to explain. "I was scared and desperate. I was stupid. Are you going to hold it against me for the rest of my life?"

The ghost of a smile touched his lips and he shook his head. "We probably have enough obstacles to surmount without piling another one on top."

Brodie regarded him levelly through the steam curling from the mugs. "No, we haven't. Not from where I'm sitting. Daniel, when I thought I wasn't going to see you again, I couldn't believe how much I'd lost over how little. I'm sorry I handled that so badly. Dead or alive, the Daws girls weren't worth sacrificing our friendship over. If that's what I've done, if you can't forgive me, I won't try to change your mind" – she flicked him a sad little smile in return – "but I will regret it as long as I live."

Daniel didn't answer at once. Brodie told herself this was a good sign. It was who he was: he thought about everything, tried to get things right. Brodie hurt people she cared about with smart remarks she was clever enough to think of and too stupid to hold back, but Daniel never did. He never said anything he wasn't prepared to stand over. And when he did take a stand, dynamite wouldn't shift him. Not in one piece.

At length he said pensively, "I didn't tell you about my family not because I'm embarrassed but because it's complicated, and there seemed no point. You can't start afresh if you're going to take your ghosts with you. But we're all products of our history – who I am was shaped before I was born by who my mother was, what she wanted, and how much. With another family I might have been another man. I might be married now, have children, a steady job. You and I might never have met."

He looked at her then, both strong and defenceless in the candour of his gaze. "What I'm trying to say is, I don't wish I was that other man. There have been things in my life I'd wish undone, but not many. Even... " His eyes flicked down his shirt front where the scars lay pale and shiny beneath. "Of course I wish that hadn't happened, those were the worst hours of my life. But you can't take things in isolation, and from that came you. You and Paddy and Marta: people I cared about who cared about me. Maybe it doesn't sound much, but it made me happy."

He swallowed. "And I thought it was over. I thought we'd reached a point where we could only hurt one another the more we tried. I thought it was best to walk away before we ripped each other's hearts out. I still thought that an hour ago when I went to your house. I wanted to tell you to your face – it seemed the honest way."

A tear spilled down Brodie's cheek and met the long-fingered hand cupped across her mouth. She ignored it. "Is that still what you want?"

Daniel didn't answer. "When I went to see Simon I

was thinking of going back to Nottingham. I thought I was done here. I thought if I went back, maybe I could pick up the threads where they were still intact. I went to see my old school."

She waited, her heart split in two. What she wanted for him and what she wanted for herself. If he could return to a time and place before he was damaged, where the horror that changed him had yet to cast its shadow, she would lose him. She knew she ought to want that. She cared enough about him to hope there was a way back, but the cost to herself would be high. She would pay it to see him whole again; but maybe it wasn't wicked to hope she wouldn't have to.

He saw the dilemma in her eyes, shook his head again. "I only got as far as the gates. I stood there for an hour – I'm sure they took me for a pervert. But I couldn't go inside. By the time I saw Simon I knew I'd made a mistake. We made small-talk for an hour, he bought me lunch, he took me back to the station.

"I didn't have a return ticket. I looked to see where the trains were going. I ended up in Penzance. I had a holiday there once, it seemed easier going somewhere I knew. All I really wanted was somewhere to be quiet and think for a few days. You see, I'd thought I was going back. And now I knew I couldn't, and I had no idea what to do instead."

He sighed. "Maybe you never can go back. Not because the past is different but because you are. Events change you, you no longer fit the slot you left. There was nothing for me in Nottingham. I could no more teach there than here, and my family...well. Let's say I embarrass them more than they embarrass me. The past is another country. And it's got my face plastered up at all the airports, and it won't take me in even as a refugee." He smiled, piercing her heart.

"You're talking as if you don't belong anywhere," said Brodie softly. "You do. You belong here, now. You don't have to go anywhere. Dimmock's a small town but it's big enough for two people, even two people who'd rather not meet. If you want me out of your life, I'll go. But I'd a hundred times rather think you're knocking around nearby than not know where you are.

"Don't do something you're going to regret. If you still want to leave in a month's time you can sell the house then, but if you sell now it'll be too late to change your mind. Keep your options open till you're sure."

Daniel nodded gravely, went on watching her. Brodie couldn't read what was in his eyes. "You thought I might kill myself?"

"I... " She shook her head. "Daniel, I didn't know. It sounded like you were tying up loose ends. I was afraid. You should have called me."

"Yes. I'm sorry, that was cowardly." It was as strong a censure as his vocabulary ran to. He thought cowardice was a mortal sin. If she'd considered it calmly she'd have known he'd feel the same way about suicide.

After a long time in which they just sat in silence, sipping coffee and healing, Brodie said quietly, "I keep wondering how you feel about her."

Daniel didn't understand. "About who?"

"Your sister. Samantha? Do you feel you had a twin sister? Or does it feel like it was nothing to do with you?"

It was hard to interpret his gaze. She didn't think he resented the question. He said, "I don't think anyone's asked me that before."

Brodie believed him. "Who in your family could risk doing so? They didn't dare ask the question for fear what the answer would be. Damage limitation must have taken all the energy anyone had to spare."

Something in Daniel's eyes seemed to say that, however imperfectly she understood him, she still did it better than anyone else. "You mustn't think I had a miserable childhood. I didn't. I loved my grandparents, and there was a lot of laughter in our house. I didn't even realise how weird it all was until I was eight years old. I didn't know about Samantha until then. I didn't know she ever existed, let alone that people blamed me for her death.

"How do I feel about her? Like I've lost something and I can't quite remember what. I feel very slightly incomplete."

Chapter Fourteen

By the time Deacon located him, John Farrell was sitting on a hospital trolley with a dazed expression and five stitches in his scalp. The x-ray showed no fracture: A&E wanted to keep an eye on him overnight but expected he'd be going home in the morning.

The man was still too shaken to give a statement. But Deacon wanted the essence of what he knew while the events were fresh and the perpetrator might still be close enough to find. "Tell me what you remember."

He'd watched Brodie go up the front steps and seen the lights come on. He'd been about to turn the car when someone tapped on his window.

"Did you see who?"

"A man," said Farrell. "I couldn't see his face, just the shape of him standing by the car. I thought it was you."

"Me?" frowned Deacon.

"The police. No one else had any reason to be there."

"I didn't leave anyone on watch." Deacon regretted that now.

"I realised my mistake," said Farrell gently, "when I got out to speak to him and he floored me. Jack, is Brodie all right?"

Deacon nodded. "She's fine. She's at your house, with Paddy. Daniel's there too."

"Daniel?" Farrell wasn't expecting that.

"He turned up at Brodie's place while all this was going on. I think that's what scared the intruder away. He thought, when he'd dealt with you, he'd got Brodie on her own. He couldn't handle two people at once."

Farrell breathed steadily for a moment, absorbing the information. "I'm sorry, Jack. I thought she was safe while I was watching the house."

"It's not your fault," said Deacon – which was something of a first: he was a great distributor of blame normally. "It's not your job to protect her, it's mine. I'm sorry you got hurt."

"Are you any the wiser as to who it was?"

Deacon shook his head. "Unless he introduced himself before hitting you."

"'Fraid not," said Farrell.

"You didn't see his face?"

"Just stars."

Julia elected to stay at the hospital with him. She asked Deacon to put her house at Brodie's disposal. He found himself warming to the second Mrs Farrell. Until now he hadn't begun to understood what Farrell saw in her, but now he did. She might wear gathered skirts and the last twin-set in England, but there was a fundamental kindness to her that was rare enough to be noticed. She wasn't a bit like Brodie. Oddly enough, she did remind him of Daniel.

First Deacon swung by the house in Chiffney Road. Voss had found nothing alarming. Sergeant Mills was once more dusting for prints in the near certainty that he would find nothing helpful. Which meant doing it the hard way: hunting through the files for someone who might bear Deacon this much enmity and had the nous to do what was done.

"An electrical engineer," suggested Voss.

Deacon's unlovely face was downright grotesque when screwed in thought. "Not necessarily. There are all sorts of applications for electronics – you don't have to be a pro to know about printed circuits. People strip systems down and rebuild them for fun. Lego was cutting edge technology when I was a kid: these days ten-year-olds build robots. If you could do that, or wire up a radio-controlled plane, or put a computer together from a box of parts, you could probably hijack a lift."

"So it's a paper-chase after all. Can I help?"

Deacon squinted along his nose at his sergeant. It was a generous offer – there's not much pleasure to be had trawling through ten years' worth of files – that shouldn't have been taken advantage of. On the other hand, there's no point being a superintendent if you can't take advantage of sergeants. "Indeed you can, Charlie Voss. I'll go so far as to say I couldn't do it without you."

Voss was easy to get on with, easy to like, but he was nobody's fool. The eyes narrowed either side of his freckled nose. "You're going to make me do it all, aren't you?"

"I am, Charlie," Deacon nodded, unabashed. "You should always play to a man's strengths. You are a swot and know how to operate the computer. I, on the other hand, have a natural talent for bullying people."

Deacon had gone through a number of sergeants in a short space of time before DS Voss arrived. Although he hadn't liked any of the earlier ones, his heart sank. Voss was twenty years his junior, which is a big gap between two men working this closely. Deacon took an immediate dislike to his ginger hair, to the fact that he looked smarter in casual clothes than Deacon did in smart ones, and to his open, attentive expression as if he'd have listened to Deacon even if he wasn't being paid to.

It was only as time passed that he realised Voss really did want to learn from him. It wasn't flattery: he'd listen as long as Deacon would talk. With any encouragement he would talk back, and Deacon was disconcerted to find that his thinking was pretty smart too. Deacon started to appreciate his sergeant at the point at which most senior officers would have become suspicious of him.

Now they enjoyed a relationship that crossed the boundaries of rank without challenging them. Voss knew he could still learn a lot from Deacon; Deacon suspected that he'd learned a certain amount from Voss. He also suspected that Voss knew him better than anyone else, including Brodie. Voss was the only officer in Battle Alley – not excluding Superintendent Fuller – who knew that sometimes Deacon was just being himself, but sometimes he was being a satire on himself. Why this amused him Voss wasn't sure, but he knew it did.

Voss lowered a sandy eyebrow and committed an act of unprovoked grammar. "Bullying whom?"

Deacon smiled nastily. "Oh, I never have much trouble finding someone."

This was pure evasion: he knew exactly who he wanted to talk to. He drove up onto the Firestone Cliffs and stopped in front of Terry Walsh's wrought iron gates.

They were high and wide, heavily ornamented, but the main thing about them was that they were locked. They weren't actually there to look expensive: they were there to keep people out. Deacon didn't believe honest people needed that much security. He thumbed the intercom and, when a woman's voice asked him to identify himself, just thumbed harder.

She was a Scot, probably the housekeeper. She said with asperity, "If you keep that up much longer, young man, I'll call the police."

"Good idea," snarled the visitor. "Ask them to send Detective Superintendent Deacon."

There was a chuckle at the other end and a man's voice cut in. "Is that you, Jack? Come on up. Just give me a minute to put the good spoons away."

Terry Walsh wasn't exactly a skeleton in Deacon's cupboard. They'd been friends growing up in the East End of London, then they'd gone their separate ways. The next time they met Deacon was a Detective Inspector at Dimmock CID and Walsh was moving into his new cliff top property: seven bedrooms, four reception rooms, three bathrooms, snooker room, jacuzzi, triple garage, hot and cold running housemaids. Deacon knew there was no lawful way he could have made it that big. More than that: he knew there was no lawful way of making it small that would appeal to Walsh. But the man had thus far managed to elude criminal charges. As far as anyone could prove he turned Norwegian trees into paper for a living. Deacon had heard him referred to as the Teflon Cockney. He suspected Walsh coined the nickname himself.

Walsh took the policeman into the garden room on

the south side of the house. In daylight it commanded an extensive view of the Channel; at night the inky blackness was punctuated by the navigation lights of ships. He was proud of his house, got considerable pleasure from his ill-gotten gains; got as much pleasure from knowing that Deacon knew they were ill-gotten and couldn't prove it.

He pressed a drink into Deacon's hand. "What can I do for you, Jack?"

Proof or none, Deacon didn't make a habit of drinking with criminals. This was an exception. "Somebody's having a go at me, Terry. It's personal – he's hurt my lady. Tonight he was in her house. Someone happened by and scared him off, but he'll be back. I think he'll keep coming until either I catch him or he kills her. And I don't know who he is. Have you heard anything? Anything that would give me an idea where to start looking."

It took a lot to startle Terry Walsh but that did it. Deacon wouldn't have asked him to fill a bucket if he was on fire. But there was a lady involved. Jack Deacon had a lady he cared about enough to abase himself before a man he despised. Deacon. It was like finding Mother Teresa had a toy boy.

All his instincts were to laugh out loud. Deacon expected him to laugh. He hadn't come here until he'd run all the likely scenarios through his head and decided he could live with them, and all of them involved being laughed at.

But actually, Walsh wasn't amused. He was a family man – Deacon's predicament ceased to be humorous the moment he put himself in the policeman's shoes. He'd upset at least as many men as Deacon in the course of his own career, and a lot of them were vicious too. Any of them could have targeted his wife or daughter to pay him back. Despite the security, any of them could have broken into this house and terrorised his womenfolk when he wasn't here. There was no funny side to it, even if it was Jack Deacon.

"Is she all right?" he asked.

Deacon blinked. He'd been ready for jokes – he hadn't expected honest concern. "A few bumps and bruises, and she's scared, but so far she's been lucky. But I don't know how long I can keep her safe. I need to find him. Find him and stop him."

"And you've no idea who?"

"Terry," sighed Deacon, "if I had, do you really think I'd have come cap in hand to you?"

"No," said Walsh quietly. "Well, I haven't heard a thing. But I will try to find out. I don't move in those circles myself" – there was the faintest hint of a smile in the man's voice – "but I have a wide acquaintance, I'll find someone who does. If there are people in this town who know what's going on, I'll find one for you."

Deacon was not a gracious man. Even in normal circumstances he found it difficult to say please and thank you, and getting him to apologise was like drawing teeth. This was harder still. He believed Walsh would help him if he could, and he should be grateful for the favour. But he also knew, even if the Old Bailey had yet to be convinced, that Walsh was a villain and would use his criminal contacts to get the information. It was the only way, and the only reason Deacon was here. Thanking him for that was almost like profiting from his crimes. Deacon might be driven to doing it, but he didn't have to like it and he wasn't about to acknowledge it.

He said gruffly, "You'll call me?"

"As soon as I've something to report. Till then, be careful. This isn't how pros operate, you know that. It's the work of a crank. And cranks are dangerous because they're unpredictable and sometimes they have nothing to lose."

"Find me the bastard who's doing this and I'll show you unpredictable!" Deacon left with a bad taste in his mouth that, if he'd had more experience of it, he'd have recognised as humiliation.

He meant to tell no one, not even Brodie, but in the end he told Voss. It was partly pragmatic – if Walsh called when Deacon was unavailable he'd be put through to the sergeant – but also because he wanted to see Voss's reaction. He knew what he'd done bordered on unprofessional. He knew it could backfire and leave him with difficult questions to answer. He also knew, from a career way marked with difficult questions, that he'd find answers that would do. What he wasn't sure about, what he wanted Voss's opinion on, was whether he was making a terrible mistake.

Voss heard him out in silence. If that had been Brodie it would have been a bad sign but Voss was polite: he might just have been waiting for Deacon to finish.

When he had, and Deacon lifted one eyebrow to invite comment, still Voss held his tongue. Deacon hoped he was thinking, was afraid he was thunderstruck. At last Voss said quietly, "If this pays off, you'll have put yourself in debt to a crook."

Deacon nodded. "Yes."

"You're sure you want to do that?"

Deacon blew out his cheeks explosively. "Of course I don't! But I don't want to have to identify the contents of a body-bag either. Brodie's life's at stake: I can't afford to play by the rules if that means losing."

Voss understood. "I'm not saying you're wrong, I just want to be sure you've considered all the implications."

"I have."

"Including Walsh's price?"

Deacon cast him a hunted look. "He didn't ask for anything."

Voss bit his lip and kept his voice low. "That doesn't mean he won't want something sometime. There's always a price. You know that."

And Deacon did. He looked away. "Then I'll pay it. Whatever it is."

Chapter Fifteen

They slept in Julia's chairs. Brodie could not face the extreme weirdness of sleeping in either Julia's bed or the spare room of the house where she had been mistress. She toyed with the idea of squeezing in beside Paddy, but it was a child's bed and very small compared to the very large chairs downstairs. She found a quilt to wrap round herself – then went back for another when Daniel also declined the spare room, out of misplaced gallantry. They dozed more than they slept but the night passed.

A shriek like an excited parrot jerked them awake on Friday morning, and what landed on Daniel's quilted knee felt like a one-ton baby elephant on a half-ton bungee rope. Having enjoyed an uninterrupted ten-hour sleep, Paddy had wandered downstairs to discover that sometimes wishes come true. She ate her breakfast crammed so close against him that he had to eat with his left hand, and when he went upstairs to shave he had to forcibly eject her from the bathroom.

They took her to school at nine and then, with John and Julia due back, had to decide where to go next. The house in Chiffney Road was out; but if Deacon was his target the stalker must know about the jail as well.

"My house?" suggested Daniel.

There was no reason why not. They had seen nothing of one another for weeks before this started: possibly the stalker was unaware of Daniel's existence. Short of protective custody, she and Paddy would be as safe on the beach as anywhere in Dimmock.

So that wasn't what made her hesitate. It had been a rough night, she was still groggy with lack of sleep, and the memory of being afraid of him surfaced a moment before the knowledge that that had been a mistake. She hoped he hadn't seen her waver, or that if he had he hadn't guessed why; but experience told her he probably had.

"Yes," she said brightly. "Fine. I'll let Jack know."

If he'd thought he'd get her to accept protective custody Deacon would have pressed the idea. Since he knew a dead horse when he was flogging one, he settled for Daniel's house as the next best thing. "But stick together, and keep your wits about you. The one thing we know about this man is that he likes springing surprises. He only took John on because he was alone and unsuspecting. Rather than face you and Daniel together he left the back way. He needs to make it easy. If you make it hard for him, you'll keep him at bay."

"Any names yet?"

"No." He sounded weary. He and Voss had been up all night, ploughing sterile soil. "I've got feelers out that may come back with one, but I don't know when and time's pressing. So we've pulled every file I worked on in the last ten years." His voice took on a note of wonder. "I had no idea how many people hated my guts."

Brodie chuckled affectionately. "Round here? Chuck a brick: you'll get one and the ricochet will find another."

* * *

Daniel had taken advantage of the rebuilding work to enlarge his home. The planning permission restricted him to the same footprint, height and general appearance as the original netting shed. But having no great need to store oars and lobster-pots he incorporated the boat-house on the ground floor into the dwelling, providing himself with a second bedroom and a study. He'd also made the budget stretch to a gallery round the top storey, wide enough for a couple of chairs or a telescope.

"What do you think?"

Brodie felt it like a fist under her ribs that she hadn't been inside since the builders moved out. Once she'd come here on an almost daily basis – it was a five minute walk from her office, if she was free for lunch she'd bought sandwiches and they'd eaten them curled up on Daniel's sofa or, on sunny days, sitting on his steps. Even through the long months of the rebuild she'd been by a couple of times a week to monitor progress. The rift, when it came, disrupted every aspect of her life, right down to where she ate lunch.

"I'm impressed," she said quickly. "From the esplanade it looks like it always looked, like the others look. But you must have doubled the space."

"The gallery," he prompted. "What do you think of the gallery?"

He was like a child with a new toy, needing someone to share his pleasure. It smarted like a paper-cut, knowing how little she had to do to make him happy, and how she'd managed to fall short even of that. She linked her arm through his. "Perfect," she said simply; and he glowed, and she fought back tears.

When he'd given her a guided tour Brodie sat on the gallery rail and watched the satisfaction in Daniel's plain, amiable face, and kept watching until, feeling her scrutiny, the grey eyes behind his thick glasses came round to meet it. "What?"

"You aren't really going to leave here, are you?"

He'd forgotten. Pain lanced through his expression. "I was. I couldn't see any alternative."

"Daniel, this place was made for you. Well, of course it was, you planned the rebuild from the ground up. But it's not just that it's the perfect home for a guy with a telescope. You put your heart and soul into it. I know the trouble you went to getting the right wood for the cladding. It came from Sweden, for God's sake!"

"Norway," he murmured.

"All right, Norway. You didn't have to do that. It's painted black, it could have been old floorboards or plastic for all anybody'd know! But you wanted the real thing even if it took longer and cost more. This house has the words Labour of Love written all over it.

"And as soon as it was finished you put it up for sale. Did you think the buyer would care that the weatherboarding came from Norway? Or even notice that you can see every inch of the night sky from somewhere on the gallery?"

Daniel's voice was low. "It's only a thing. I was never a

slave to possessions. It's not good to think there are things you can't do without. Feel that way about something and you end up doing things you'll regret to hold onto it."

"And the other danger," Brodie retorted sharply, "is that one day you'll throw away something important just to see if you can."

He regarded her for what felt like a long time. "Are we still talking about houses?"

Brodie sighed. "Not only houses, no. I'm sorry, Daniel. I let you down and I'm sorry. But what you did was pretty low too. You let me think I'd lost you. With everything else that was going on, that was the unbearable part. That you'd gone and I couldn't find you. That you could be dead, and it was my fault."

Her fists gripped the rail either side of her, afraid of falling. Daniel saw the tautness of her body, half-angry, half-defensive, silhouetted by the sea. He reached out a tentative hand and bent a lock of her hair around his finger. As if he'd sprung a trap Brodie's arms were round him, her head on his shoulder. He breathed in her scent. It had been a while. He was struck by the warmth of her body, she by the narrowness of his. The embrace put an end to a long cold time and they made it last.

But finally, noting the smirks of passers-by, they drew apart with a wry chuckle and straightened themselves out. Daniel headed inside. "I suppose, if I'm staying, I should tell the estate agent." He hesitated. "I suppose you should come with me."

Brodie shook out her dark hair luxuriantly. For the first time in weeks her body felt free of tension. "I'll stay here. I'll stay inside and keep the door locked. How long will you be – half an hour? I'll get some lunch on."

"There's nothing in the fridge."

"I'll open some tins. Pick up milk and bread on your way back."

"Shall I collect Paddy from school?"

"No, she's finishing later now. I'll go for her after lunch." Paddy had started a whole new chapter in her life – the five-hour school day – in the weeks Daniel had been absent from it.

Edwin Turnbull's pleasure at seeing Daniel evaporated like spit on a hot pavement when he said he'd changed his mind.

Mr Turnbull thought he didn't understand. "I have a buyer lined up," he explained carefully. "A cash buyer. He's offered the asking price. It's possible he'd be prepared to dig a little deeper to secure the property."

Daniel shook his yellow head. "Tell him I'm sorry but my circumstances have changed. I'm staying."

The estate agent bit the end off his biro in his agitation. Two percent of a seafront property, even in Dimmock, was not to be sneezed at. Then a crafty look stole over his face. If there's one thing better than two percent it's four percent. "Can I interest you in another property in the area? You're an imaginative young man – can you see yourself living in a tide-mill? Still got the wheel and everything. Roof's a bit dodgy – well, missing, mostly – but you're no stranger to a bit of renovation, soon have the place up to scratch. Been on the market a while, I can get you a good price. What do you say – shall we take a look?"

Daniel admired optimism but he wasn't going to waste any more of the man's time. "I'm sorry, Mr Turnbull, my mind's made up. It was a stupid mistake. I didn't go to the trouble of rebuilding it to live somewhere else. I'm sorry to have wasted your time."

"Still got the millstones and everything," said Mr Turnbull hopefully.

Before she started hunting through Daniel's cupboards Brodie phoned John's number. Julia answered.

"I just wondered how he is," said Brodie. "How you both are."

"I'm fine," said Julia, with restraint. "John's on the mend too. He's gone to bed but he'll be all right to-morrow."

"I am sorry for dragging you into this," said Brodie. "I never imagined for a moment he could get hurt."

"It's not your fault," said Julia; so far as Brodie could tell she meant it. "Jack said you stayed with him. That you came out of the house with the stalker behind you, and you could have run but you wouldn't leave John. Thank you for that."

Brodie was taken aback. At the sheer decency of the woman, but also by the idea that she could have run, leaving John unconscious on the gravel. She hadn't considered it an option. Some things you can't do if you want to look at yourself in the mirror next morning, and that was one of them. She'd have stood by the injured man who turned her life inside out if what had come down the steps behind her had been not Daniel but the hounds of hell.

When she put the phone down it rang again so quickly she thought Julia must have remembered something else she wanted to say. But it wasn't Julia.

For a moment she couldn't work out who it was. There was a lot of silence punctuated by little knocks and rattles as if the phone was being juggled from hand to hand. There were also odd words, but at first she could make nothing of them beyond the fact that it was a man's voice. It wasn't Daniel and it wasn't Deacon, and John was safely tucked up in bed with his wife watching over him, and after that she really didn't much care who else was in trouble.

Because someone was. The fragmented nature of the call would have told her that even without the words. And the words were "please" and "oh dear God" and "help me".

She'd thought she didn't know the voice. But now she thought she did, and it was only the sheer distress tearing it apart that had confused her.

"Geoffrey Harcourt? Geoffrey, is that you?"

The sound of his name seemed to help the man get a grip on himself. Still his voice shook with fear; and even through that she could hear deep, mortifying embarrassment. "Mrs Farrell, I'm so sorry to bother you. I couldn't think who else to call. I've been so stupid... "

His voice petered out, defeated by the enormity of his situation. In the background Brodie could hear the tinny echo of a platform announcement.

"You're at the station?"

"I know," he mumbled miserably.

"Is someone with you?"

"Bloody hundreds!" he wailed.

"What are you doing there? I thought you couldn't leave the house. You paid me good money because you couldn't leave the house!"

"Someone called me," he whimpered. "About a Spinning Jenny. I've been looking for one for years. I couldn't call you, not after last time. So I thought I'd try to go myself. This is as far as I got."

"How long have you been there?"

"About half an hour. It feels longer."

"All right," said Brodie, taking control, "this is what you do. Put the phone down and go to the taxi rank outside the main entrance. Get in a taxi and give the driver your address. You'll be home in fifteen minutes."

"Yes," said Harcourt faintly. "Fifteen minutes. Yes."

"Can you do that?"

"Yes," he said again.

Brodie waited. Then she said patiently, "Geoffrey, you haven't put the phone down yet."

"No," he whined.

"Have another go."

But the background hum of the station concourse continued unabated. She thought she could also hear him crying, the sound muffled as if he was trying to hide it, retain that last fragment of his dignity.

Finally she sighed. "OK, Geoffrey, I'm on my way. Stay where you are, I'll be there in five minutes."

Chapter Sixteen

Superintendent Fuller asked Detective Superintendent Deacon to step into his office for a minute, and wouldn't take no for an answer. "I know you're busy. This is important."

Deacon was tired and worried, and when he found himself being ushered to a chair and offered cream and sweeteners for his coffee he was no distance from suggesting an alternative use for a sugar cube.

Battle Alley's senior officer looked up, catching his eye just in time to stop him. Around Deacon's age, he was a quiet, self-contained man, neat of figure and mannerly of mien – too mannerly for some colleagues who mistook quiet for soft and polish for lack of substance. In his five years in Dimmock Peter Fuller had disabused those who took him for a paper tiger, but he never quite knew where he stood with Deacon. The detective's seniority was close to his own, his experience arguably greater, his temper notorious. The two men had never had a major public argument yet, largely because both had seen the wisdom of avoiding one, but Fuller was aware that the time might have come.

"I know," he said, forestalling Deacon's objection, "you think you have more pressing business than coffee and biscuits with Sir. You may be right. But I'm wondering if it should be your business at all."

That got Deacon's attention. He lowered himself careful into the proffered chair and eyed Fuller guardedly. "I don't know what you mean."

Fuller poured the coffee. "I mean, I think you may be too close to this inquiry to continue leading it."

"Who else?" demanded Deacon. "Who knows as much about my enemies as I do? Who has the same incentive to get to the bottom of this?"

"If you've kept your paperwork up to date," said Fuller pointedly, "it's all a matter of record."

That was disingenuous and both men knew it. The files would show who said what and who did what: they could not record the look in an eye that could tell an experienced officer how much significance to vest in what was said and done. For that you had to be there.

Deacon said tersely, "I've been threatened on a daily basis since I got my first truncheon. I've been threatened by amateurs and professionals. I've been threatened by men and women, by children and pensioners, by people in wheelchairs and those so short they'd have had to stand on a chair to take a swing at me. I'm world class at being threatened.

"I know when it means something and when it doesn't. Of the hundreds of files downstairs that contain threats against me, I can dismiss three-quarters out of hand. I know, because I knew the people involved, that most of them were just mouth. You put anyone else onto this and he'll waste weeks chasing people I know had no real desire to hurt me, or had the desire but lacked the bottle. This is no time to drop the pilot."

Fuller regarded him speculatively. "I take your point, of course. I wonder if you can see mine? That you're too close to be objective. That you're running on anger when you need a clear head. That someone to whom it's a duty rather than a crusade might do a better job of protecting Mrs Farrell."

Deacon knew that if he couldn't bridle his temper in this office he would never persuade Fuller he could do it anywhere else. His big body was rigid, as if he was sitting on a powder-keg.

"Of course I understand. I can see that if there was any chance of me decking a suspect you'd want someone else doing the interviews. But we don't have a suspect – or else we have too many, which comes to the same thing. I'm not making bad decisions because I'm emotionally involved. There are no decisions to make right now. When we arrest someone I'll hand him over – to you, to DS Voss, to anyone you want to interview him. But you need me to find him. Whatever the relationship between Mrs Farrell and me, she's a member of the public and she's in danger. Neither of us wants to see something happen to her because you didn't trust me."

Fuller sipped his coffee reflectively. "That's exactly the issue, isn't it? Trust. Jack, I would trust you with my life. I don't know if I can trust you to take a step back if the need arises."

"You can." Deacon had to unclench his teeth to get the words out.

"Your word?"

"You have it."

"I'll hold you to that, you know. If I see a problem developing, I'll ask you to step down."

"Do it," nodded Deacon. "I won't fight you."

"Jack," said Fuller patiently after a moment.

"What?"

"Put the cup down. You've broken the handle."

As Deacon was with Superintendent Fuller when the call came in, Voss took it.

"Jack?"

"DS Voss," said the sergeant. "Mr Walsh, I know what this is about. Maybe I shouldn't but I do. If you have a message for Mr Deacon I can pass it on."

"Er...yes," said Terry Walsh, momentarily wrong-footed. "A message, and a word of warning. I don't know, maybe I should wait till I can talk to him?"

"Someone's life is at risk," Voss reminded him gently. "I don't think we should waste too much time."

"No." It wasn't like Walsh not to know what to do next. If he'd been talking to Deacon he'd have dumped everything he knew in his lap and let him make the decisions. The involvement of a third party complicated things.

But if Deacon had taken his sergeant into his confidence perhaps it wasn't for Walsh to second-guess him. "OK. You know he came to see me? That he was looking for a name?"

"Have you got one?"

"Not exactly. But I've had a bite on the line and he might want to follow it up."

"Someone else has the information he needs?"

Again Walsh's voice was oddly unsure. "Probably. Yes, I'm pretty sure he has, I wouldn't be bothering Jack otherwise. But he's going to have to be careful. I don't need to tell you, Sergeant, there are people in this town who would get huge satisfaction from seeing Jack Deacon bleed in a gutter. I'm not one of them, but Joe Loomis is."

Voss felt his pulse quicken. "Joe Loomis is behind this?"

"I don't think so, no," said Walsh. "But I think he knows who is. I think he'll talk about it, but only to Jack. He wants a meet."

"When? Where?"

"Hold on a minute," said Walsh sternly. "You do know who I'm talking about? Joe Loomis?"

Voss clung onto his patience. "Of course I know, Mr Walsh. He's a thug and a pimp, and one day soon we're going to take him down. I don't expect he's trying to help us out of the goodness of his heart. But if he's in a position to help us any way at all, we can't afford not to meet with him."

Walsh was thinking. "I'm guessing," he said slowly, "that if he's told you about coming to see me, Jack Deacon takes you into his confidence a lot of the time. I'm going to do the same. I believe Joe when he says he has the information Jack needs. I don't believe that he's had a sudden change of heart about his way of life and is doing this to clear his conscience. He knows Jack's close enough on his tail to bugger him. Whatever Joe has for him, it'll cost. I want Jack to understand that before he goes anywhere near Loomis."

Deacon would understand perfectly. Voss understood too. Joe Loomis wasn't the biggest criminal in Dimmock but he may have been the nastiest: Hence CID's recent drive to get him off the street. When Loomis went down, the local drug's trade would halve over night. He supplied doormen to half the clubs on the south coast and escorts for half the conferences. Both his bouncers and his toms peddled drugs, but when they were caught they took the fall and never implicated Loomis. This was due less to a notion of honour among thieves than to the certainty that he'd have their kneecaps if they did anything else.

Walsh was right to be wary. Loomis intended to trade his information for something of value to him, and nothing Voss knew about the man suggested it would be the warm glow of having done good. "Why do you think he's telling the truth?"

"He told me how he got the information. A man was showing a photograph of Mrs Farrell and asking questions about her in a club. The bouncer was one of Loomis's. He recognised her, didn't know if he should say, so he checked with Loomis. Who naturally reckoned that anything that might make trouble for Detective Superintendent Deacon was worth encouraging. So the bouncer took fifty quid off the guy in return for her name."

Which was interesting but Voss couldn't see how it helped. "Unless he signed a cheque for the fifty quid, I doubt that's going to lead us to him."

"Patience, Sergeant Voss," said Walsh reprovingly. "Point is, the bouncer recognised him. Bouncers go a lot of places, see a lot of faces. He'd seen this one before. He had a name to go with it."

"But Loomis didn't give you the name."

There was a slow smile in Terry Walsh's voice. "Don't be silly, Sergeant. He said he'll be in The Rose for an hour. But I'm not saying Jack should go. Right now, nothing in the world would suit Joe Loomis so well as getting a hold over him. If he's offering to trade it's because he can see a percentage in it. I don't see Jack cutting a deal, but I can see him taking damage trying to get what he needs and give nothing back.

"I wasn't going to call," admitted Walsh. "Then I thought, it's his decision. Just tell him to be careful."

"I will," promised Voss. But in his mind he'd broken the promise before he'd even put the phone down.

Entering the station Brodie kept her eyes peeled. She was looking for Trevor Parker, though the intervention of the man on the London train had all but cleared him of suspicion. He was probably in his office right now. In any event, he wasn't here.

She found Geoffrey Harcourt huddled in the phone booth, trying to ignore the passing travellers. When she tapped his shoulder his whole body spasmed. "Car for Harcourt."

At the sight of a familiar face his eyes flooded with relief and the rigidity drained from his body – so much so she was afraid he was going to faint. Quickly she linked an arm through his. "Come on, let's get you out of here. Unless, of course, you want to go and see that Spinning Jenny?"

"Stuff the Spinning Jenny," muttered Geoffrey Harcourt.

* * *

For a moment, when he got back from the estate agents and found the house empty, fear hit Daniel like a train. But it only lasted a second. Brodie had known what his reaction would be and left a note by the phone where he'd find it before he could raise the alarm.

"Had to pop out after all. Nothing to worry about – I'll be right back. I'll pick Paddy up on the way so don't hold lunch."

He glanced at the clock. It was quarter to one: Paddy would be out of school soon after two, and mother and daughter would be back here soon after that. He decided to wait.

He still hadn't stocked the fridge. There was a corner shop one block behind the esplanade. By the time he'd bought enough to feed two adults and a five-year-old who cared more about the cartoon characters on the outside of tins than the food on the inside, he thought Brodie would be back.

It wasn't a long drive to Cheyne Warren: Brodie could take Harcourt home and be at Paddy's school with half an hour in hand. Once clear of Dimmock she lightened her foot on the accelerator and let the car cruise. She glanced sideways at her passenger. "How do you feel?"

He couldn't meet her gaze. The side of his face was ridged with strain. "I don't know how to apologise, Mrs Farrell. It's not the first time I've made a fool of myself, but it's certainly one of the more memorable ones!"

"Don't exaggerate," she said. "You're a client and a friend – I'd have been offended if you hadn't felt you could ask for my help. It's no big deal, really."

"It is to me," he mumbled into his chest. "I don't know what I'd have done if you hadn't come for me."

"You'd have called someone else."

"I don't know anyone else! No one I could ask favours of. If you never go anywhere, you never meet anyone." He risked a glance at the passing scenery: it seemed to make him more uncomfortable than distressed. "Do you think we could pull over for a minute? I'm a little dizzy."

Brodie found a lay-by off the Guildford road where they could sit undisturbed and just talk. "Take a few deep breaths. You'll feel better soon. You've had a busy morning."

"Tell me about it," moaned Geoffrey Harcourt. He had a canvas bag across his knees like an old lady's handbag, and he folded his arms on top of it and dropped his forehead onto his wrists.

Brodie thought the best thing she could do was keep him talking. "How long have you lived in Cheyne Warren?"

He straightened up, loosening his tie with a finger. "About four years now. I left Dimmock after my wife died. I couldn't bear living in our house alone. Every time I opened a door I expected her to be on the other side; every time I woke I expected to find her in bed beside me. I thought a change of scene might help."

"But it didn't."

He gave a broad-shouldered shrug like an apologetic bear. "Yes and no. It certainly altered how I live."

"That's when the agoraphobia started?"

"The funny thing is," he said, "at first I didn't notice. I didn't want to go out; I didn't want to see people. I thought it was my choice. I found a store that delivered so I didn't have to go shopping, and I'd sold the business by then so I didn't have to go to work, and I thought I was just taking some time out and would get back on track once I'd got my head sorted. Only the longer it took, the harder it got. My life had closed in around me while I wasn't looking. And the rest" – he darted her a fugitive smile – "you know."

Brodie nodded sympathetically. "But you are getting better."

He couldn't see it. His eyebrows canted sceptically. "How do you figure that? I lost it today. Totally. I got a taxi into town, and I was pleased with that. I just needed to get the train as far as Chichester, he was going to meet me at the station. But suddenly the enormity of it hit me. The people – the noise, the bustle. I needed to buy a ticket but I couldn't get myself to the booking office. I know it sounds absurd – I can't explain. I stumbled into the phone-booth mostly to get away from all the people."

"But you got there," she insisted. "And when you got into trouble, you dealt with that too. Geoffrey, when you first contacted me two months ago, it took you three phone-calls to introduce yourself and say what you wanted. Do you remember? When I came to your house to talk about it, it took you ten minutes to open the door.

From there to even thinking you could visit someone in another town is a quantum leap."

Harcourt hadn't looked at it like that. Brodie saw him consider and begin to draw a little comfort from it. "I hadn't realised. You've been good for me, Mrs Farrell."

Brodie was glad he thought so. "I have another friend who has panic attacks, so your condition is nothing new to me. It doesn't embarrass me. I'm happy to help."

"You're very kind." Harcourt thought for a moment, then he unzipped the canvas bag. Brodie saw the gleam of oiled brass. "All the same, I want you to bill me for your time. No." He stopped her protest with a lifted finger. "I insist. If you won't let me pay for your time I won't be able to call you again, and if I can't come to you for help I wouldn't know where to turn."

Brodie was used to being paid for her time but not like this. It made her uncomfortable, that she couldn't perform an act of simple kindness without putting a price on it. There was a fine line between businesslike and mercenary, and sometimes she worried that she didn't tread it as surely as she should. "Put your money away. Next time I find something for you I'll factor it in, all right?"

He smiled. "All right."

"What's in the bag?"

He opened it a little more, so she could see. "The man with the Spinning Jenny – I was taking this to show him."

Brodie recognised it. "That's the one you showed my daughter."

"I just finished it," he nodded. "The old Solitude tide-mill, on the Windle. He asked what I was working on, I said I'd bring it to show him. I was showing off, I'm afraid. But it is a pretty good model. Of how it used to be – now it's so derelict you can hardly make sense of it. I wanted to record the automation before it was impossible to work out how it was done."

"Automation?"

"The most important part of a tide-mill," Harcourt assured her, warming to his favourite subject. "The wind blows day and night, and rivers run round the clock. But high tide only comes twice daily, the times vary with the moon, and for half the year at least one high tide will be during the hours of darkness. You had to make it more convenient – by storing the energy of the tide until you were ready to use it, and with automatic systems that could run while you slept."

He pointed out the tiny brass features with a finger that looked too thick for such delicate work. "Rising tide filled the lagoon through one-way sluices. Another sluice sent the water down to the mill, turning the wheel from about half-tide until the lagoon was empty. You could mill for up to eighteen hours a day.

"But some of that would still be at night. Things were rigged to start up automatically. As long as the miller refilled the grain hopper, emptied the flour-bins and reset the sluices, the mill would start work again at the next rising tide. Flour mills were capable of the highest degree of automation. It's harder to pour spades."

Brodie looked at him, puzzled. Harcourt gave a sad smile. "Sorry. Engineers' jokes tend to be rather obscure."

"I had a t-shirt once," said Brodie helpfully. "It said, 'Engineers do it with precision'."

The way Harcourt looked at her, she thought he was going to ask: "Do what?" Instead he just nodded.

"Milling was hard and dangerous work," he said, faintly reproachful. "One or two men were harnessing enormous natural forces to run heavy machinery: there were some dreadful accidents. Runaway wheels were common. If you were lucky they just stripped the teeth from the pit-wheel. If you weren't they ripped your arm off."

"You should add that to the model," suggested Brodie. "A tiny miller being torn apart by a rogue wheel. Paddy would love it."

Harcourt did the sad smile again.

"How did you get into all this?" she asked.

"I've been interested in machinery since I was a little boy. My father was a locksmith. I had my own business by the time I was twenty-five: people told me what they wanted and I designed and constructed a lathe or a loom or a press or a specialist security lock: whatever they needed. I had a certain talent," he said wistfully.

"And then you lost your wife," murmured Brodie.

"And then I lost Millie," he agreed. "And nothing else mattered. I let customers down, I let the business fail, I wallowed in misery for two years. By the time I realised I had to get a grip on myself, that Millie wouldn't have wanted me to waste my life in mourning, the business was gone and I was no longer a recluse from choice."

"And now," Brodie said positively, "you're mending. You're going to get over this, Geoffrey. You've come so far already. Get your breath back, then when you're ready try again. Only this time call me first and I'll come with you."

He regarded her sombrely. "You're quite something, you know that?"

She smiled. "I can bear to hear it again. Listen, we have to move. People will be wondering where I've got to." She started the engine.

"Of course." He drew the canvas bag up round the model and zipped it closed. Then he opened it again and took a handkerchief out.

Chapter Seventeen

When Deacon left Superintendent Fuller, Voss was out of the office. He'd told DC Winston he had someone to see in town and would be back soon. Deacon gave him fifteen minutes, then tried his phone. It was switched off. He waited ten minutes longer and tried again, with the same result.

He prowled into the long CID room where half a dozen Detective Constables worked, often ate and occasionally slept, and which in consequence resembled a pigsty, and lowered one haunch onto the desk in front of Winston's. "Where did Charlie say he was going?"

"He didn't," said Winston. "A phone-call came in, he took it and he said he was going out."

"On his mobile?"

"Your office phone."

Deacon called the switchboard. Yes, a call had been put through to his office some forty minutes earlier and answered by DS Voss. The caller gave his name as Walsh.

Deacon was looking up Walsh's number when the mobile warbled in his pocket. He didn't recognise the number but he always found it hard to ignore the peremptory summons of a ringing phone. There was no knowing what fun a man could miss that way.

It was Voss's fiancée, Helen Choi. "Charlie asked me to call you."

"He did?" Deacon scowled at the phone. "I've been looking for him. Do you know where he is?"

"He's here. At my flat, in the nurses' building behind the hospital. Can you come? I'll meet you at the main door."

Jack Deacon didn't get invited to young women's flats so often that he knew the protocol. "You want me to come there?"

"Yes, please," she said. "I think you should."

"Put Charlie on."

"No, Mr Deacon," the girl said quietly. "I want you to come here, as soon as you can. You can talk to him then."

Two-metre rugby players with broken noses and police-issue semi-automatics didn't say "No, Mr Deacon" to him. For a moment he couldn't think what came next. "Er ... all right," he conceded weakly. "Give me five minutes."

She was waiting for him, compact and businesslike in her blue uniform with her glossy black hair scraped back in a bun. "I'm sorry to be so mysterious. But Charlie needed to see you before anyone else finds out what's happened."

Deacon stared down at her. "What has happened?"

"This is my flat." Helen opened the door.

When his eyes fell on Sergeant Voss, Deacon's jaw dropped and then clamped tight shut. So tight that he had to force the words out between his teeth. "What fell on you?"

The Rose in Rye Lane was an old pub – bits of it dated back to the original Tudor inn. The lane was narrow, the windows small and the low ceilings carried on dark oak

beams so that even in the middle of the day there was
barely enough light to read by. Conveniently, The Rose's
patrons were not big readers on the whole. Page Three,
the sports section and the statutory declaration on a Legal
Aid form: a man who could read those could, they reckoned, read enough. And low lighting has advantages in a
villains' pub. When men in pointy hats ask what you've
seen, it's nice to be able to say in all honesty that you saw
nothing.

Charlie Voss took a deep breath before he went inside
but he didn't linger in the doorway. A man with enemies
waiting in the dark is better not silhouetting himself
against the light. He moved calmly towards the bar. "I'm
looking for Joe Loomis. He's expecting me."

The man behind the bar and two customers leaning
on it looked at him as if someone had found him on a
shoe. "Mr Loomis is?" The barman's voice was a heavy
blank with undertones of disbelief, just about as offensive
as a man with illegal substances about him wants to be to
a police officer. If he'd used that tone with Deacon he'd
have been scraping his nose off the bar by now. "Are you
sure, Mr Voss?"

"Tell you what, Wally," said Voss amiably, "why don't
you ask him?"

Whatever reason Wally Briggs had to stop short of
picking fights with the police paled into insignificance
beside his overwhelming need not to annoy Joe Loomis.
It wasn't just that his livelihood might depend on it: his
neck might too. However unlikely it seemed to him that
the nastiest thug in Dimmock wanted to see a police

officer, he couldn't afford to trust his instincts when the consequences of being wrong could be grave. "I'll ask." The man ducked under the bar and disappeared into a back room.

A minute later he returned, holding the door open. "He'll see you."

His heart in his boots, Voss managed a good-natured nod. "I thought he might." He left the comparative safety of the public bar and entered the secret bowels of the old building, and the oak door shut behind him.

Joe Loomis was not a big man, would never have hired himself out as a bouncer. He was shorter than Voss and though he was ten years older he was no broader. He was a local man down to the accent, but legend had it that his people were from Ireland. His black hair was thinning alarmingly, and he glued it down with gel and drew the eye away from it with a thin moustache.

"Mr Voss," he said – politely, cautiously. "I wasn't expecting you."

"Mr Deacon couldn't come."

One thin black eyebrow arched in surprise. "Doesn't he think what I have to say is important enough?"

"It's not that," Voss said evenly. "I didn't tell him."

For a moment Loomis said nothing. Then the ghost of a smile crossed the neat dark features, fastidious and cruel as a cat's. "Why not?"

"Because you'll want paying for your information, and I don't want Mr Deacon having to choose between his career and his lady."

Now Loomis was smiling openly. "You think you can

– what? – treat him? We're not talking about a round of drinks and a tandoori chicken afterwards: we're talking about information that could save somebody's life. You think it's going to come cheap?"

"I doubt it," said Voss honestly. "But then, Jack Deacon's my boss and my friend. And I don't come cheap either."

Loomis wasn't sure what he was being offered. His smile was uncertain around the edges. "What are you suggesting? I tell you what I know, and sometime when I really need a favour you'll lose me a parking ticket? No offence, Mr Voss, but sergeants are ten a penny. But a detective superintendent would be worth getting chummy with."

"You were never going to get chummy with Mr Deacon," Voss said with certainty. "He wouldn't sell out to you or anyone like you. But if this goes badly he could spend the rest of his life wondering if he should have done. Me, I'm open to offers. I won't always be a sergeant: the time may come when the knowledge that you can end my career may be worth something to you."

Loomis was at least thinking about it. Already he'd spotted the flaw. "For what? You ask for information in connection with a police inquiry and I give it to you. What's my hold over you? You've done nothing wrong. Jesus, I've done nothing wrong!"

Voss nodded. "Then I'll do something wrong. Don't get your hopes up – I won't give you a get-out-of-jail-free card. Prison's the right place for you, I won't help you stay out, not even for this. But who knows what the future holds? There may come a time when you'd give your eye-teeth for a handle on me – for the ability to make a phone call and know it'll result in my suspension. That's why I'm here. Prove this meeting took place and whoever I am by then, however senior, I'm history. And the proof is what I'm about to tell you. If Divisional HQ ever learn that when I was a DS in Dimmock I passed on operational data to a prime suspect, they won't care how trivial it was, they'll hang me out to dry. That's what I'm offering you. That's all I'm offering you."

"What proof?"

"Our codename for you. The label on any intelligence we receive about you, any action we plan against you."

"I could get that anywhere," said Loomis dismissively.

"No, you couldn't. If you could you would have done, and you'd have told me what it is by now.

"Police stations aren't very secure places – you put your pen down and it's gone, you put your wallet down and someone treats the office to tea and buns with your fiver. But some secrets we're good at keeping, and the reason is that people who can't keep them don't stay. You can't have Jack Deacon at any price. You can't have me in your pocket. But you can have me in the garbage disposal with your finger on the button. For information of no value to anyone else, that's a good deal."

Joe Loomis had one of those smooth, closed-in faces which ration out expression like a taxi-driver giving change. Even people who knew him well could rarely guess what he was thinking. A minute ticked by and still he said nothing.

Voss waited. He had no illusions about this. He was mortgaging his career to a man he wouldn't have lent his car to. If he'd thought about it any longer, maybe he wouldn't have done it. But maybe he would, because there was a lot at stake and he wasn't a man to stay safe while other people were getting hurt. He'd risked his life to protect the paying customers before now, he expected to do it again. Beside that, the chance this might one day cost him his job seemed an acceptable gamble.

Depending on how his career – and Loomis's – developed he might never have to pay up. But if he did it wouldn't have been for nothing. Brodie Farrell's welfare concerned him, both because it was his job to be concerned and because he liked the woman. But that wasn't why he was dancing with the devil. He was doing it because Jack Deacon couldn't, and if it came to a straight choice he put a higher price on Deacon's professional survival than his own.

Finally Loomis came back from whatever mental counting-house he'd stopped off at and his smile broadened. "Mr Voss, I can't see the day coming when that would do me any good. The moment you thought it might you'd go to your superiors and say what you did and why you did it. Maybe you'd have to resign anyway but that wouldn't stop me going down. I don't think what you're offering is worth squat to me.

"But then," the little thug went on, "I never expected to come out of this with Dimmock CID in my pocket. It's a nice thought but a man has to be realistic. You're right: Mr Deacon wouldn't sell me his soul even to save his fancy piece. He wouldn't have offered as much as you have. That's not why I suggested meeting. I wasn't hoping to leave here with his future in my hands. Just his blood on my boots."

Loomis watched his words register in Voss's face. He saw the younger man stiffen, then deliberately relax. This wasn't a fight-or-flight situation. Voss could leave any time he wanted, just open the door and walk out. He didn't because he'd come here for something and he wasn't leaving without it.

Slowly Loomis nodded his approval. "All right. Well, I'll tell you what we're going to do. I've got a bit of business to attend to. I'll be back in – oh, let's say ten minutes. If you're still here I'll tell you what I know."

Voss said nothing. Nor did he move. Loomis left the room, closing the door behind him.

After twenty seconds it opened again.

"Never mind that," said Voss wearily. "I got it. The name. The man who was asking questions about Brodie in the Shalimar Club. Only I hope it rings more bells with you than it did with me. French. Freddy the bouncer said his name was French."

"French." Nothing much was happening in Deacon's brain either. But then, it was still struggling with the evidence of his senses: what he could see and what he could infer. "French?"

"You know him?" A thin trickle of blood ran from Voss's nose down his broken lip. It was an effort to raise one hand and wipe it away.

Deacon shook his head. "I don't think so. I've never arrested anyone called French..." It was no good, he couldn't keep his eyes off Voss's face, and he couldn't look at it and talk about anything else. Helen had cleaned him up before Deacon got here, so there was less blood than there would have been half an hour ago but more swelling. His best friends would have had trouble recognising him now: in another half hour it would be a matter of dental records. "You should be in hospital," Deacon said, his voice both soft and rough.

Voss shook his head, wincing. "I couldn't. I couldn't have kept a lid on it once people had seen me. Same way I couldn't turn up at Battle Alley. I had to see you first."

"Charlie," said Deacon fiercely, "you could be bleeding inside. You can beat a man to death, you know – well, this is what it looks like. How many were there?"

"I'm all right," muttered Voss. "They knew what they were doing – it wasn't in anybody's interests to have me pass out and wake up in A&E. Nothing's broken. I'll be stiff for a few days, after that I'll be able to show my face back at work."

"That face? We'll need to come up with a bloody good explanation!"

Voss already had. He'd been thinking about it since Helen picked him up in her car from the alley behind Rye Lane. The secret to thinking clearly when you're in pain is to concentrate on one thing at a time. "I fell off a motorbike. A mate let me have a go on his scrambler and I wasn't very good. Chief, you shouldn't still be here. Get back to the office, find out who French is. Find out where he is."

Deacon nodded, numbly. He still couldn't believe what had happened. Not that Voss had got a thumping: that had happened before, would happen again, it was an occupational hazard. What left him gobsmacked was how and why it happened. It wasn't a fight, it wasn't even an ambush. He'd stood still and taken it, and he'd done it for Deacon. Jack Deacon had had no idea he inspired that kind of loyalty.

He got halfway to the door, then turned back. Propped on the sofa, his ginger hair lank with sweat, a woman who loved and was furious with him swabbing his bloody face with a wet cloth, Charlie Voss had already let his eyes slide shut. The bruises were a splash of shocking colour against the pallor of his skin. Deacon felt something like a hand gripping the base of his throat. "I shan't forget this, you know."

"Good," mumbled Voss.

"How many were there?"

"There were four, Mr Deacon," said Helen Choi with the quiet fury of someone who knows there is a time for vengeance, and it's after the injured have been attended to. "Four. And there wasn't a mark on any of them."

Chapter Eighteen

French. The name meant something to him. But it wasn't in the One-day-I'll-be-free-and-then-we'll-see-Mr-Deacon file. It was...it was...

Charlie Voss had stood and taken a thumping from four men, and when he couldn't stand any more he'd let them pick him up and thump him some more. And he'd done it not for the job, and not because he had no choice, but for Deacon. He didn't understand. It wasn't that he was ungrateful, just that he was more angry. So angry he could barely think straight. So angry that if anyone looked at him the wrong way in the next few minutes he could blow the career Voss had protected at such cost by flooring them. And the thing that confused him as much as anything else was that it wasn't Joe Loomis he was angry with – it was Charlie Voss.

OK, French. Not a collar he'd felt. And – actually not a man. Millie French was the complainant – years ago: what, four, five years ago? She claimed she'd been raped, the man said she consented. No evidence either way and it never went to court. No, he was on the wrong tracks – it wasn't Millie French asking about Brodie in the Shalimar Club. Some other French, some other time.

With all the damage to his face – and these were professionals, they weren't concentrating on his face, mostly they were powering blows in under his ribs, into his belly and onto his kidneys – Voss's knuckles were unbloodied. Deacon had looked. He hadn't attempted to defend himself. A deal was struck and he kept his side of it. So did Loomis. Which left Deacon ... out of the loop. Side-lined. He wasn't used to being on the periphery of events and he didn't like it. He'd got what he needed and it had-n't cost him a penny, but the humiliation was like ashes in his throat.

Millie French wasn't doing this. For one thing, she was dead. Months after the episode she walked into the sea. Which was sad but rather confirmed what Deacon suspected: that the girl was neurotic and her version of what happened couldn't be relied on. No one behaved well that night but Deacon thought she'd probably got herself into a situation she lacked the know-how to get out of. The man said he believed she was available. It might have been true; in any event he'd have said it with conviction and the jury would have believed him. Millie would have mumbled, played with her hankie, forgotten what she said in her statement, made mistakes that would sound like lies, and generally come across as a bubblehead who couldn't be trusted. Not when she said "Take me" and not when she screamed "Rape!"

Deacon was in his car now and driving – not very well, he gathered from the fisted horns and startled faces that way-marked his passing. Damn them. If anyone wanted to make an issue of it they could follow him to the police station.

Think as he might, he could recall no more Frenches. Just Millie. And her husband, of course. The more Deacon dug, the more details surfaced and the slower he drove. Now people were hooting because he was holding

them up. Their concerns did not trouble him; in fact he
did not notice them.

The husband. Michael? He and the other man were
doing some business together. They were all going out for
a meal, only something stopped French going. Millie
came home distressed, and when French found out why
he called the police.

The last time Deacon saw French he was identifying
his wife's body in the morgue at Dimmock General.
Deacon struggled to remember him. He was a few years
older than Millie and solidly built. Whey-faced, tears
streaming down his cheeks, unable to string three words
together, confirming the identification with a spastic nod.
Michael French. Whatever happened to him?

Deacon parked in the yard behind the police station
and hurried up the steps, shouting as he went. He wanted
the file on the French case. He couldn't remember the
name of the accused.

As he surged up the stairs to his office, messages followed him. Someone had been phoning for him.
Someone else was waiting for him downstairs.

Deacon thought quickly. It wouldn't be Brodie downstairs
– she believed waiting-rooms were for other people – but it
might have been her on the phone. Usually, though, she'd call
his mobile. He asked the switchboard, "Who was calling me?"

"Daniel Hood."

Not until Julia Farrell phoned had Daniel made the tran-
sition from mild unease to real anxiety.

She was a polite woman and it was a polite call but

clearly she was annoyed. She asked for Brodie: when Daniel said he was expecting her back Julia asked him to convey a message.

"I know things are difficult at the moment and she's having to prioritise, but some things you have to take care of regardless. It's not as if I've nothing else to do. I have my husband in bed with concussion thanks to – " An eminently reasonable woman, she fielded the thought in mid-air. "No, that's not fair: what happened to John isn't Brodie's fault. But saying she'd collect Paddy and then not doing is. Suppose I hadn't been here when the school called? Who'd have collected her then?"

Chills were racing up Daniel's body from below his ribs to the base of his throat. "Is Paddy with you now?"

"Yes, she is. But – "

"Can you keep her?"

"Yes. But Daniel, that isn't ... " Her voice petered out mid-plaint. She whispered, "Oh Daniel – you don't think something's happened to her?"

"To leave Paddy alone in the playground long enough for the school to try to contact her, fail, and then phone you? Yes, I think it may have done."

He knew the seriousness of the situation, really didn't need Deacon shouting at him to underline it.

"You said you'd stay with her! You said she'd be safe with you!"

"I thought she was safe. I left her at my house, there was no reason for anyone to look for her there. I was only gone forty minutes. But she went out."

"Went? Or was taken?"

"Went, I think. The note she left seemed normal enough. I was expecting her back about twenty-past two. At half-past Julia called."

"Try your phone," said Deacon, "see if anyone called while you were out. Call me right back."

Daniel did as he was told. "No one."

"All right." He held the phone away from his ear for a moment, shouted for Voss, remembered, shouted for Winston, told him what to do. He told Daniel, "We'll get onto the phone company, access her mobile records. If someone's got at her, that's probably how – phoned her and lured her out."

"If –?" His voice was faint.

"Just being tactful, Daniel," growled Deacon. "Of course someone's got at her."

He got the information he needed but it wasn't much help. Brodie's mobile was last called from a public phone on Dimmock railway station at 1.02 pm. The call lasted a minute and a half. She must have left the netting shed just minutes before Daniel got back. That was an hour and a half ago.

DC Winston had found the file. The accused man was called Saville. Deacon took it without a word of thanks, hunting for the Frenches' address. River Drive – no. 22. Perhaps French was still there, perhaps he wasn't. Deacon could make enquiries or he could go round there and pound on the door.

Jack Deacon always took the pounding option.

The house in River Drive was empty. It looked to have been empty for some time, for the lawn was overgrown and the furniture gone. But there was no For Sale sign.

Deacon found a neighbour. "Yes," said Mrs Haynes, "poor Mr French moved out a couple of months ago."

"Poor Mr French?"

"He was never the same after his wife died," she confided.

"Where did he go? Did he leave a forwarding address?"

Mrs Haynes shook her blue rinse regretfully.

"Did you see the removal van? Was it a local firm?"

She brightened. "Yes. What are they called – Watkins? Watsons? Navy blue van with white letters."

"Warwicks," said Deacon, and Mrs Haynes beamed agreement.

But the trail ended at Edward Warwick & Sons' depot in the small industrial estate on the eastern fringe of Dimmock. They had no new address for Mr French either. He asked them to clear the house and store his furniture and paid for three months' storage in advance. There was still a month to run.

Moments like this Deacon missed Voss. There's a lot of thinking involved in being a detective, and recently he'd noticed that he did his best thinking aloud. Unless a man wanted to be considered for early retirement this involved having someone to think aloud to, and for some reason Voss seemed good at it. (Any year now Deacon would make the leap of intuition and recognise that this was because Voss didn't just listen, he contributed – quite substantially, just subtly enough that Deacon hadn't noticed.)

Mulling things over in the privacy of his own head didn't work as well. But lacking an alternative, he gave it a try.

Two months ago Michael French put his furniture into storage and left his house. He told no one where he was going, but he thought three months would be enough for what he had in mind. He didn't put the house on the market because he didn't want estate agents bothering him, but he didn't expect to return there or he'd have left his furniture where it was. A nice house at the better end of Dimmock, it could be worth half a million pounds. And he'd turned the key and walked away, and put the furniture into storage to save someone else the trouble. A neat man who tied up loose ends, who didn't leave others to pack up his life after he'd finished with it.

A man bent on suicide? Or one with no hope of being able to return home after he'd done what he'd spent the last five years planning?

Deacon hurried back to Battle Alley. Daniel was waiting. "Any news?"

"I know who's behind this." He summarised what he'd learnt in a few sentences.

"Michael French has Brodie?"

"I'm pretty sure."

"Why?"

Deacon looked at the younger man. Then he looked away. "I can't imagine."

Daniel's light brows gathered behind the thick glasses. "There must be a reason. He's gone to a lot of trouble. He had a photograph of her but he didn't know who she was, so he went round asking in bars until someone recognised her. Why would he want to hurt a woman he didn't know?"

Having Daniel on your case was like being tracked by a spaniel: he never looked like he was going to bite but he never gave up. Deacon knew he might as well come clean. "To get at me," he gritted.

Daniel blinked. "All right. Then why does he want to hurt you?"

"He blames me for what happened to his wife. It wasn't my fault, but maybe he thinks it was."

"What happened to his wife?"

He drew a long breath. "She killed herself."

Daniel's eyes saucered. "Because of you?"

Deacon's lip curled at him. "Of course not. But French may think it was because of decisions I made."

"What decision?"

"Not to take her case to court. She claimed she was raped, I didn't think there was enough evidence. If Michael French is doing this, that's why."

There was a long pause. Then Daniel said, "Was it a good decision?"

Deacon looked surprised. "Actually, yes. There was no chance of a conviction. The defending counsel would have torn her to shreds and the jury would have thrown the case out. I don't know for sure what happened. I do know we couldn't prove it was rape."

Daniel believed him. "So what can I do?"

"Nothing," said Deacon. "Really – there's nothing you can do. Go home. I'll call you when there's some news."

"How are you going to find her? How are you going to find French?"

"We'll find them." Deacon had no idea how he got that note of confidence into his voice. "I'll look at his furniture for starters, see what that tells me. If he has another property somewhere, we may find a reference to it."

"Another property?" Then Daniel understood. "Somewhere he could be keeping her."

"A lock-up, a house, a warehouse. He owned a factory once – I'll establish whether it's still in business and where the premises are."

"He'll hardly have taken her back to his office!"

Deacon scowled at him. "In fact, stranger things have happened. But what's more likely is that there are out-buildings somewhere that he has access to. If I can find his books there may be an entry for rental or something."

"That could take hours!"

Deacon forbore to tell him it would certainly take days, maybe many of them. "It'll take what it takes. Daniel, you're not the only one who wants to see Brodie safe. I'm not going to be cooling my heels. I'm not going to be taking tea-breaks. Now do what I say and go home. If I'm talking to you I'm not looking for her."

When Daniel had gone Deacon put his head through Superintendent Fuller's door to bring him up to date. He said he would need a warrant to examine French's furniture. He told him DS Voss had fallen off a motorcycle and asked for some help.

"A motorcycle," echoed Fuller.

Deacon couldn't tell if the man knew he was being lied to. "So I understand."

"Is he in hospital?"

"It was a nurse who called me," Deacon replied, dead-pan.

On the way back to his office Deacon finally remembered someone was waiting for him downstairs. He called the front desk to say he was free for a minute if they could make it quick.

"He gave up twenty minutes ago," said Sergeant McKinney. "He said you were obviously busy and he'd catch you another time."

Deacon wasn't sorry. "Did he leave a name?"

"French," said the duty sergeant. "Michael French."

Chapter Nineteen

Where she was it was cold and dark and dank, reeking of time and rot. Her clothes were wet with it, slimy against her skin. Her hair hung in rat-tails around her face and she'd lost her shoes.

She didn't know where she was and she wasn't sure how she'd got here. The last thing she remembered clearly was being in her car with Geoffrey Harcourt. He'd had his bag across his knees and he'd gone to blow his nose. Only something unexpected happened. And now she was cold and leaden-limbed, and her head ached and felt like it didn't belong to her and wasn't her size. Which suggested ... yes. He hadn't felt a sneeze coming on. He'd pulled out a handkerchief soaked in chloroform and clamped it to her face, and her first startled gasp had drawn the gas deep into her lungs.

Sometime after that she was vaguely aware of movement – of being dragged around the way Paddy dragged Howard. She must have been at least half-conscious: enough that he didn't have to carry her, not enough to have any idea where he'd brought her or how long it had taken or why it was so dark. Only in the last few minutes had her brain-cells started phoning round the neighbours and reached some sort of consensus as to what was going on.

Harcourt had pushed her across the car-seat and got behind the wheel. After driving for a time he hauled her from the car and steered her, staggering, in here. They walked some distance and it involved steps. Finally he let her slump in this corner. He fastened her wrists behind her and also to the wall, then he left. She had no way of judging how long he'd been gone, couldn't remember if he'd said he was coming back.

She tried to work out how long she'd been out of touch. If the darkness meant night it had been hours. But if it had been that long, she should have wandered longer in the twilight zone between sleep and waking. She thought she'd been fully conscious about ten minutes, and was perceptibly clearer now than at first. She didn't think she'd been AWOL for hours.

So it wasn't dark outside, just in here: not enough daylight penetrated to dissipate the cold and the damp. And by God it was cold – even with her coat on she was shivering. She might be underground – a cellar, an air-raid shelter, a sewer even. It smelled bad enough.

But as she strove to assess her situation calmly she realised that there was a minimal amount of light present: a hint of grey in the blackness that enveloped her, as if a few persistent photons got in here by bouncing around determinedly until they did. Which meant it wasn't dark outside, and she hadn't lost hours, and service to her brain had been suspended only temporarily.

This was good. It didn't improve her situation but it did make her feel marginally more positive about it. Of course she was afraid: she wasn't stupid. But with her brain back in business she knew she was capable of things no one ever expected. If she waited, clear-headed and patient, her chance would come and she'd be ready to take it.

* * *

Armed with the search warrant Deacon led his team to
Warwick & Sons' depot to carry out a detailed inspection
of everything Michael French had left behind. The
accumulated detritus of two people's lives was packed into
crates and piled in a corner module of the storage facility.
Spread out it would cover the warehouse floor. Deacon
had brought extra people because he knew he hadn't
much time.

The only absentee, apart from Voss, was Detective
Constable Winston who'd gone to the railway station. He
phoned as Deacon supervised the unpacking.

"She was here, all right. About ten past one. She met a
man and they went down the steps and got into her car."

"Description?" said Deacon.

"Unremarkable," said Winston.

"Slightly fuller description, Constable," Deacon prompted tersely.

"Sorry, sir, there isn't one. A middle-aged man in a
tweed jacket. Thickset, thinning on top. Aged anywhere
between thirty-five and forty-five. A bit of a stoop. Someone thought he was distressed. Mrs Farrell went into the
station, met the man at the phones and they left together."

"In what direction?"

"Into the traffic," said Winston wryly.

At least they knew where she'd gone when she left the
shore. She'd collected a man from the station and driven
him away in her car. It didn't sound like an abduction.

So the abduction came later. Because come it had: abduction and wild horses were the only things that would have stopped her being at the school gates when Paddy came out.

A thickset, balding, stooped middle-aged man in a tweed jacket who seemed distressed. He didn't sound much like an abductor. He didn't sound much like Michael French, although Deacon's recollection of the man remained vague.

But whether the man on the station was French or an accomplice, Deacon was now convinced that Brodie was in French's hands. Assuming she was still alive. Strong fingers gripped his heart and kneaded.

But this wasn't about Brodie, it was about him. About hurting him – punishing him for Millie's death. French went to Battle Alley because he wanted to tell Deacon what he'd done and didn't give a damn what happened after that. But he hadn't waited. Why not? He was going to prison for most of the rest of his life – could he really begrudge an hour spent in a police station waiting room? No, his presence was required elsewhere. And Deacon didn't see how that could be if Brodie was already dead.

He knew he could be kidding himself. He knew you can want something so much that any alternative seems impossible. But he couldn't make sense of French coming to see him and then leaving because he was busy if he'd already accomplished everything he purposed. Maybe he did mean to kill her, but he hadn't killed her yet.

He had to find French. He had to find out where French would go if he couldn't go home.

"What exactly are we looking for?" asked PC Huxley. Everyone in the warehouse was thinking it, but Huxley had the immune system of a bull buffalo and never suffered from tact.

"We're looking for a missing person," Deacon told the room at large. "That means a secure place. Keys. Bills or other paperwork referring to premises other than River Drive. Correspondence. And photographs – I still need a good picture of Michael French. Not that picking him up is likely to be a problem," he added bitterly, "the guy's tried to turn himself in once already."

But not now, he reflected in some confusion. An hour ago was fine, no doubt he'll be back later, but right now isn't good for him. Why not? What is it that changes?

A metallic clang away to her left warned Brodie she was no longer alone. Then she heard footsteps, and then that rumour of light was eclipsed by a shaft of brilliance that made her flinch. Her belly tightened with fear.

A voice said cheerily, "I'm back. Listen, I have something to do outside. I won't be a minute. Then we'll have some tea. Well – milk and cake, actually, there's no way to boil a kettle, but I don't expect you'll mind. You must be starving."

She wouldn't give him the satisfaction of knowing she was afraid. "No," she said haughtily. As her eyes adjusted to the glare of his torch, for the first time she could see something of her surroundings. It wasn't a room exactly, more a bay. The floor was covered with years of rubbish, wet-rotten. Behind him, lost in shadows, was a corridor of sorts. The way out.

"Nonsense," he said briskly, "you've got to keep your strength up. I don't want anyone thinking I mistreated you."

"Whatever would give them that idea?" she snorted.

Harcourt chuckled. She'd never heard him chuckle before. He came closer. "It's a pity about all this. I like you, Mrs Farrell, I wish we could stay friends."

"We were never friends, Geoffrey," she said dismissively. "You were a client. I took your money in payment for my services and never gave you another thought. My friends cost me money on the whole, but they don't lie to me, they don't drug me and they don't tie me up in damp cellars. You want a friend, Geoffrey, buy yourself a dog."

Without the sad bear stoop, and now he'd stopped combing his hair to emphasise his bald spot, he looked ten years younger. That wasn't the only change. "And you're fairly getting on top of the agoraphobia, aren't you?" she added sniffily.

Geoffrey Harcourt smiled – not the wry self-deprecating smile that was his trademark but something altogether more confident. Physically he was as she had always known him. He was wearing the same tweedy brown clothes. But everything else about him – his manner, the way he moved, the way he spoke, the very space he occupied – was so different that if the circumstances had been more ambivalent she might not have recognised him. And the reason for that was, as she now realised, that he'd been playing a part for as long as she'd known him.

"I owe you an apology," he said calmly. "Well, several probably, but one in particular. I obtained your services under false pretences. I did suffer from agoraphobia once, for about three months, but that was years ago. Now I go anywhere I want. But I needed a reason to hire you. I had to make myself part of the furniture of your life. I needed you to think of me as harmless."

"Until now," said Brodie tautly.

"Until now," he agreed. "How's your head? I'm sorry about that, too. I thought you might get hurt if I had to wrestle you all the way here."

"My head's fine," she growled, though there was still an odd thickness behind her eyes. "Where's here?"

"A place I know," he said off-handedly. "Somewhere we won't be disturbed. It's not exactly salubrious but you'll be safe here."

"Until?"

He didn't understand. "Until what?"

"Until you knock me out again? With a shovel this time?"

She'd managed to wipe the smile off his face. "I won't hit you." He sounded a little offended that she'd wondered.

Her chin came up pugnaciously. "Then this is your idea of a love-nest. I don't mean to be picky, Geoffrey, but shabby chic is so last year."

He straightened, taken aback. "Mrs Farrell – I didn't bring you here to rape you!"

"So what does that leave? Ransom? My friends might pass a hat round, that's about the best you can hope for."

"No," he said slowly, "I think your friends will care more than that. I think Jack Deacon will care far more than that."

So Deacon had been right: he was the target all along. But why?

Why depended on who: who the man in front of her was. "I keep calling you Geoffrey," Brodie said roughly, "but I don't expect it's your name. Who are you? What's this all about?"

For a moment he regarded her without reply. He seemed to be weighing his options. Then he said, "My name is Michael French."

She searched her memory but there was nothing there. "I don't know you!" she exclaimed petulantly.

"No, you don't." His voice had lost the irritating heartiness without resuming the hang-dog tones she associated with Harcourt. The transformation was complete. He was a different man: younger, stronger, more decisive and much more dangerous. "I will explain," he promised. "But there's something I have to do first. Otherwise we're going to be eating our cake waist-high in water."

When he came back French freed her left hand so Brodie could feed herself. If she'd seen half a chance to break free she'd have kneed him somewhere sensitive and taken it, because even if he caught her she'd never be more at his mercy than she was right now. But he knew better than to give her a chance. There was never a moment when both her hands were free. She might have hurt him but she could not have escaped. She bided her time, hoped an opportunity would come.

"So Geoffrey Harcourt wasn't real. The man with the model in the Woodgreen estate wasn't real either, was he? You gave me an address that would take me under that walkway, and I told you when I'd be there. You dropped the brick on me."

French nodded. "I didn't mean to hurt you – I was aiming for the back of your car. I was never any good at ball games either – no hand/eye co-ordination."

"What were you trying to do when you burnt my car?"

"Funnily enough, that wasn't me. I suppose it really was the local yobbos. You shouldn't have gone back asking questions. They didn't know it wasn't one of their own they were protecting."

"My handbag?"

French gave a slow smile. "Yes. I followed you into town. I had coffee and croissants at the table behind you and you never even noticed."

"Why did you want my handbag?"

"I didn't. I wanted to unsettle you."

"And it was you at the library. And in my house."

"Yes," said French again, "that was me."

"You put my husband in hospital!"

"Ex-husband." He said it as if it made a difference.

Brodie was getting angry enough to forget the danger she was in. "Will you tell me what it's about? Or is keeping me in the dark part of the fun?"

French sliced the cake, keeping his knife out of her

reach, and poured the milk into two plastic mugs. He looked up sombrely. "Believe me, Mrs Farrell, none of this is fun. But it is necessary. I owe it to someone."

"Jack Deacon."

The man shook his head. "My wife. Millie."

Brodie sounded surprised. "Millie was real? Among all the lies you told me, Millie was real?"

French nodded.

"And she really is dead? Or was that part of the fiction and actually she ran off with the milkman?"

"She's dead," French said in a low voice. He resented Brodie's bitter levity but not enough to break his word and hit her. After all, she was entitled to be annoyed. "She killed herself. Things happened to her that she couldn't live with. I promised that some day, somehow, I'd get justice for her."

"By kidnapping me?" Brodie's voice soared.

"Yes."

"Jesus!" she swore, "it's the Christmas presents all over again. Men have no bloody idea what women want!"

"Well, that may be true," French acknowledged with a smile. "And no, if we could ask her I doubt if Millie would want this. But I want it for her. I'm sorry to involve you. It would be naïve to ask your forgiveness, but I am sorry. I never wanted to hurt you."

"Hurt me? You damn near killed me, Geoffrey! – Michael, whoever the hell you are. Now you've got me tied up in a damp cellar and it's a toss-up whether pneumonia or Weil's Disease will get me first. What do you mean, you don't want to hurt me?"

He accepted her rebuke. "Then let's say, if I did want to hurt you there've been plenty of opportunities. I know this is hard on you, Mrs Farrell, and I know it's undeserved. Life is unfair sometimes, and right now it's being unfair on you. Accept the situation. It won't be for long."

Her ears sharpened at that. "How long?"

He shrugged. "That rather depends on Mr Deacon. I called on him an hour ago but he was too busy to see me. Admittedly, I didn't announce the purpose of my visit."

In Brodie's eyes his face had acquired a sort of duality, as if split by a prism. She knew it; it was quite familiar to her, she'd paid several visits to Geoffrey Harcourt. She'd liked his kind, sad eyes and self-deprecating sense of humour. She'd thought him a decent, unlucky person and almost a friend.

At the same time, offset from that image by the least amount, a mere line of spectral light, was the face of Michael French who had spent a fortnight reducing her to a nervous wreck and then abducted her. There was nothing kind or sad about his eyes. They were steady and intelligent, and if she could detect no cruelty in them there was a degree of resolve that was almost as worrying.

She didn't know how much to fear him. Part of her thought hardly at all – that this was another of his faintly absurd pastimes, like collecting models of obsolete machinery. But her brain, now firing on all cylinders, said there was every reason to be afraid. He hadn't done this on the spur of the moment. He'd mounted a campaign of terror which he was now bringing to some kind of finale. He was untroubled by the fact that she knew who he was.

He was even prepared to talk to Deacon about it. He wasn't expecting to get away scot-free: he wanted to do it anyway. That made him a fanatic, and fanatics are always dangerous.

She kept her voice level. "What is it you want?"

French shook his head. "You wouldn't understand. There's too much you don't know."

"But you expect Jack to understand."

He didn't have to think about it. "Oh yes."

"He didn't the last time I talked to him."

"Well, that's why I need to see him. If he hasn't worked it out yet, I'll help him."

"And then he'll arrest you."

"Yes."

"Don't you care?"

He pursed his lips. "Mrs Farrell, to all intents and purposes my life ended five years ago. From the day my wife died I've been waiting to meet you. You are in no way to blame for what happened, but you are the key to resolving it. All I can do is apologise again for the inconvenience."

"But it is almost over?" Brodie wanted to be clear on that point.

"Eleven hours," nodded French. "Try to be patient for another eleven hours. I'll have to leave you alone for a while, I'm afraid, but you have my word that by three o'clock tomorrow morning it'll all be over. You'll have been found and I'll be behind bars."

"I'll freeze to death before then!"

"No, you won't." His tone rebuked her for exaggerating.

She sniffed. "What's so special about three o'clock tomorrow morning?"

"Nothing. If Deacon had seen me earlier it would all be over now."

Which was reassuring. Though it's hard to feel much confidence when you're attached to a wall by something less like a shackle and more like the master lock to the Tower of London.

Brodie gave a one-shouldered shrug. "Eleven hours is a lot of time to fill. Tell me about your wife."

She'd managed to surprise him. "Millie?"

Brodie nodded. "Tell me about Millie."

Chapter Twenty

Sometimes, when you conduct a search for evidence, you come up against the plain fact that there's nothing to find. And sometimes there's so much that the problem is separating the bright specks of investigatory gold-dust from the mountains of silt.

Deacon found himself stymied on both fronts. The house at River Drive was empty. He knew there was nothing to find before he even started – the place was bare walls and floorboards. But he didn't dare lock up and join the team at the storage depot. There could be something crucial here. The only way to be sure there wasn't was to act as if there was. He gritted his teeth and got on with it.

Meanwhile, on the ring road, most of his people were unpacking crates and opening drawers, putting aside anything that might conceivably help. They made the goal wide because they didn't dare make it narrow, so this material soon overflowed the trestle table allocated to it. Deacon had asked them to look for documents and there were documents; and correspondence, old newspapers, photograph albums, old postcards used as bookmarks, two filing cabinets, several box-and concertina-files, some bunches of keys. There was a forgotten wallet with ten pounds and some family snaps in it. There were travel brochures – if French had been to some of these places before he might go back to evade the hunt for him. There were books – stacks of books – and it was impossible to know which if any might cast light on his intentions.

At five o'clock Deacon declared the search at River Drive fruitless and moved everyone to the depot. He began to pick through the eclectic collection on and around the table. He was appalled how much there was, how much time it would take to sort it properly.

At half-past five there was the scrape of someone drawing up a kitchen chair to the other end of the table, and when he looked Charlie Voss was patiently disembowelling a filing cabinet, starting at A. One eye was swollen shut but the other was scrutinising every order, every invoice, every business card ever dropped in there.

Deacon stopped work and regarded him in silence for a moment. "What do you think you're doing?"

Voss considered carefully. "I think I'm going through these files."

Deacon shook his head. "No, you're going home. I'll get someone to take you."

"I'm all right, chief." The way he said it, it could almost have been the truth.

"You look like shit."

Voss gave a cautious shrug. "Damned motorbikes... "

"You've had a busy day, Charlie. Get some rest."

"I'll rest tomorrow," promised Voss. "When Mrs Farrell's safe."

Deacon said no more. But his heart was making notes in indelible ink.

"Tell me about your wife," said Brodie.

French was oddly reluctant, as if the memory was too

precious to share. But he knew he owed Brodie something, and an explanation wasn't a lot to ask.

"She was working as a nursery school assistant when I met her. She was nineteen. I was twenty-seven, and that's a big age gap when you're young. Also, we moved in different circles. I had my own business, with eight people on the payroll. I had a flat on the seafront and a BMW, and if you must know I had a pretty high opinion of myself."

The picture of himself at that age made him smile. Like most young men he'd thought he knew everything. It was curious how, with every passing year, he'd found more to learn. All the certainties that surrounded him then had softened and mutated since, except this. Of what he was doing now he remained unbendingly sure.

"Millie lived with her parents and cycled to work. She wore her hair in a ponytail and only put on a bit of lipstick if she was going out in the evening. She was doing an evening class in home economics and saving for a holiday in France. She hadn't been abroad before."

"How did you meet?" asked Brodie.

"At a concert. I'd never been to one before – I was only at this one to please a client whose daughter was in the orchestra. She played the French horn. It could have been a comb and a bit of tissue-paper for all I knew or cared. I was just hoping the second half would be shorter than the first."

Oblivious of the damp and garbage he sat on the floor beside her, the torch in his lap distorting her view of his face. Brodie concentrated on the tone of his voice. He sounded wistful. He still sounded like a man in love.

"But there was this girl. In fact there were two of them, sitting just in front of me. I noticed them because, while most of the audience were middle-aged and blasé, these girls were as excited as if the first violin had been a pop star. I found myself eavesdropping during the interval. They'd saved for the tickets for months.

"When we were leaving I saw them again, in the foyer. There were CDs for sale and Millie wanted one but she hadn't got enough money. She had her friend turn out her pockets to try to make up the difference. A goddamned CD, and between the pair of them they couldn't afford it."

French's smile was audible in his voice. "I don't know what came over me. You couldn't have given me a CD of the damned concert, the only souvenir I wanted was the horn player's dad's signature on a contract. But there was something about these girls and their sheer enthusiasm; and then, maybe I was still trying to impress my client. I sauntered up to the till and slapped down a twenty-pound note and told them to enjoy the thing. They were too startled to argue.

"But outside Millie caught up with me. She wanted my name and address so she could reimburse me out of her next pay-cheque. That was the word she used – re-imburse. What kind of a nineteen-year-old says reim-burse?"

"The smart kind?" Brodie suggested. Listening to him was like being with Geoffrey Harcourt again. She had to keep reminding herself that he wasn't a nice, odd, sad man who was pathetically grateful for the scraps of friendship she threw him, and that the feelings of affectionate tolerance she still harboured for him were no longer appropriate. That she was his prisoner.

"She was smart," French agreed, "in a head-girl sort of way. She wasn't sophisticated. All sorts of things took her by surprise. Wine-waiters. The smell of leather in a car. The fact that, if you have money, people want to give you things for free. She disapproved of that, believed in paying her way. If I took her somewhere nice on a date, the next time she'd bring a picnic and feed me. It was ... charming. I couldn't decide if she was old-fashioned or very modern, and anyway it didn't matter. By then I was in love."

"Yes, you were, weren't you?" There was a note of envy in her voice that startled Brodie. She'd been in love too – she married for love. But it wasn't like that. She loved John Farrell for being dependable and safe, for the home he could give her and the father he would be to her children. In the event, of course, the safe pair of hands dropped the ball. But even before that she didn't remember feeling about her husband the way French obviously felt about his wife. Perhaps she'd forgotten. Or perhaps the Farrells just weren't as good at love as the Frenches had been.

Perhaps the Frenches had been too good. "What happened to her?"

He still didn't turn the torch her way. Perhaps because if he could see her properly it would be impossible to ignore the fact that he was talking to a woman whose right wrist he'd shackled to the wall. He'd spent days designing and fashioning those shackles. He'd been pleased with the result – she wouldn't break out of them however long he left her alone, it would take cutting equipment. But the intellectual exercise was one thing: using them to imprison someone, someone he knew and liked, was another.

Finally he said, "That depends on who you ask. According to the coroner she committed suicide while the balance of her mind was disturbed."

"And if I asked you?"

"I call it murder," he said bitterly. "She'd be alive today but for the actions of two men she had no reason to fear. And what William Saville did to her was over in minutes and didn't even leave bruises. But what Detective Inspector Deacon did – I'm sorry, it's Detective Superintendent Deacon now, isn't it? – went on for weeks, and stripped her naked again and again, and left her bloody and humiliated. He was supposed to protect her. He's a policeman, for God's sake, and she was the victim of a crime. And he brutalised her."

His breath was coming fast and ragged. The sheer impotent rage had in no way diminished with time. Perhaps time had fed it. The rage had filled the gap left by the loss of his wife and he no longer had any reason to fight it. If it faded it would leave him empty.

Brodie pursed her lips, considering her response. The words she chose were important. Nothing stood between her and a man half-mad with grief except her own wits.

"I understand how you could feel that way," she said quietly. "You were both upset and needed someone to

treat you with sensitivity, kindness. What you got was
Jack Deacon. Jack has many good points but sensitivity
isn't one. He thinks crime is about criminals, not victims.
He thinks by the time he's involved it's too late to do
much for the victim – but the next victim might be saved
if he's good enough, and sharp enough, and quick
enough. I think maybe you got run over in the rush."

She could have agreed with every word he said. With
her safety at stake Deacon wouldn't have wanted her to
defend him, and Brodie had no qualms about saying anything that would get her out of here. But she didn't think
validating French's bitterness would achieve that. The
more he hated Deacon, the easier it would be to hurt her.
She thought her best hope was an appeal to reason. If
Michael French was obsessed, he was not in any clinical
sense insane. She could get through to him. She just needed to find the argument to which he was open.

"You suffered a terrible, life-altering experience. If
Millie had survived you'd have helped one another
through it, pooled your strengths, supported each other
when the going got tough. But you were left to deal with
the anger and the pain alone. Finding someone to blame
is a coping strategy.

"And let's face it, Jack Deacon's easy to dislike. He's
curt, bad-mannered, short-tempered, and he thinks the
term for someone who disagrees with him is Stupid
Bastard. It's easy to take him for a thug. A lot of people
much less vulnerable than you and Millie have gone away
with that impression."

She drew a steadying breath. "But if it's justice you

want, you need to recognise the truth. Jack Deacon isn't a thug. He isn't much of a people person, but he's a good man and a good policeman. He tries to stop dangerous people and protect innocent ones, and he'll put himself on the line in the process. I'm sure whatever distress he caused you and your wife was inadvertent."

"Really?" snapped French. "So telling her friends and family that Millie was a liar and a whore was just his little way, was it? My wife was raped twice, Mrs Farrell. Once by a man I was stupid enough to introduce her to, and then again by Detective Inspector Deacon."

Apart from the house at River Drive, French no longer owned any property. For eighteen months after his wife's death his business, neglected and rudderless, had lost direction, lost profitability, and finally lost the will to live. On the verge of bankruptcy he sold up to a competitor and since then had been living on the proceeds. But Deacon could find no evidence that he intended them to last beyond this week.

Even though they had belonged to someone else for three years he wanted to search French's business premises. He had no time to apply for another warrant but the new owner could have no objection to admitting him. Leaving Voss at the warehouse he packed his car with bodies and drove back to town.

The Wayland Foundry had been in existence almost as long as Dimmock. It dated back to the same period as Deacon's house and was no distance from it, tucked away behind the bus-station.

When he saw it Deacon's heart began to race. The place was abandoned. The purchaser had stripped out the machinery, taken over what remained of the order book and locked the door. French might not have any legal access to it now, but nor was there anyone around to keep him out.

Deacon didn't suppose for a moment that the front gate with the fancy padlock was the only way in. French would know every rat-run in the place – how to get in if you lost your key, the windows that had to be nailed shut to keep local children out, the doors that could be opened with a judicious kick. But Deacon didn't, and didn't have time to learn. He opened the front gate with the front bumper of his car, to a sharp intake of breath from the assembled constabulary who were afraid they should be stopping him.

It was a bigger place than it looked from outside, the original workshop extended by add-ons and lean-tos made of iron frames and galvanised sheeting. Age-blackened, oil-blackened machinery still occupied some of the bays, half-buried now under discarded rags and draught-blown papers – too old, presumably, to be worth the cost of carting away. Deacon couldn't identify what it was all for, though he recognised the banks of crucibles along the back wall.

But he wasn't here for the industrial archaeology. He was looking for somewhere you could imprison someone, and neither the crucibles nor the furnace pits below them were big enough. He hurried on through the building, shouldering open doors sealed by rubbish, checking above and below and behind anything big enough to conceal a body.

He found nothing. Not Brodie, and no evidence that she was ever here. No evidence that anyone else had been here recently. Thick grey dust lay like ash, undisturbed on every surface. When he saw this place Deacon had believed he'd found French's redoubt. He didn't think that now. Disappointment writhed in his stomach like a parasite.

Again he left people behind to do a thorough job, to apologise if an indignant owner turned up, and then to make the premises secure. The sourness of bile in his mouth, he returned alone to Battle Alley.

Daniel was sitting on the steps like a foundling. "I couldn't think where else to go."

Deacon looked him up and down and grunted. "Come on up. I've brought some stuff back from the warehouse. You can help me go through it. You might spot something I wouldn't."

Daniel followed him upstairs.

"So you loved her, and married her, and then you lost her," said Brodie. A detached part of her brain that was editing everything she said noticed a grain of impatience creeping in, warned her it might be better to maintain a degree of empathy with him. Although undermining his grudge could also pay dividends. "And you blame Jack Deacon. But you aren't honestly telling me he raped her, are you?"

French said roughly, "He might as well have done. He

certainly violated her. Even Saville didn't do the damage
to her that Deacon did."

"Will you tell me what happened? Or would you
rather not risk it? I mean, the last thing you want is someone convincing you that the grievance you've nursed all
these years wasn't justified."

If he hadn't heard the impatience in her voice before he
certainly heard it then. His chin came up sharply, dissect-
ing the beam of the torch. It made him look like something glimpsed from a Ghost Train. Brodie supposed she
had the same gaunt, unearthly, chiaroscuro look.

"I expect you to defend him," French said tartly. "If
you had no feelings for one another you wouldn't be
here."

"Having feelings for someone doesn't blind you to
their failings," she said pointedly. "Jack's no saint; but
he's not the monster you need him to be either. He's
done too much for too many people. Too many people
are safe because of Jack Deacon for you to be right about
him. I'm sorry about your wife, but I don't believe Jack's
done anything to deserve what you're doing to him. Or
to me."

She was only making French angry. He'd come this far
on righteous indignation. It had got him through the
bereavement and the abiding sense of loss, the crushing
loneliness; through the three months when he never
wanted to see the world again; through the collapse of the
business that was his life before Millie was, and the years
since when the hope of revenge was the only thing that
got him up in the mornings. It wasn't a campaign so

much as a crusade: there was an element of sanctity to it. And she was telling him he was wrong.

If Millie French had lived, the uncritical adoration her husband retained for her, which fuelled his very existence, would have been impossible. You don't feel that way about people you see every day, who snore and drop egg on their tie and forget to buy milk. You don't love them less for being human but you'd feel silly worshipping them. They'd feel silly letting you.

By dying in the bloom of her youth, before he had time to realise that marriage is a marathon not a sprint, Millie made it possible for him to preserve her memory in amber – unaging, unchanging, safe from assault. But it had never grown, never developed, never had its corners rubbed to a comfortable roundness; never learned to laugh at itself and discovered the power of tolerance. She'd cut him adrift in the heat of their love, and stronger men than Michael French, men with better instincts and a fuller understanding of themselves, would have struggled for equilibrium. French had struggled and failed. He'd found strength of a kind in anger, and the hatred that it spawned provided him with a stanchion, a fixed point that endured though his world fragmented around him. He needed the hatred, couldn't afford to wonder if it was warranted.

"You think Millie died because Jack Deacon was unkind to her?" asked French savagely. "That her life was so little it could be snuffed out by simple mean-spiritedness? That he made a bad call, and she was too weak and self-centred to rise above it? You wouldn't think that if you'd known her. She was full of life. It took him weeks to kill her."

He was panting with anger. He took a moment to compose himself. "You want to hear the gory details? I'll tell you. You ought to know why this has happened to you. And then, we have a little time to kill."

Chapter Twenty-One

The tale was neither long nor complex, and not – except for the ending – the Greek tragedy he seemed to think. If Millie French hadn't been young enough to believe the present more important than the future, that how she felt now was how she would always feel and that her pain wouldn't heal, the crime against her would have been all but forgotten by now. It shouldn't have had the power to spoil their life together.

Oddly, French seemed not to bear William Saville the enmity he bore Deacon. It was as if he were a force of nature that hurled through their lives and then passed like a storm. He worked for a company that made rolling-stock. French used some words that Brodie didn't know but she gathered that the Wayland Foundry wanted the contract to cast some parts. It sounded a routine enough bit of business but from French's manner, as well as what came next, it must have been a big deal to him.

Wanting to make a good impression, he had Millie meet them for lunch. He asked her to make an effort and she did: she and Saville got on well. In the afternoon the men talked specifications and costings, and in the evening French booked a table at the best restaurant in Dimmock.

At ten to eight he got a call to say there'd been an accident at the foundry and the Health & Safety inspectors wanted to see him. He left Millie to carry his hopes with their guest.

She returned home at one in the morning. It took her

an hour to tell him what had happened. It took him till daybreak to persuade her to tell the police.

"She was afraid." French's voice had fallen lower as he spoke; now it was barely audible. "Of being humiliated again. She knew there'd be examinations and questions. She knew Saville would deny it, point out that she went to his hotel room voluntarily. He offered her a nightcap and she thought it would be rude to refuse. She knew I wanted his business. Perhaps she was naïve, but it was a situation she hadn't met before. She didn't know how to rebuff him without giving offence. She thought the best thing was to have a drink and then leave."

"But he wouldn't let her," murmured Brodie.

"He acted as if it was a joke – blocked the door and said the toll was a kiss. Of course, he'd been drinking. Millie wasn't finding it very funny but she still thought it was the best way out. Better than causing a scene. She let him kiss her."

"But he didn't stop at one kiss." Brodie might have been there, watching it happen. Indeed, Brodie had been there, more than once. She'd discovered that when a kiss doesn't work, a sharp upward jerk with one knee mostly does. Millie's tragedy was that she never had the occasion to practice before she had to do it for real. "Did he hurt her?"

"He raped her!" shouted French. His voice barrelled off the damp walls and went chasing away through the darkness.

"I know. But were there any injuries? Did she fight him?"

"He was twice her size! If she'd fought him he'd have killed her."

But without injuries it was her word against his. Perhaps the man genuinely thought he was being offered more than a good meal for his custom. Perhaps polite, nicely brought up Millie was still starting sentences with "I'm not sure this is a good idea" when she should have yelled "Get the hell off me!"

And criminal charges must be proved. It's not enough that the jury sympathises with one party or the other: they have to be convinced beyond reasonable doubt. Millie French had dinner with William Saville in an expensive restaurant, then she went to his hotel room. They had drinks and she kissed him. He didn't hit her or restrain her forcibly enough to leave marks. She claimed it was rape, but there was no supporting evidence and the man's account had to be heard too. At that point it could come down to who made the best witness.

"Was Saville acquitted?" asked Brodie softly.

"No, he wasn't acquitted," snarled French. "He wasn't charged. Deacon put my wife through physical examinations, hours of interrogation and weeks of anxiety, then he phoned to say he wasn't going to charge Saville. She'd gone through all that for nothing. She didn't want revenge, she wanted to stop him attacking another woman. But a man who cared more for his batting average than the safety of young women on his streets told her he didn't believe her and no one else would either."

Brodie knew that wasn't what Deacon had said, but it

might have been what the Frenches heard. "And that's when ...?"

"Yes, Mrs Farrell. That's when my beautiful girl who'd promised to spend her life with me walked down Dimmock beach, took off her shoes at the water's edge and walked into the sea. People saw her do it. They thought she was paddling. The water was up to her waist before they realised their mistake. Some of them tried to reach her but they were too far away – by the time they got there she was gone. The lifeboat searched for two days without finding her. Her body washed up under the Firestone Cliffs three weeks later."

By painting him in highlights and shadows the flat glare of the torch stripped his face back to its core elements of bone, skin and passion. Brodie could read his helpless rage clearer on that naked scaffold than on a face seen plainly by daylight. He had become a surrealist portrait, the distorted lines and colours serving to focus attention on the distilled essence of him, the seminal purpose.

His voice was a whisper. "I had to identify the body. My wife's body. My beautiful girl, who'd been three weeks in the English Channel. It's one of the busiest waterways in the world, did you know that? With Atlantic traffic passing east and west and local shipping heading north and south. Something had run her down – chewed her up. Then the crabs got to work. The woman at the hospital pulled back a sheet and said, 'Is this your wife?' And I didn't know. It didn't look like a human being."

Despite everything Brodie was moved to pity for him.

"You have to remember," she said quietly, "all that happened after she was dead. None of it touched her. She drowned in just a few minutes. Nothing that happened afterwards could hurt her."

"It hurt me!" yelled French, his face tracked with silver tears. "He did that – Jack Deacon. Took my lovely girl and gave me fish-food in return! I hated him more that day than I ever hated anything before. And I hate him more today than then."

Among the items Deacon brought back to Battle Alley was a cardboard box full of photographs. Feeling like a voyeur, Daniel picked through them.

He pushed one across the desk. "Is that Millie?"

Deacon glanced, nodded, looked away. Then he made himself look again. All this was happening because he hadn't given the girl the consideration she deserved. The decision he'd made on her case had been correct: he couldn't have persuaded the Crown Prosecution Service to proceed, and if he had the case would have failed. But he could have given her more time, more care. He could have made sure she understood that not charging Saville didn't mean he thought she was lying. The girl might be alive now if he had, and Brodie wouldn't be in the hands of a man dehumanised by grief.

So he looked at her. At first she looked entirely un-familiar. It was only a snap-shot, like the other snaps of smiling people posed against picturesque back-drops, and in all the time he'd spent with her she hadn't managed even a wry grin. She'd seemed broken by her experience, never began getting over it. It was as if her life stopped in that hotel room and nothing afterwards meant anything to her. So when she finally mustered the strength to take command of her situation, the action she took was entirely predictable. It hardly counted as suicide when her life was already so shrunken and etiolated.

But if her death had been so predictable, Deacon wondered now, why hadn't he prevented it? He must have seen how vulnerable she was, how the effort of going on had worn her almost to transparency. Her death wasn't inevitable. She was twenty-three years old – every cell in her body was burgeoning with life. Only the soul-deep hurt made it possible for her to contemplate a state of un-being. He should have guessed. He'd seen enough victims in his time. He should have helped her. Held her, kept her from falling.

And not only because Brodie would have been safe if he had. Millie French would have been safe too. The girl with the long, straight, fair hair posing self-consciously by the river would be alive and well and raising a brood of children by now. Her husband would be running his company, working to balance the demands of a business he loved and a family he loved more, instead of stoking the furnaces of hatred in a desperate attempt to cauterise his misery. He'd served them all badly. His failure had already cost one young woman's life. At this moment there was no way of knowing how much was yet to pay.

Daniel said, "Where is that?"

Deacon had hardly looked at the scenery. He'd

thought it was a river but perhaps it was a pond, with some old building behind. "I don't know."

Daniel didn't recognise it either. "Maybe they were on holiday."

Deacon wasn't interested in the Frenches' travels. He needed something that would lead him to Brodie. "Look out for a country cottage or maybe a beach-house. Somewhere quiet, somewhere he could go now he needs privacy."

Daniel thumbed through the photographs, shaking his yellow head. "I can't see anything. But that doesn't mean there isn't a cottage – it could be just out of shot. How would we know?"

"If there was somewhere they kept going back to," ruminated Deacon, "they'd keep photographing the same scenes. Look out for duplicates. The same trees in spring and autumn; Millie sunbathing on the rocks in summer, and sitting on the same rocks wrapped up in her winter woollies."

Daniel nodded and kept looking. But he found nothing. He thought there was nothing to find. "Is there any mention of a weekend cottage among his papers?"

"No," grunted Deacon, his shortness masking despair. "They may have rented a place." He pushed the papers away with an angry gesture. "But I'm damned if I know where."

"Or maybe he just found somewhere he could use for this," suggested Daniel. "An empty house, a derelict factory, a barn – somewhere he had no connection to until he took Brodie there. Maybe he just looked round till he found a place. Maybe that's what he's been doing for the last five years."

Deacon's eyes flared like kicked coals. "Don't say that. This is the best chance we have of finding her – don't tell me we're wasting our time!"

"I didn't mean to," said Daniel, chastened. "I just – " He looked up, the emotion naked in his face. "I'm scared, Jack. Brodie's in danger and I'm afraid we're not going to find her in time. Isn't there something more we can do?"

Deacon glowered at him across the desk, eyebrows beetling. His voice was harsh. "You blame me, don't you?"

"No." Daniel sounded honestly surprised. "Only for being who you are. I mean, this wouldn't have happened if you were a bus-driver. But I don't think that makes it your fault."

The policeman wasn't mollified. "Yes you do. Decisions I made five years ago are the reason Brodie's in danger now. Of course you blame me. I blame myself."

"Well don't," said Daniel stoutly. "Jack, you've done nothing wrong. You couldn't anticipate what's happened to Brodie any more than you could have guessed what Millie French would do. People are responsible for their own actions. Millie killed herself, and her husband kidnapped Brodie. Not because of what you did – because of who he is. The blame lies squarely with him. I know you're doing all you can to find her. Brodie knows that too. Knowing that is what's keeping her alive."

Deacon was not a man easily touched by kindness, he had no feminine side to get in touch with. He stared at Daniel Hood across the scratched surface of his desk and struggled, not for the first time, with the conflicting feelings the younger man stirred in him. He knew he should like him. He knew it was unreasonable not to. He knew Daniel was a good man, a decent and generous man. He'd seen what he was prepared to do to ease other people's pain. He thought it remarkable that, worried as he was about Brodie, he could find compassion for the man any reasonable person would blame for her predicament.

How could a man like Jack Deacon not hate the guts of someone like that? "We don't even know she is still alive," he said roughly. And he tried to tell himself there was some satisfaction in watching the pain crash through Daniel's eyes.

Michael French cocked his wrist to look at his watch. "That time already?" He stood up. "I have to go."

It was a guess – her own watch was gone, pulled off when he was dragging her in here – but Brodie thought it was mid-evening and French had been with her some four hours. In that time he hadn't laid an unkind hand on her. So the bizarre situation – picnicking with her captor while chained to a wall – had slowly acquired a normality of its own. It wasn't that she was no longer afraid, more that the fear had found its own level and settled there. As time passed without further drama it became possible to ignore it. To talk to him as she'd talked to Geoffrey Harcourt – not exactly as friends but with an ease, a frankness, a degree of mutual understanding. By not taking advantage of her helplessness he'd encouraged her to think that way.

When he said he was going, the balance shifted again. The reality that she wasn't free to do the same was unavoidable, as was the fact that he had an agenda to which she was not privy. She still didn't know what he meant to do with her. The fear that had lain dormant for four hours surged into her throat like bile.

"Go where?" She heard the shake in her voice and wondered if he'd heard it too.

"To the police station. I think perhaps Mr Deacon will make the time to see me now."

"You'll tell him where I am?"

"Yes," promised French. "But not immediately. I'm afraid you're going to be here a little while yet."

"How long?"

"Six hours. That's all. You can manage six hours, can't you?"

Six hours. Alone, in the cold and the dark. Brodie nodded. It could have been worse. "Leave me the torch."

He was contrite. "I'm sorry, I need it. I should have brought another one. You're safe enough – there's nothing here to harm you. There's nothing in the dark that isn't there in the daylight too."

She bit her lip. "Six hours?"

"Six hours," he assured her. "Then it'll be over."

"You know you're not going to get away with this, don't you?" said Brodie.

He nodded and smiled. "I don't expect to get away with it. I don't need to get away with it."

She stared at him, confounded. "Then what was it all for?"

He thought about that for a moment. "The look on Jack Deacon's face."

"God damn you, Michael French," she hissed as he backed away from her.

"I imagine so," he said bleakly. Then he turned, the beam of the torch swinging in a broken arc, and then he was gone.

Chapter Twenty-Two

The envelope was among the travel brochures: probably French had forgotten where he put it. There was no rent book or other paperwork, just a cutting from a newspaper and a leaf of a notebook on which he'd jotted down the gist of a telephone conversation. Together they told Deacon that Michael French had rented a small house in Cheyne Warren for three months, paying in advance two months ago. This then was where he went when he left River Drive.

Like River Drive, it was empty now. Past waiting for warrants, he put his foot through a panel of the back door and turned the key. Everybody keeps a key in the back door lock, even after they've moved out.

It took him three minutes to establish that Brodie wasn't there. Neither was French, and he didn't seem to be coming back. There was no food in the house, the bed had been stripped, the fire put out and no coal left ready. He'd finished with the place and moved out, leaving only the landlord's furniture and some clothes hanging in a wardrobe.

Deacon found it hard to believe they were French's clothes. The photographs had kick-started his memory, and what he remembered best about Millie's husband was his self-esteem. He drove a BMW coupé and dressed to match. He was a talented engineer and a successful businessman, and he liked people to know. He was proud of what he'd achieved. He said people like us a lot, and only just stopped himself asking if Deacon knew who he was dealing with.

These were not the clothes of a thirty-six-year-old style-conscious executive. They were old-fashioned, brown and tweedy, and some of them were knitted. Either French was so reduced in circumstances as to be shopping at Oxfam now, or they were a disguise. A new persona to do things and go places French could not. And they accorded with the descriptions given by witnesses at the railway station.

The only trace of himself French had left behind was in the parlour. Oil-cloths were spread on every shelf and table, and every surface was occupied by a little machine.

DC Winston was fascinated. "Do you think he made these, sir?"

Deacon looked closer. "Some of them are pretty old – older than him. The newer ones he probably made. It's what he did for a living – he designed and built machines."

"An engineer and model-maker," said Winston thoughtfully. "We were looking for someone who could rig a remote control system for a lift. If he can build these I bet he could do that."

It was another link in the chain. But all Deacon said, sourly, was: "Why, were you in some doubt?"

All police officers need thick skins. Those working for Deacon needed armour like a rhinoceros. Winston was undeterred. "There's one missing."

These models were important to Michael French. He'd brought very little of his old life to this house but he had brought these. He'd set them up carefully, each in their own space, and attended to them lovingly – and judging from the lack of dust – on an almost daily basis. But one of the oil-cloths was vacant. Something had stood there until recently, and it was possible to judge from the impression it left that it was heavy and half a metre in length, but of the model itself there was no sign. They searched the property without finding it.

"He must have taken it with him," said Winston.

Deacon thought he was right but wanted to know more. "Why? Why leave all these behind but take that one?"

"Maybe it was his favourite," hazarded Winston.

"They're not teddy-bears," growled the Superintendent. Yet French must have had a reason to encumber himself with something so large and awkward. He hadn't just slipped it in with his shaving gear: it had been a conscious decision to take this one though the others could remain. Why?

Answering his own question, thinking aloud, Deacon said slowly, "Because he didn't want us finding it, and he couldn't bring himself to destroy it. He thought there was a chance we'd find this place, but if we saw that particular model it would tell us something he didn't want us to know. So he took it with him."

DC Winston was suitably impressed. "How do we find out what it was?"

"When we find him," said Deacon shortly, "we'll ask him." He couldn't imagine there was another way. It never occurred to him to get a little girl out of bed and ask her what she knew about it.

* * *

Before Michael French started this he knew there could
be no turning back. He knew what the end result would
be and deliberated whether what he stood to gain was
worth what he stood to lose. And it was. Deciding to proceed, with all the risk that entailed, lifted a five-year-old
burden from his shoulders. A tide of recklessness swept
through him. The certainty of ultimate defeat left him
nothing to lose, freed him to follow the demands of his
heart without any regard for the consequences. To walk
calmly into the lion's den, though he knew he wouldn't
walk out again. To note with amusement that the reception he got at Battle Alley was quite different this time to
last.

There was no talk of waiting rooms. The sergeant on
the desk was eyeing him warily even before he gave his
name: when he did he was conducted to an interview
room, and two constables stayed with him while Deacon
was informed. The radio room called his mobile: he
answered as he was coming up the back steps on his
return from Cheyne Warren.

Deacon entered the interview room like a bull entering
a ring: as soon as he was there, no one was looking at the
matador. He crossed the room in two strides, lifted
French from his chair by the lapels and slammed him
against the wall. "Where is she, you bastard?"

The constables fluttered round him like a couple of
programme-sellers trying to stop the bull mid-charge,
unsure how to prevent him hurting French without get-

ting trampled in the process. But French was unruffled. He said – drawled, almost – "For the tape, that was Detective Superintendent Deacon entering the room."

Deacon didn't care what the tape was recording, what the constables were seeing, what complaints French might bring. Right now he didn't care if he'd have a job tomorrow. All he cared about was getting an answer to his question. "Where is she? What have you done with her? If you've hurt her I'll see you in hell if I have to take you there myself ... "

Suddenly someone else was in the room. Peter Fuller wasn't a heavyweight in Deacon's class but he was accustomed to wielding authority. His voice cut through the scuffle like a diamond saw. "Detective Superintendent Deacon, put that man down immediately. Constable Vickers, see Mr French to his seat. Constable Batty, summon the police surgeon. Jack – outside, now!"

But that wasn't what French had come for. He didn't mind a few bruises, he didn't mind a bloody nose; he'd endure broken bones rather than let them stretcher him away for treatment that would rob him of vital time. He'd come to watch the comprehension grow in Deacon's face – the knowledge of what he'd done, what it had cost, what it was costing still. He wanted to see the fury turn by inches to fear and finally to grief. He had five hours in which to extract the price of Millie's life from Jack Deacon's soul, and he didn't mean to waste a minute of it completing complaint forms for the custody sergeant.

His voice was level. "I'm sorry, Superintendent Fuller, but I won't talk to anyone but Detective Superintendent

Deacon. You may remain if you wish, you can provide me with bodyguards if you think it's necessary. But this is between Mr Deacon and me, and that's the only way it'll be resolved. If you want me to sign a disclaimer I will. I'll take full responsibility if Mr Deacon can't keep his hands in his pockets."

Fuller was momentarily lost for words. But it was only momentary. You don't get command of a police station just by being a good police officer: you get it by being a good manager of men. Anyone with the courage to face Jack Deacon in full spate was unlikely to be thrown by mere thugs and murderers.

"No, you won't," he said to French. "You're under suspicion of committing a serious crime: if nobody's got round to arresting you yet, I'll do it. I'll take responsibility for your safety here. And I, not you, will decide who will interview you. Now Jack, if we might have that word outside... "

Deacon followed him; not exactly like a lamb, more like a wolf who has unaccountably been mistaken for a lamb and is wondering whether he should eat very fast or try bleating.

"This is the situation we talked about," said Fuller when they were out in the corridor. "You've found him. Now it's time to hand him over to someone else."

"I didn't find him," gritted Deacon. "I couldn't find him – he covered his tracks too well. He's here because he wants to be. You heard him: he wants to talk to me. He wants to – I don't know – lecture me, gloat over me? OK, if that's the price for getting Brodie back, I'll pay it. I won't thump him, I promise. But he's not going to talk to anyone else, and until he talks we're not going to find her. Let me do what he wants. Once she's safe you can do anything you like."

"I can do anything I like now," said Fuller pointedly.

"Of course you can," agreed Deacon. "And you can make a mistake. It's easy, believe me. You can make a reasonable decision that has totally unforeseen consequences, that other people are still paying for five years down the line. No one will blame you but you'll know. You'll know you had a chance to prevent a disaster and you let it go. Peter." It was the first time he'd used Fuller's Christian name. "Don't let it go."

People show distress in different ways. Some freeze, some weep, some shout. Deacon was a shouter, but he wasn't shouting now. The low urgent monotone of his voice was harder to ignore than if he had been. In his eyes Fuller saw not fury but fear. Compassion for the big man flooded his veins but still he hesitated, wrestling with the implications of whatever choice he made. Brodie Farrell's life was the most important consideration but it wasn't the only one. And it wasn't clear to him that it could best be protected by doing as her abductor wished.

On the other hand, he couldn't claim with confidence to know a better answer. He was burning no boats by granting the suspect's request and allowing Deacon to proceed. If he didn't pull him out now, he could pull him out in ten minutes' time. If he did pull him out it would be harder to put him back if French clammed up.

"All right," he decided. "Stay with him. But by God, Jack, if he has a pimple at the end of this that he didn't have at the start you'd better be able to prove it wasn't your doing!"

Still shackled to the wall by her right wrist, unable to move more than a little, cold and damp and profoundly oppressed by the darkness, Brodie hung onto her sanity by a succession of devices. She told herself that when a man who's dropped a brick on you, violated your home and kidnapped you leaves you alone somewhere, that's good news. She told herself the darkness only seemed this absolute because she'd got used to the torchlight, and that as her eyes adjusted she'd be able to see a little again. She told herself French had no reason to lie when he said it would all be over in six hours' time. Though she had no way to check she thought the first of those hours must already have passed. One down, five to go.

But six hours alone in the dark leaves too much time for thinking. Ten minutes after French left she knew that moonlight couldn't penetrate this deep and she'd see nothing more until after dawn tomorrow. She was as good as blind.

As with any void, her mind worked to fill it, to compensate for the missing sense and furnish the missing data. She started seeing shapes, movements, the outlines of things that weren't there. For now she knew they weren't there because she wouldn't have been able to see them if they had been. But the night stretched ahead of her, and as time passed that brave thread of logic would grow thin and finally fail. When it did she would be alone in the dark with monsters.

And then, a man who's done all French had done clearly has few inhibitions about hurting people. He was no longer here with her, talking in that martyred way about his unhappy wife, but did that in fact mean she was safe from him? He'd managed to frighten and hurt her unseen before and could do so again if his plan required it. That plan was the instrument of his vengeance against Jack Deacon, designed to cause him as much anguish as possible. Would twelve hours of not knowing where she was accomplish that? The more Brodie thought about it, the less likely it seemed that the climax French was building up to was for Deacon to rush over here in five hours' time and find her sitting damp and snivelling in the dark.

He'd said she'd be all right, that she'd be rescued early tomorrow. Could she count on that? If French had no reason to lie, he had no overwhelming need to tell her the truth either. Perhaps he was just being kind. And now she thought about it, that wasn't quite what he'd said. He'd said he never wanted to hurt her. He'd said it would all be over when Deacon got here. All that could be literally true without ensuring her safety. He could have left her here to die. The satisfaction he demanded of Deacon might be nothing more elegant than the discovery of her dead body.

There was no way to know. Somewhere in the next few hours, if French was to be believed, events would take one course or the other. Rescue or...not. Or Deacon would find her, by his own efforts and overthrowing French's plan, and she'd be out of here before the bell tolled for anyone. He was a detective, after all. How difficult could it be?

In the darkness she heard two kinds of movement – both quiet, secretive. One, she was horribly afraid, was a rat pattering round. The other just sounded like running water.

"All right," said Deacon, restarting the interrupted tape and taking the seat opposite Michael French. "You want to talk to me, here I am. You want my full attention? You have it. You've been offered the right to have a solicitor present and declined. Now let's get down to business. Where's Brodie Farrell?"

But that wasn't what French had sacrificed his liberty to talk about. Not yet. He said, "You killed my wife."

"Of course I didn't kill your wife," said Deacon brusquely. "Your wife committed suicide. I'm sorry if there's something you think I could have done to prevent it, but I'm not to blame for her death. And Brodie sure as hell isn't."

Now he had what he wanted – Jack Deacon across a table, unable to ignore what he had to say – French relaxed. There had been moments in the last fortnight when he'd wondered if he'd ever get to this point, or if his careful plans would collapse as soon as the players he'd been manoeuvring in his mind for so long stepped off his mental stage and into their own reality. He'd thought he'd foreseen their motives, their reactions, how they would handle the drama created for them, but he could have got it wrong. If he'd misjudged one critical response he could have found himself here before anything worthwhile had been achieved.

Amazingly – and looking back it was amazing, there were so many points at which the train could have derailed, the odds against bringing it in safe had been ter-rifyingly long – right now he was exactly where he'd hoped to be. He'd out-thought them all, and Deacon was at his mercy.

But he hadn't waited five years to be merciful. This interview wasn't an end so much as a climax: he had five hours to enjoy his success. It wasn't that long, not com-pared with five years; but it would be long enough to make sure that Deacon, who hadn't thought much of Millie when she was alive and probably hadn't thought of her at all since she died, would never forget her. And then, while most of this was for Millie, French was honest enough to admit that some of it was for him. Retribution. Payment for what he'd lost. He meant to feed on Jack Deacon's despair for the next five hours. Nothing after that mattered.

"This isn't about Mrs Farrell," he said. "You know that. She's a pleasant enough woman who never did me any harm – actually, she was kind to me. The only mistake she made was to take up with you."

Deacon nodded slowly. "So you've been terrorising a woman who was kind to you because you were too cow-ardly to face me. Jesus, Michael, Millie would be proud of you!"

That wasn't his temper slipping: he was trying to

provoke French. To crack his resolve, tempt him to an indiscretion. Deacon knew who was in charge. This suspect wasn't tracked down by brilliant detective work and dragged in here kicking and screaming: he presented himself at the front desk and Deacon was here because of it. This room, this table, even the softly hissing tape were not Deacon's today. Today they were French's – props on his stage, witnesses in his court. He held the initiative, and the massive advantage of knowing how this was supposed to end, and Deacon needed to shake him. Right now, French angry was less dangerous than French in iron control.

The desire to surge to his feet and grab Deacon by the collar raced through Michael French as a tremor races through the earth, engaging then abandoning each muscle in turn, leaving him essentially where he had been, only disturbed-looking. He spread his blunt hands on the table-top, staring at them and breathing hard. "Nothing you say," he panted. "Nothing you say alters the facts. You didn't know Millie. You didn't take the time to get to know Millie. You have no idea what she found in me to be proud of."

That caught Deacon up short: because it was true but also because it resonated with his own uncertainties. He and Brodie had been together for five months, and he had no more idea what she saw in him now than he had at the start. There must be something. She was a handsome woman, if she wanted a man she could walk into the street and point. The initial euphoria that she'd pointed at him had, as the relationship developed, spawned puzzlement and unease. If he didn't know what she saw in him, how could he believe it would last?

He grabbed his straying attention and hoped French hadn't noticed. "No," he agreed quietly. "But I think she was a good person. I don't think she'd have wanted you to harm another innocent woman, whatever the reason. She might understand where it came from – the pain, the loss, the loneliness – but I don't think she'd have stood by and let it happen. Do you? You knew her better than anyone. Can you see her watching while you destroyed Brodie Farrell out of hatred for me?"

But a man can do a lot of soul-searching in five years. French had asked himself that before, and found an answer. There were no questions Deacon could ask that French hadn't dealt with a hundred times. "No, I can't," he said softly. "But then, if she was here I wouldn't be doing this. She isn't here, she's dead. Because of what you did to her."

"I never touched her!"

This was why French was here: to hear Deacon's increasingly desperate arguments and demolish them. He went on remorselessly. "My wife was a virgin when we married. She never had another man, except the one who raped her. She was frightened, hurt and humiliated. But that didn't kill her.

"She dreaded coming here. But it was the right thing to do and she did it. Men who behave that way don't just do it once: she wanted to stop him before he hurt other women. It wasn't lack of courage that killed her either.

"What killed her was that it was all for nothing. Because you didn't believe her. Or maybe it was worse than that – you believed her but didn't think it was worth the trouble of obtaining justice for her. You chewed her up and then her spat out, and you didn't leave her enough self-respect to live on. That's why she died."

"I did believe her," said Deacon quietly. "I believed she was telling the truth, that she didn't want to have sex with William Saville. But I knew what neither of you did – that in a rape trial the woman's actions are scrutinised at least as closely as the man's. Saville would have bought himself a good, tough barrister and he'd have taken her apart. Publicly and protractedly. She'd never have stood up to that. I was doing her a favour by not asking her to."

But French had anticipated that argument too. "If she couldn't face the prospect of a trial she'd never have come to you. It wasn't for you to judge what she could stand. He raped her, and his defence was that he took her for a slut, and you accepted that. Can you imagine how that made her feel?"

Deacon raised both shoulders in a gesture that was meant to convey sympathy but looked like a shrug. "I know it was difficult for her – "

"Difficult?" yelled French, leaning forward so the gale of his breath blasted Deacon's face. "You think it was difficult for her? You labelled her a slut and a liar, and everyone who knew what happened knew that was your opinion. You're surprised she didn't want to live that down? You robbed her of her self-respect, left her feeling soiled and worthless. After that every day was an ordeal. Do you know, she came to believe you were right? That she must have encouraged Saville, given him a reason to think she was willing. That she was to blame all along. That she let me down. Can you believe that? She was afraid she'd let me down!"

Deacon felt his brows gathering of their own accord. He felt to be on the edge of a truth. "Michael – is that what this is about? You're afraid you let Millie down? Not me but you? You think you should have seen what was happening to her and found a way to stop it. God almighty, Michael – you blamed her?"

Chapter Twenty-Three

For an instant longer French stared into Deacon's eyes from a range of inches, the rage boiling off him. Then he flung himself back in his chair.

But in that instant Deacon knew what had happened. The couple had survived the initial trauma, and the painful days and weeks that followed, by supporting one another. But they got tired. French got tired enough to say something he didn't mean, that he could never have meant, that Millie would have known he didn't mean if she'd had any reserves left. And Millie got tired enough to walk down the beach rather than reason with him.

Which didn't excuse the things Deacon did, or didn't do, around then. He should have taken the time to explain to the Frenches what it meant that he wasn't going to charge Saville – more precisely, what it didn't mean. It didn't mean he thought Millie was lying. A prosecution would fail because the jury would think Saville might also be telling the truth. There was a grey area where a misunderstanding could have arisen, and they wouldn't jail a man for rape if they weren't sure that was his intention.

"Oh God, Michael," Deacon said thickly, "I'm sorry. You'd taken a hammering too – you can't blame yourself for letting one unkind remark slip out. It went on too long. You can be a rock for somebody, but only so long. Eventually even rock weathers. Is that what happened? You finally ran out of patience, and in an unguarded moment you said something you'd never have said if you hadn't been so bloody exhausted.

"It shouldn't have mattered. She should have burst into tears, or thrown the kettle at you, and you should have screamed at one another for a minute and then grabbed hold of one another and hung on. Neither of you was to blame for the situation. You were doing the best you could.

"But instead of chucking the kettle she ran out of the house, and you never saw her alive again. You never got the chance to apologise. That's why you hate me. Because if it isn't my fault she's dead it's yours, and no one should have to carry that burden."

French looked up then. There were no tears. He'd done all the crying he was capable of five years ago. His eyes were like polished agate, shiny and hard. "You're letting your imagination run away with you, Superintendent. I loved my wife. I would never say anything to hurt her."

There was a pause. Deacon had thought he was making progress. He knew where he had to be, wasn't sure how to get there. "Michael – how are we going to resolve this?"

French shrugged, settled back in his chair. "You tell me. I'm at your disposal, it's your problem now. How are you going to resolve it?"

Deacon chewed his lip. Shouting would get him nowhere and for once he recognised the fact. "Have you hurt her?"

French paused before answering, for no better reason than to let dread gnaw a moment on the other man's vitals. "No. A whiff of chloroform kept her quiet while I got things organised. She's fine. Not comfortable, not happy, but fine."

"Where is she?"

French laughed aloud. "Come on, Superintendent! You don't really expect me to answer that?"

Deacon forced a rueful smile. "You might. Now you've put the fear of God into me you might think this has gone on long enough, and the sooner somebody rescues Brodie the better. You don't want her to come to any real harm, after all. Do you?"

French smiled, cat-like with idle cruelty. "Don't I?"

Deacon kept his hands on the table in front of him, where he could see them. "I wouldn't have thought so. Not when you're going to stand trial for it. Unlawful imprisonment is one thing, murder's another."

The smile faded leaving French's face sombre. "Yes, it is."

"Tell me where she is, let me go and get her. Then we can talk."

French's eyes were scornful. "Superintendent, the only reason you're talking to me now is that I know where your lady friend is and you don't! I think we'll leave it like that until I've had everything I want from you. It's quite hard to get your undivided attention. Believe me, I've tried."

Deacon dipped his head in what might have been a real apology. "I am aware I didn't give you and Millie the time I should have. I didn't look after you as well as I should have. It wasn't that I thought it didn't matter, I just didn't see victim support as my responsibility. Even when she died, I didn't realise it was anything to do with me. I thought I'd done all I could, when it came to nothing I moved on. It's what we do – close one case, for better or for worse, and start the next. There's not much time for inquests. If you made mistakes you try not to make them again; if you got it right you enjoy the warm glow while it lasts – which is generally that night in the pub because tomorrow's headlines will have police being baffled about a whole new set of mysteries."

French gathered his brows in a frown. "Let me get this right. You think I should be sorry for you?"

Deacon bristled – and immediately every muscle at his command locked rigid. He absolutely could not afford to lose his temper with this man. He couldn't spare the time, he couldn't risk Fuller pulling him out, and he needed to get a grip on this interview which was different from any other he'd conducted.

People had walked in off the street to confess to him before. But that wasn't what French was doing. He'd come for his pound of flesh. Deacon had to regain the initiative if he wanted answers to his questions – but gently, because French held the ultimate sanction of withdrawing from any proceedings which didn't serve his agenda. It was like a game they were playing: each anxious to defeat the other, to outmanoeuvre his pieces and demolish his strategy, but also aware the game would end if the other left the table.

French knew that if Deacon took a swing at him he'd be down the corridor faster than he could say PACE. That was the last thing he wanted. He wanted to see Deacon suffer. He wanted to watch him grow increasingly desperate as the machinery of power failed him, as he discovered that his authority and the code of law underpinning it would not serve him now. That it was just the two of them, and this time French had nothing at stake and Deacon had everything. He wanted to be there when Deacon finally understood what losing everything felt like. He had to be there to see the hope turn to ashes in his face.

In months to come there would be arguments about his sanity. In fact he knew exactly what he was doing, wouldn't demean himself by claiming otherwise. He wasn't mad, just very, very angry. He'd been angry so long it no longer affected his capacity to function, reverberated in his voice or made his hands shake. What it mostly did was stiffen his resolve to a steely determination. No pressure Deacon could bring to bear would bend him. He would break first.

Both men needed to keep this dialogue going. It made them infinitely careful about every word they said.

Deacon unknotted his fists knuckle by knuckle. "No, I don't want your sympathy. I'm trying to explain how it happened. But you're not interested in how it happened, are you? You think I shouldn't have let it happen. Of course, you're right.

"What do you want from me, Michael? My resignation? You can have it. Tell me where Brodie is and as soon as she's safe I'll go. I'll make a public statement saying why. I served you poorly and I'll pay for it. But Brodie's not part of this. Let her go. Don't soil Millie's memory by using her as an excuse to hurt another woman."

French regarded him without expression, the very stillness of his body a kind of threat. It seemed to suggest that when he finally moved the sky would fall.

He broke the spell with a tiny shrug. Deacon was watching so intently it made him start. "Call it an excuse if you like. I call it a reason. Millie, and what happened to her, is why all of us are where we are today. You, me and Mrs Farrell. And why none of us is going anywhere for the next" – he glanced at his watch – "four hours."

"What happens in four hours?"

Michael French's lips curved in a faint knowing smile. "The big reunion."

"You give me your word?"

The smile broadened. It was impossible to take any comfort from it. "Oh yes."

It was most certainly a rat. There were crumbs left from the picnic: it had caught the scent and was screwing up the courage to investigate. In the crowding dark it ventured nearer, its progress marked by the tiny skipping patter of its claws on the floor. Brodie yelled and flung her free arm in its direction, and was rewarded by a diminuendo skitter as the creature fled. But ten minutes later it was back.

A soft touch on her breast where her collar was open gripped her with a momentary horror so great she couldn't even scream. But as the cool spot migrated down the curve of her body she realised what it was: a tear fallen from the end of her nose as she sat huddled in the dark. She hadn't even realised she was crying.

She couldn't know how desperate her plight was, whether it would end in a few hours in tears and hugs or if she was meant to die down here. She wouldn't know until one thing or the other happened. Nor had she any way of measuring time. But if the cold relaxed its grip that might mean it was day, and past the deadline French had set for her rescue. Which could mean she was in for a long haul.

It would not mean she was as good as dead. Deacon was looking for her, drawing on the full resources of his force. She was unhurt, and had eaten and drunk within the past few hours. It was cold here but not freezing – she could survive like this for days. Longer, if she could find the source of that trickling sound and a way to reach it. Among the rubbish there might be a stick: she had a handkerchief, and water wrung from a rag would keep her alive while the search continued.

That was her first priority: to try to better her situation. She should have used the light while French was here to scan her surroundings for anything she could use. She hadn't been thinking that far ahead. Now the torch had gone a finger-tip search was the only option. She gritted her teeth and told herself the rat was no keener on a close encounter than she was. Still it took an effort of will to reach into the blackness and begin to map the refuse strewn across the floor.

But her right wrist was still shackled to the wall, and in the arc of her reach she found nothing helpful. Mostly what she found was rubble, slimy with algae. She thought again about the trickling sound. There must be times when a fair bit of water got in here. If it rained, would she find herself sitting in a puddle?

"What do you want from me?" Despite his best intentions, as near as damn it Deacon was shouting now. Even by his own standards: by anyone else's he'd been shouting for a while. "How can I bring this to an end? What is it you're waiting for?"

French knew the answer to that. "For you to accept your responsibility for Millie's death. To admit that it wasn't suicide – that you forced her into a position, and a state of mind, from which there was no other escape. That you killed her. Tell me you killed her."

Only the safety of someone he cared for would have made Jack Deacon humble himself before this man. He knew he'd made mistakes, should have done better by the Frenches. But he didn't believe he was responsible, either legally or morally, for the girl's suicide. Someone who walks into the sea months after an attack on her may be depressed, may be despairing, but is responding to internal not external pressures. He hadn't treated her well. But he hadn't treated her so badly that suicide was a legitimate response.

But finally this wasn't about Millie. It was about Michael French – what he believed, what he'd accept as the price of Brodie's life. "All right. I killed her," said Deacon, his voice low.

French shook his head like a teacher correcting a sullen student. "Not just the words, Mr Deacon. Feel it. Know it. You killed her. You put her through hell, then you lost interest and that's why she died. She came to you for help, and you wiped your feet on her. You tossed her into the gutter and she drowned there. Say it."

"I killed her," Deacon said again, tersely. "I killed her, Michael. I'm to blame for the death of your wife. All right? I'll say it as many times as you want, as many different ways as you want, in front of anyone you want. I killed Millie French."

"But you don't believe it," murmured French. Disappointment was bitter on his tongue. He'd thought, when he got to this point, there'd be a sense of achievement. But it was meaningless if it was just the words. "You'll say anything to save Mrs Farrell."

"Of course I will!" exploded Deacon. "Damn it, that's why you're here – because you can make me say things I wouldn't say otherwise! If that isn't enough for you, I don't know what else I can do."

"You can believe it! You can feel remorse."

"I do feel remorse," said Deacon. "That much is true. The rest...I'll tell you anything you want to hear, but if there's a part of you that's still in touch with reality, that knows the truth when it hears it, and if that part is telling you that I don't believe the words you're putting in my mouth, maybe that's because you don't believe them either. Because they aren't credible. Because we both know the difference between a tragedy and a murder. What happened to Millie shattered her confidence, and what she did because of that shattered your world. I don't think you're an evil man. But what you're doing is evil. I'll do anything in my power to help you stop."

For minutes the silence in the little room was broken only by the faint hiss of the tape. French studied Deacon's irregular features as if the answer to a puzzle might be written there. His brows knit in a frown and he looked at his hands, folded in his lap.

Deacon said nothing more. He dared not. He thought it just possible French was reconsidering his position. That he was coming round to thinking he'd already had all the satisfaction he was going to get out of this and it was time to talk terms.

After an agonising wait French looked up again and met his eyes. "I don't want to stop. This is all I have left. All you left me. I'm not interested in making it easier for you."

Deacon said, choking, "Brodie... "

French leaned forward over the table, peering into his face. "Now do you understand? Are you beginning to get some inkling of how it feels? To have something you'd gladly die for and watch it die instead? Have you the least notion what you did to me, Mr Deacon?"

Deacon was restraining himself by sheer iron determination. But some kind of a nexus was coming: he could feel it. "Are you telling me Brodie's dead?"

French shook his head. "No. She isn't."

"Is she going to die?"

Sometimes, an absence of reply is reply enough.

A little after eleven someone sat on the bench beside Daniel, waking him. He was amazed that he'd fallen asleep. But he'd been sitting here, up the corridor from the interview room, for a couple of hours now, with nothing to do but the sure conviction that he dare not leave, and the mental exhaustion that came of being worried sick and also quite helpless had gradually settled on him, weighing down his eyelids, slowing his breath.

There hadn't been time for the rest to do him any good. He woke with a start, staring round wildly before his eyes focused. Of course, his glasses hanging off one ear didn't help.

When he'd pulled himself together he looked at the new arrival and his eyes widened. "What happened to you?"

DS Voss gave a minimalist shrug that didn't hurt too much. "I fell off a motorbike."

"In front of a truck?"

Voss managed a rueful smile. He pointed up the corridor with his nose, bloody and swollen. Helen had thought it probably wasn't broken. But then, Helen had thought he was going to A&E for X-rays. "What's happening in there?"

Daniel raised a pale eyebrow. "You think they tell me? I know Jack went in, then Superintendent Fuller went in, then they both came out and argued a bit, then Jack went back in. That's two hours ago. Nothing's happened since. I tried to tell myself that was a good sign."

Charlie Voss didn't understand the relationship between Brodie and Daniel but he knew it was something real and strong. The man needed as much compassion as if his wife or perhaps his sister was missing. "If French had killed her and come in here to confess, there'd be no point not saying where he'd left the body. And if he knew that, the chief wouldn't still be here." However many promotions Deacon earned, he would remain The Chief to a man who first served under him as a chief inspector.

Hope twisted a knife under Daniel's ribs. "You think she's alive?"

Voss knew he could be wrong. But it was kinder to be optimistic and wrong than pessimistic and right. "I think so. If he wanted her dead he could have done it days ago. He went to some trouble not to. And why kill Brodie? He doesn't even know her. This is about the chief. About taking his revenge. He can do that without making himself a murderer."

Daniel was desperate to believe him. And it sounded plausible. Voss knew about criminals and murder and stuff. Probably he was right. As recently as a couple of days ago Daniel had been ready to sever whatever tied him to this woman. Tonight he'd have given his right arm – and that was the literal truth – to see her safe.

Chapter Twenty-Four

Deacon got to his feet, stretching muscles rigid with tension. "I don't know about you but I need a break. Let's whistle up some tea and try again in half an hour."

Whatever he was expecting, French's reaction surprised him. The man rocked quickly forward in his chair, leaning across the table, his expression urgent. "No! I didn't come here for tea, I came so you and I could talk. With everything that's happened, this is the first time we've really talked."

"But you're not saying anything, Michael," said Deacon wearily. "You've told me what I did to you, what my mistakes cost you. I've told you I'm sorry. I've told you I'll resign if that's what you want – I've told you I'll do anything that you want – but apparently that isn't enough. I don't know what would be. I want to know where Brodie is and you don't want to tell me. What else can we talk about?"

"I haven't said I won't tell you," insisted French, "only that I'm not ready to tell you yet."

"Fine," said Deacon. "So let's order some tea."

French glanced at his watch again. "We can drink it while we're talking, can't we? We can't stop when we're starting to get somewhere."

Deacon stared at him. "Are we starting to get somewhere? Michael, we're going round in circles. If you're ready to tell me something, yes, we'll keep going. Are you?"

French hesitated. Deacon turned away. "That's what I thought. Listen, I need a break. I'll pick up some tea, then you can tell me if you're ready to take this forward or if you're just going to faff me around some more. Because if you are, Michael, there are more important things I could be doing."

French didn't reply. His mouth was a straight line, yielding nothing. "Fine," growled Deacon. He stopped the tape and left the room.

The men on the bench stood up – Daniel more easily than Voss – and came to meet him. "Well?"

But Deacon shook his head. "Nothing. He didn't come here to talk. I don't know why he did come. To tell me it's all my fault, of course, but he could have done that over the phone. I don't know what it is he wants. But he can hardly take his eyes off me. And there's a deadline: he keeps looking at his watch. Something happens at three o'clock tomorrow morning." He checked his own wrist. It wasn't tomorrow any more.

"The tide turns," Daniel said automatically.

The policemen looked at him. What they knew and what they guessed and what was possible reeled through their eyes like the tumblers on a one-armed bandit: when they stopped there were four in a row, which meant some kind of a pay-out.

Voss said quietly, "High tide or low tide?"

"High tide."

"How do you know?" frowned Deacon.

Daniel shrugged. "I live on the beach. I know what the tide's doing."

"And it's high at three o'clock this morning?"

"Ten past."

"In two and a half hours."

"Yes." Daniel wasn't a detective, he hadn't put it together yet. He didn't realise he was talking about a death sentence and the instrument of execution.

Those who did immediately cut him out of the conversation. They knew something now that they hadn't known two minutes ago but they still didn't know the whereabouts of Brodie Farrell. They rattled through the options.

"A boat?" said Deacon tersely. "One of those hulks on the Barley River that cover at high tide?"

Voss was nodding. "That's why he went away and came back. There was too much going on here, you weren't going to see him in time."

"He wanted to be with me while Brodie was drowning!" grated Deacon.

"Like Millie drowned," said Voss softly. "He wanted to tell you about it when it was too late to save her. He wanted you to see her body the same way he saw his wife's."

They were already heading down the corridor. Deacon wouldn't waste time gathering manpower from around the station: he used his phone, wanted all available hands in the car park five minutes ago.

Daniel bobbed along in his wake like a pram-dinghy behind a battleship. He still wasn't sure what they were talking about. "You know where she is? Is she all right?"

Deacon broke his stride just long enough to swing round on him. "No, Daniel, she's not. She's sitting in the bottom of a boat with the bung out. She's up to her waist in water now: as the tide rises it'll go above her head. We don't know where this boat is, and we won't know it when we see it. We'll have to search every derelict on every mudflat up and down the coast, and we have two and a half hours to do it. We need to be searching, not talking about it. Stay here. I'll let you know when there's some news."

Then he was gone, leaving Daniel alone in the corridor with his mouth open and his eyes bottomless with shock.

Given enough manpower you can search a lot of garages, sheds and lock-ups in two and a half hours, at least well enough to find someone who's been unlawfully imprisoned. Boats are different, and boats that take the ground hardest of all. You can neither walk out to them and peep through the portholes nor row out: all you can do is scramble into waders like old men's trousers, with the waist up under the chin, and struggle through mud like the Mississippi: too thick to drink, too thin to plough.

When the police cars reached the Barley estuary their headlamps picked out a score of neglected hulks in assorted shapes and sizes but all the same colour as the mud they lay on. These were not the only derelict boats in the area but they were the largest concentration: it made sense to start here and only proceed elsewhere if they drew a blank.

Considering the scene, Deacon saw the problem immediately. As the tide crept in the mud slipped, sucking, beneath the surface which gleamed with dull rainbows as if the clams had struck oil, and the boats became all but unreachable from the bank. There were a couple of dinghies pulled above the high-water mark, but they would have to be manhandled over the mud and would have capsized as the policemen tried to clamber in. It was possible; it would have been desperately slow.

"Now what?" he exclaimed, caught between anger and despair.

Voss was listening. "Just a minute."

What had sounded at first like the buzzing of an insect soon hardened and deepened to an engine note, and a moment after that a light appeared around the hem of the land and the RNLI's inshore lifeboat, normally kept in a garage in Dimmock, rode up the Barley on a V of moonlight.

Deacon turned slowly and looked at his sergeant. "You thought of this?"

Voss shrugged. "It seemed the best way to get out there."

"I didn't know there'd be a problem."

"You'd have called the Coastguard when you saw there was."

"And we'd have lost twenty minutes."

Neither man said anything more. There is no precedent in the British police force for senior officers thanking their sergeants, and if there had been Jack Deacon was not a man to be bound by tradition. But he knew that if they found Brodie with less than twenty minutes on the clock she'd owe her life to Charlie Voss.

A thought occurred to him. It was a bit like bringing

the after-dinner mints when someone else has cooked a four-course meal, but it was better than nothing. "I should call for divers. Just in case." He reached for his phone.

Voss cleared his throat. "I – er – asked them to bring a diver with them."

There was a jetty reaching out into the river – or rather the remains of a jetty, not much more now than a few posts with some decking clinging drunkenly to them. The orange boat took half the police contingent aboard and dropped them, two at a time, on the rotting hulks sliding perceptibly beneath the waves. It went first to those at the seaward end of the estuary. If Brodie was on one of the upstream boats she had a few minutes' grace.

Deacon went with the first contingent. Voss stayed on the jetty, meaning to go with the second. But when the boat came back he was sitting on the deck with his feet dangling above the water and his forehead leaned against a post, and he looked to be asleep. PC Batty climbed over him carefully and told the coxswain not to wake him. "He fell off a motorbike."

"He's not going to fall in the river, is he?" asked the man, concerned.

Without opening his eyes Voss mumbled, "No, he's fine where he is. Pick him up on the way back."

No one told Michael French that the interview was over but after ten minutes PC Vickers conducted him to a cell. He was puzzled and concerned. "Where's Detective Superintendent Deacon? I'm happy to continue. I told him I was happy to continue."

There are formulae for every situation in a police station. Vickers slipped into the appropriate one without even having to think. "Something came up. He hasn't forgotten you – he'll see you as soon as he's free."

French's face was appalled. "But that won't do! Time's passing. Time matters!"

Perhaps there isn't a formula for everything. Vickers pursed his lips. It was always better to say nothing than too much, but still... "I imagine that's how Mr Deacon feels too. Listen, Mr French, I'm just here to see you to your cell and bring you some tea, but you might want to give a bit of thought to your next move. You can change your mind and see a solicitor any time you want, but either way it might be a good idea to make a statement now. I think they've found her."

As French went on staring at him, Vickers saw the man's world collapse from the top down and fall through his eyes, taking his heart with it. "No," he whispered, stricken. "He has to lose."

"How about it?" asked Vickers diplomatically. "Do you want to talk to someone? Superintendent Fuller's still in the building – just about everyone else has gone to the river."

As soon as he'd said it he realised he probably shouldn't have. But the lack of a reaction from French reassured him that the search-party wasn't wasting its time.

French blinked uncertainly. For five years the prospect of having Deacon at his mercy, of paying him back, had been what held him together. With that gone it was almost possible to see his personality fragment. "Why would I want to see Superintendent Fuller?"

Vickers hung onto his patience. "To make a statement? To get your account on record before Mr Deacon comes back and says his girlfriend's safe, and no one's interested in anything you have to say."

"They've found her?" It was as if the idea had simply never occurred to him.

"They will have by now," said Vickers. "There were a dozen of them, they'll have searched everything on the river, floating or sunk, by now."

Something extraordinary was happening behind French's eyes. The debris which had tumbled there, the building-blocks of his world, were slowly reassembling themselves and mounting up, like film of a demolition run backwards. His face and his body were very still, his expression frozen, but behind his eyes a new edifice was growing. He said – and his voice was still too but the kind of still that vibrates, that is the only possible alternative to an explosion – "Boats. They're searching the boats. In the mud-berths on the Barley."

Vickers knew now he'd said too much. Or perhaps not, because if French was about to tell him they'd got it wrong, that was something Deacon needed to know. "You're saying they aren't going to find her?"

And French smiled. "Of course they're going to find her," he said with a kind of avuncular calm. "Just not there, and not in time."

They'd come to a halt in the middle of the corridor. Now Vickers got things moving again. He hustled French to his cell, shouting to the custody officer, and headed for the radio room at a run.

For a few seconds longer Daniel remained glued by thought to the bench where he'd been sitting unnoticed by the two men debating Brodie's life three paces away. Then he rose and went upstairs, and let himself back into Deacon's office.

On the third boat he tried, Deacon's shouts were answered by a frantic hammering deep within the hull. It was a steel boat – possibly some kind of a landing-craft, then a pleasure-boat, now a derelict vanishing twice daily beneath the English Channel – so the sound came at him like drums. His heart leapt in concert and he turned, muddy and triumphant, to those behind him. "She's here. We've found her."

The stern of the craft was already under water. But the bows stood a little higher and the hold wouldn't fill until the creeping tide reached an open hatch in the forepeak. When it did the sea would pour in like Niagara. The decks were awash as far as the waist.

Deacon ran, his boots sliding from under him in a mousse of mud and water, keeping his feet by grabbing what was left of the handrail except for twice when there was nothing left. Then he measured his length in water up to his ankles. It hardly slowed him. He surged forward, on his hands and knees when he couldn't stand, racing the incoming tide.

The hammering from below had stopped. Deacon shouted her name again but Brodie didn't answer. But he reached the hatch before the sea did and he thought she was safe.

As he thrust his head through the hatch there was an explosion of white immediately below him and something at once soft and muscular hit him in the face and bowled him backwards, rolling once more in the liquid mud. Startled and uncomprehending, it took him a moment to focus on the swan rowing away up-river, a metre above the waves.

Then his heart hit rock-bottom. He stood up, trembling with reaction, and gestured DC Winston towards the hatch. His voice was rough and cracked. "Check it anyway. But I doubt that bird would have been in there if anyone else was."

They kept searching, the orange boat ferrying officers between the disappearing hulks until nothing remained above water but masts. Somehow they'd managed to check every boat before it was covered. Brodie was on none of them. There was no sign that she had been on any of them.

Unsurprisingly, Deacon's phone wasn't working. Voss's was. It was PC Vickers, calling from Battle Alley. "I don't think you're in the right place. I thought French was going to give it up, but when he realised where you were he backed right off again. He didn't say much, only that you'd got it wrong, but I believe him. I saw his face. He didn't reckon he was beat."

Edwin Turnbull of Turnbull, Fitch & Stewart had been asleep for three hours when his wife Doreen prodded him in the ribs and hissed in his ear, "There's a drunk in the garden."

It wasn't so much a garden as a front step with a few pot-plants. But Mr Turnbull liked living in town. He could walk to work and didn't spend every Sunday mowing the lawn. The only drawback to living close to his office was that occasionally people looked at the photographs of houses for sale in his shop window and couldn't wait until he opened for business.

Grumbling, he rolled out from under the quilt and went to the window. At the same time the lion's head knocker on his front door began to thunder. The estate agent pushed up the sash and stuck his head out. "Go away! It's two o'clock in the morning, for pity's sake!"

The yellow head beneath him turned until he could see a round white face in the glow of the street-lamps. "Mr Turnbull, I'm so sorry about this. I tried to phone but I got your answering machine. I wouldn't be here if it wasn't a matter of life and death."

Turnbull grunted, somewhat mollified by the politeness of the disturbance but with no intention of opening his door. "Matters of life and death are the province of the police," he said loftily. "Do you want me to call them?"

"I've just come from there. Mr Turnbull, I have to speak to you. You know me – Daniel Hood. Please let me in."

The estate agent blinked in surprise and peered closer. He hadn't been expecting that. But he was, first and foremost, a businessman. There was a hopeful note in his voice. "You've decided to sell after all?"

"Let me in, Mr Turnbull," Daniel begged desperately.

"Just a minute."

* * *

The sound of running water was stronger now, and closer. Brodie groped in the darkness around her but couldn't find the source. She put her ear against the stone wall behind her and thought she felt a kind of vibration, as if a stream ran on the far side. But it hadn't run there before. What kind of a stream only flowed sometimes?

And when she put it that way, the answer was obvious. It was tidal. Her heart sank. However close it came it would do nothing to sustain her. The only thing seawater does for thirst is magnify it.

So she was near the shore, a big derelict building within the tidal range. Big enough to have cellars. A warehouse? Something to do with the fishing industry which petered out here thirty years before? She pictured her way along Dimmock's seafront and east and west along the coast, puzzling what it might be, but nothing fitting that description came to mind.

So had she been unconscious longer than she supposed? Had there been time for French to drive beyond the area she knew? If so, the chances of Deacon finding her must be much diminished. He would start looking where she was last seen. If she was nowhere near Dimmock, the search could last a very long time.

Except that French said it would be over by three o'clock. She didn't think that could be much more than an hour away. She could stick it that long. If he was telling the truth. If that was what he meant, that she could expect rescue by three o'clock.

There were, of course, other possible endings.

And once she'd thought that there was no going back. Independent of will, her mind put the pieces together. The stream that only flowed sometimes. The dank walls and damp floor of her prison. Her jailer's ability to say with such precision, hours before, when she might expect her ordeal to end.

She wasn't here to be rescued, she was here to drown. Wherever she was, the rising tide would fill this space and, chained in place, she would die here. Only the rat, free to move, would leave and live.

She wanted to scream but her throat was too tight. She wanted to cry but the tears wouldn't come. If she'd been a praying woman, or a swearing woman, now would have been the time. She had perhaps an hour to live, and after that a few desperate minutes to die, and the fact that people were looking for her was scant consolation. There was little chance of them stumbling across her when even she didn't know where she was. This was the furthest extreme, the deepest despair, of her life, and she knew what was coming, and she couldn't find an appropriate response.

Until she thought of Paddy. That she wouldn't see her child again. That the last goodbyes they said were only little ones, good for the length of a school day at best, in no way adequate for two people whose existence, centred in one another, was about to be sundered. That she was leaving a five-year-old motherless, and if it wasn't her fault it was because of choices she'd made.

Then the tears came. Tears poured from her, flooded down her cheeks. Broken sobs racked in her throat, and she gave herself up to despair.

Chapter Twenty-Five

Mr Turnbull couldn't find his glasses. He remembered reading the paper in bed and went back upstairs for them.

Doreen was sitting with the quilt pulled under her chin and she clamped his wrist in a grip of iron as he reached for the bedside table. "You've let him in?" she hissed. "You've let a drunk into the house in the middle of the night?"

"It isn't a drunk," Mr Turnbull explained patiently, "it's a client. At least – " It was too complicated for two o'clock in the morning. "I know him, he's harmless. But he is very upset. Someone's in trouble and he thinks I can help. I couldn't send him away."

"You? Help? How?"

Mr Turnbull was an estate agent and so not a naturally sensitive man, but it was difficult to take that as a compliment. He sighed. "I'm not sure, dear. If you'll let go of me I'll go and find out." He went back downstairs with his glasses.

It was a photograph he was being asked to look at: nothing elaborate, just a holiday snap, and he didn't recognise the woman in it. She might have been in her early twenties. Apart from Sharon in the office, he didn't know any young women. "I'm sorry, I've never seen her before."

Daniel knew he wasn't making much sense. Anxious as he was, he was still deeply embarrassed at getting someone from his bed at this time of night. "Not her. The place. The building. You told me you had a derelict mill on your books – a tide-mill. Is that it? No one in the police station recognised it but I hoped you might."

Mr Turnbull frowned and took back the photograph he'd been returning. He tried with his glasses on and he tried with them pushed up his high and wrinkled forehead. "I don't think so. That's quite pretty, isn't it, a bit of a beauty-spot. The place we're selling – I shouldn't tell you this, but you're really not planning to buy it, are you? – is derelict. It might have looked like that once but not for years. It's all overgrown and neglected."

Daniel felt his last hope spiralling away. Disappointment clenched on his insides like talons. "Are you sure? That could be ten years old – a lot of weeds can grow in ten years."

"Really?" The estate agent looked again. "We've had it for about two years. There was someone living there till the nineteen-eighties, I think. There was talk of restoring it, but the cost was prohibitive and the owners finally decided to sell. Ten years?" He pursed his lips, tried to picture it before the paths closed over and the weather-boarding began to rot. "It could be the same place. I'm not sure. I never saw it looking like this, but that could be Solitude."

"Solitude?" echoed Daniel faintly.

"The Solitude Mill, on the River Windle. I think maybe it is."

"Can you take me there?"

Mr Turnbull's eyebrows rocketed. "Now?"

"You know the way," Daniel said miserably. "Searching for it will take too long. If my friend's there, she's in mortal danger. High tide's in an hour's time and I think she'll be dead by then. Minutes count. Please, Mr Turnbull, I need your help. No one else will do."

Edwin Turnbull sighed again: not this time the resignation of a little man who knows the world wouldn't miss him but the quiet pride of someone who can do something no one else can. "I'll just tell Doreen."

He threw some clothes on top of his pyjamas, then he picked up his keys and led Daniel out to his car. As he drove past the house the bedroom light snapped off indignantly three floors up. But Turnbull didn't care that his wife could hold a grudge for months. Tonight Edwin Turnbull the estate agent was racing to save someone's life.

"This friend of yours," he said when they were on their way. "Is it Mrs Farrell we're talking about?"

Daniel was taken aback. "How did you know?"

It was quite hard to come up with a tactful answer. "How many friends have you got?" was bound to cause offence, so was "You two are a standing joke in every pub in Dimmock." "We talked when she was trying to find you. Also, I take the Dimmock Sentinel."

"Oh. Yes," said Daniel. "I suppose we've had our fifteen minutes of fame this last year."

"You could say that," murmured the estate agent. "And now she's in trouble?"

"Yes." Daniel smiled wanly. "It was her turn."

Turnbull gave a sympathetic chuckle. But he knew it wasn't a joke, not to the young man slumped in the seat beside him. The aura given off by misery is unmistakable and Daniel Hood was sick with it: miserable and scared.

For the first time in years Turnbull thought, Speed limits be damned. "We'll be there in fifteen minutes."

Daniel looked at his watch. "Two twenty-six. High tide's at ten after three."

"Three-quarters of an hour," said Turnbull stoutly. "Plenty of time to find her."

"I hope so. Oh God, I hope so." Suddenly Daniel sat bolt upright, eyes wide behind his thick lenses. "I haven't called Jack. Jack Deacon – he's the investigating officer, he thought he knew where she was but he's gone to the wrong place. The wrong damned river! I need a phone. Have you got one of those...mobile...thingies?"

Turnbull regarded him for so long he almost left the road. "You mean, you haven't?"

"I live alone, I haven't got a job, who the hell needs to contact me in a hurry? Please, can I use yours?"

Turnbull passed it to him. Then, seeing his difficulty, without a word he took it back and switched it on. "Just dial the number."

Daniel was a mathematician: numbers he could do. He could remember the phone numbers of people he'd only ever called twice. He dialled Deacon's mobile.

He got the unobtainable message, which was pretty restrained in the circumstances. If there'd been a recording to say "The silly sod dropped it in the sea" he'd have got that instead. So he called Battle Alley and they patched him through to DS Voss.

Voss was asleep in the front passenger seat. Deacon stopped the car and extricated the phone from his jacket without waking him. "He isn't here," he growled softly; which as an alibi works rather better with static phones than mobile ones.

"Jack? It's Daniel. Where are you?"

"I'm just taking Charlie to the hospital. We didn't find her, Daniel. She wasn't there."

"I know where she is. At least, I think I do. I'm on my way there now. You have to meet me."

"Meet you where?"

"Solitude Mill, on the River Windle. Mr Turnbull can give you directions."

"Mr – ?" Then he thought, Don't even go there. "The Windle? That's a whole other river."

"But subject to the same tides. It's a tide-mill, Jack. And French knows it – he and Millie went there, it's where that photograph was taken. And now it's derelict. It's been empty for years. He could have Dagenham Girl Pipers tied up down there and nobody'd know."

A detective for more than twenty years, Jack Deacon had good instincts and knew to trust them. Common sense told him it was a long shot, that in a coastal region there must be many places that would inundate with each tide and a derelict mill was only one of them. But instinct said it was exactly the sort of place French would choose. A forgotten beauty-spot, neglected and overgrown; a place where he was once happy with his young wife; a place where a man could conscript the forces of nature to do his dirty work while he sat resolved and complacent in a police station, watched the face of his enemy and waited for comprehension to dawn.

With less than an hour to high tide it was instinct or nothing. He knew if he returned to Battle Alley Michael French would not give him the information he needed in time to save Brodie's life. He'd wait until it was too late and then tell him. If Daniel was wrong about this, probably it would be too late to save her any other way. Even if he was right they might be all out of time. All he could do was hurry and hope.

A taxi was coming from the hospital. Deacon stopped it, flashed his warrant card, apologised briefly and insincerely to the fare who'd thought she was going home, and poured Voss onto the seat beside her. "Accident & Emergency, and tell them to keep him in." As the taxi headed back the way it had come he shouted after it: "Tell him I've got his phone."

The rare impulse to behave like a Good Samaritan had paid dividends. From the ring road adjacent to Dimmock General Hospital he was ten minutes closer to the Windle than if he'd returned to Battle Alley with the rest of the team. Once he'd got Turnbull's directions he called for back-up but he had no intention of waiting for it.

He turned the car by crashing across the central reservation and headed west again, his foot hard down on the accelerator, ignoring speed limits and traffic lights and the occasional other vehicle. At its end the bypass filtered into the old Shore Road and still he drove hard, registering as a different kind of road-song where his wheels crossed the bridge over the Barley. He'd come this way two hours before and turned left towards the sea. Now he drove on, watching his dashboard. Another mile, another

minute; another mile, another fifty seconds. At this
speed a few wet leaves under a tree would put him off the
road. But speed was the only thing he had to give her, the
only thing that might help, and he wouldn't stint it to
save his life.

The River Barley drained much of the Three Downs
and emptied closer to Dimmock by a couple of miles.
The River Windle emptied the western flank of Menner
Down, never reached the same volume, lost itself among
the trees of Windle Coombe and finally reached the sea
on a stretch of coast unfrequented except by waders and
the odd twitcher. Most people, even those who'd lived in
Dimmock all their lives, didn't know there was another
river.

Deacon found the lane where Turnbull had said; without detailed instructions he'd have missed it. It looked no
more than an overgrown farm-track, but it veered off
south and if Deacon's sense of direction was true he was
within a mile of the Channel. She was less than a mile
away. At first he hardly eased up on the accelerator. But
driving at speed down a rutted track is a good way to
explore the freedom of flight, if only briefly, so he slowed
down and fumed instead.

After a few minutes, suddenly the tangle of briars and
hawthorn that had made a tunnel of the lane parted and
moonlight poured into the bowl of Windle Coombe, illu-
minating a scene both magical and oddly sinister. The
lagoon he found himself driving beside was too black, too
flat, the moontrack across it too steely-bright. The building ahead was too big, towering against the star-dusted

sky. A sea of grass washed its walls. Sometime in recent years the abandonment of the place had ceased to be a fact and become an entity. What inhabited it now was a silence so real that for a moment he hesitated to break it, unsure what the repercussions might be.

Then he saw the other car parked neatly by the wall and remembered why he was here and what was at stake, and he fisted his hand on the horn and slewed to a halt in the grass, his headlamps pinning two figures to the looming edifice of the wheel. One was tall and bald, the other was short and blond and raised a hand to shield his eyes from the light.

"Daniel." A couple of strides brought Deacon to his side. He stared up at the great wheel, hung on a beam as high as his head, and up further where the rotting clapboard, silver by moonlight, rose like a cliff above him. "Have you found her?"

They'd been a bare minute ahead of him, hadn't yet found a way inside. The main door was beside the wheel and had been reached by a bridge over the water-channel until it had rotted away. Mr Turnbull's pocket-torch hadn't yet discovered an alternative.

In Deacon's car was an eclectic toolkit from which he pulled, like a rabbit from a hat, a torch of an altogether more robust design, as big as a shoe-box, waterproof to five metres and capable of pin-pointing a low-flying zeppelin. He flashed it over the face of the building and then along the side where it found a ragged hole low down in the masonry.

The estate agent remembered it now. "Some of the

machinery was sold off when the mill shut. That's how they got it out."

"And that's how we're getting in. Except you," Deacon told Turnbull. "Stay here and wait for my team. They're maybe ten minutes behind – unless they get lost. Tell them where we are and to look for another way in. Me and Daniel'll start searching at this end."

Turnbull gave Daniel his torch. "Be careful. It's rough in there, and the cellars can flood."

Daniel shivered.

They hardly needed telling. As soon as they were inside the mill the stench hit them: stagnant, weedy, oddly sweet with the scent of rotted grain. The torches picked out timber struts as thick as trees, the massively complicated structure that harnessed the drive from the great wheel to turn stones the size of cartwheels, and elongated chutes slanting through the space like petrified sunbeams.

The machinery that had been removed had had a value elsewhere. But all this was part of the mill: removed, it would have been just so much kindling. So it stayed where it was built, old and strong and capable of doing its job again if anyone wanted it to.

So the water didn't reach this level – the timbers would have rotted if it did. Around the ragged gap in the wall the stones were mossy from rain penetration but ten feet into the mill the flag floor was dry.

"She's lower down," said Deacon tersely. "Somewhere the tide reaches."

"That's not how it works," objected Daniel. "The sea doesn't come into the building. The sea fills the lagoon, the lagoon empties down the leat, the wheel turns, the water gets away down the tail-race. The sea never came into the mill."

"Well, maybe it didn't used to," snarled Deacon, "but I'll bet my car to your telescope it does now. Hell, we got in through a hole in the wall. You're telling me water can't?"

It wasn't a bet Daniel felt safe taking. The smell alone was evidence the policeman was right. The building hadn't been watertight for a long time.

He looked at the great flat grindstone, cracked and broken now, picturing how it had worked. "If this is the stone floor, the meal floor's below us and the cellars are below that, in the lowest part of the mill. The part that floods."

Deacon nodded. "That's where she'll be."

No stairs were obvious but there was a wooden hatch in the floor. The trapdoor, split in half with a hole in the middle for the rope, identified it as a sack-hoist. The grain that came down here by gravity returned to the storage lofts as sacks of flour.

"That'll do," said Deacon, relieved, throwing open the hatch and hoping it wouldn't be too much of a drop. "Damn!"

After the mill stopped working some resident, tempted by the convenience of a large hole in his floor, used it to dispose of unwanted domestic goods. There was a fridge in there, an ancient washing-machine with a mangle, a rolled mattress which the rats had got at, lengths of wood which may have made up a bed, several suitcases, a mirror with a cracked glass, a model yacht with a broken mast and a wooden bench two metres long. These were only the things they could see. They rested on a whole lot of other things which they couldn't.

Everything that went into that hole could come out again. Even with just the two of them, they would have cleared an access to the lower floors eventually. But not in the next half hour, and after that there would be no hurry. Deacon let the hatch fall back. "There must be another way."

They only found it when Daniel stumbled over a length of corrugated iron and it shifted just enough to reveal the edge of an aperture. Deacon gave a muted grunt of triumph, seized the thing in both hands and yanked it aside.

The satisfaction drained instantly from his face and voice. "Well, that's the way he took her. I don't know if we can follow." The torch showed them a flight of stone steps descending into the bowels of the mill. But an iron grille had been fitted across the top of the steps. If it had been part of the original mill workings, rusted and weak, it might have yielded to a good kick. But this was new, stoutly made, bolted into the floor and secured with a padlock that would have had career cracksmen weeping into their Ovaltine.

"Now what?" Daniel's voice broke with despair.

"Hacksaw," said Deacon. He dropped the toolkit and began to rummage. But when he found what he was looking for his gaze travelled from the blade to the pad-lock and back and he made no attempt to use it. Daniel could see why. A hacksaw wouldn't open that padlock, not in the time available. Semtex mightn't.

"We have to find another way," gritted Deacon. "There must be another way." The beam of his torch slatted round the wooden machinery, fracturing whenever it met an obstacle, reassembling on the other side.

"Jack."

Deacon sought him with the torch. Daniel was standing beside the great beam of the axle where it pierced the wall, and his voice sounded hollow. There was another odd sound which Deacon could not immediately identify.

When he followed Daniel's frozen stare he realised what it was. The grindstone was starting to move. Seawater running down the leat had built up the energy necessary to turn the wheel.

Chapter Twenty-Six

He knew it mattered, he suspected it mattered a lot, but for a moment Deacon couldn't see how. He watched the great axle slowly turn, heard the trundle-wheel groan as it meshed its wooden teeth with those of the horizontal wheel, traced with his eyes the transfer of force across to the lantern-gear and down a short vertical shaft to the grindstones. His ears separated the wooden moans of the gear from the anguished grinding of one broken stone on the other, and still he failed to make the connection between the mill coming slowly to life and the fate of the woman captive in its depths.

"What's happening?" he asked suspiciously. "Who turned it on?"

As the night deepened, the darkness continued unabated and the cold hardened its grip, Brodie slumped in a reverie of hopelessness. Nothing touched her, nothing penetrated the cocoon of her misery. Distantly, almost uncaring, without trying to make sense of it, she was aware that the faint trickling sound had altered its note, belling fuller as a head of water began to stream past her, the thickness of a wall away. If she'd heard two cars pull up at the other end of the building it would have put new life, new hope, into her. But she did not.

The first thing she registered, that grabbed her by the heart and squeezed, was like nothing she'd ever heard before – a great grinding, creaking sound like a tree being tortured, a deep monumental groan that reached her partly as sound and partly as a thrill in the damp stones she sat on. And her first thought – curiously, given the fact that she'd been kidnapped by a man mad for vengeance and chained to a wall where she might never be found – was, "Now I'm in trouble!"

"Who turned it on?" demanded Deacon.

Daniel shook his head, fast. "The sluice is open. The rising tide tripped it. That's how French could be in Dimmock – talking to you, so he thought – while the mill did his job for him. High tide triggers the sluice, the lagoon empties down the leat, the wheel turns."

The detective stared at him in blank astonishment. "How do you know?"

"How do you not?" retorted Daniel with the unthinking arrogance of the scientist. "Forget the wheel, that isn't what kills her. What kills her is water from the tail-race getting into the cellars through cracks in the wall. That whole lagoon is going to funnel through the bottom of this mill. The cellars will flood, and they won't empty again till the tide drops. We need to get her out, now."

"If he went to the trouble of securing the steps it's a safe bet he's blocked any other way down." It sounded as if Deacon was beaten. But he wasn't. He was dismissing ideas that wouldn't work to leave a clear view to something that might. There wasn't time to waste agonising over the impossible.

"Jack." If anything, Daniel's voice sounded odder than before. "Come here."

He was watching the stones grind together with the kinetic energy of tons of running water. Once the twin stones, each a foot thick, had been enclosed in a wooden tun that stopped the flour from flying; now they were surrounded by matchwood. Daniel played Mr Turnbull's modest torch on the topmost stone. "There's nothing underneath."

A segment had broken off the runner-stone; and when its turning lined them up there was a similar gap in both the bedstone and the floor beneath. For a brief moment every turn, torch-light shone through to the lower level.

Daniel was running fast, incomprehensible calculations, and he was doing it aloud for the same reason Deacon theorised at Voss. "That's the meal floor. It's an undershot wheel so the water in the leat isn't deep – maybe about the level of that floor. But the cellars will flood to the ceiling if enough water gets in. There'll be a flight of steps down to the cellar. With the way down to the meal floor blocked, probably French didn't worry about the cellar steps."

Deacon understood that. "But we can't get down that far. Not without cutting equipment."

Daniel flicked the little torch upwards and seemed to change the subject. "Something fell from up there. Maybe a piece of machinery when they were selling it off. It shattered the tun, smashed clean through both stones and took a chunk out of the flags beneath. What used to be a small hole for the flour to fall through is now – " With his hands he hazarded the size, like an angler remembering a fish.

Deacon couldn't see why it mattered. "So?"

Daniel's unremarkable face was rigid with determination. "I can get through there."

Deacon looked at him, then at the stones, then back. "Don't be stupid!"

"I can do it, Jack. You couldn't fit, I doubt if Brodie could, but I can. I know I can."

Deacon looked again. The stone wasn't turning at milling speed but it was inexorable. Maybe he could have got through – there wasn't a lot to him, anywhere you could poke a stick Daniel Hood could probably wriggle through – but the gaps lined up only fleetingly each turn. A ferret would have been taking its life in its paws.

The policeman dismissed it out of hand. "It'd cut you in half."

"I'm not going through while it's moving!" exclaimed Daniel. "Credit me with some sense. We have to stop it. For just a few seconds, then I'll be through. I'll find Brodie, cut her free, and we'll wait on the meal-floor till you can shift that grille."

Deacon was looking for an off-switch. "All right. How do we stop it?"

There never was an off-switch. There were stone-nuts engaging the runner-stone with the drive shaft. When Daniel failed to shift them Deacon tried. There was neither movement nor the promise of movement, though he strained till the muscles knotted in his shoulders and the tendons stood out in his neck and the blood-vessels at his temples. Then he stood back with a breathy curse. "It's seized solid."

Daniel frowned. "That isn't possible. If the stones had been grinding every high tide since the mill was abandoned they'd have worn away. Ah... " The answer formed behind his eyes. "They haven't been grinding – there wasn't enough water coming down to turn the wheel. The sluices were silted up. French dug them out. He knew from the state of the walls that once there was water in the leat again it would flood the cellars. It's almost high tide: it won't be long before it starts dropping again, but longer than Brodie can hold her breath."

Deacon didn't care how it all worked. It was enough for him that Daniel understood. He took the younger man by the shoulders and shook him. "So what do we do? How do we stop it? Daniel, she's dying down there! How do I stop the water?"

Daniel nodded swiftly, his quick brain prioritising. "You need to stop it, but you can't stop it in time. There's too much water in the system." He tented his fingers in front of his mouth, panting softly through them. "You have to stop the wheel. Just long enough for me to get through the stones. Then you have to find the sluice and shut it off. Follow the leat up to the lagoon. There'll be a ratchet operating the paddles. He may have removed the handle – have you got a wrench?"

Deacon unslung the tool-kit and extracted a wrench as long as his forearm. "So how do I stop the wheel?"

The finger of Mr Turnbull's torch pointed. "With that."

Archimedes reckoned that, given a long enough lever and somewhere to stand, he could move the world.

Deacon didn't need to move the world, only to contain the force latent in a pond of salt water trying to find its way back to the sea. For a few seconds, Daniel had said. There was no knowing if he could do it except by trying, and if he tried and failed Daniel would die. And if he didn't try Brodie would die.

He lifted the wooden beam from where it lay forgotten against the wall. It wasn't clear what its purpose had been, but it was long and strong and it was all he could do to lift it. Braced against the shaft it might stop the wheel turning, if only for those few vital seconds.

When the reality of what he was considering struck him, Deacon turned cold. "You want me to hold the machinery still while you crawl through it? If it slips it'll crush you!"

"I know," said Daniel. And clearly he did because his voice shook. "Jack, we can do this. We have to do this or Brodie's going to die. We've found her, but she's still going to die if you don't help me reach her."

"We don't even know she's down there. Not for sure."

"Of course she's there!" snapped Daniel. "You think French thought he'd do a bit of mill restoration to pass the time while he waited for his shot at you? He put a lock on the stairs because that's the only way to reach her, and he dug out the sluices because that's how he meant to kill her, and if we argue about this any longer it's all going to happen just the way he planned!"

It wasn't that Deacon didn't believe him. There was no other way to read it; but still. "I'm not risking your life. We'll find another way."

"There isn't time," cried Daniel. "That whole lagoon is coming down here right now. It'll fill the cellar to the ceiling. Brodie's tied up down there. She's helpless, alone in the dark with the water rising round her. Either we do this or we stand by knowing she's drowning under our feet.

"I know what could happen. If this goes wrong – if you can't hold it long enough – it's my fault, not yours. But if we don't try we will lose her. She's saved my life before now, and she's saved my sanity, and I'm not going to stand here and listen to the water that's killing her."

"It's not your job to save her," roared Deacon in an agony of indecision. "It's mine!"

"Then do it!" yelled Daniel. "Do your part. You can't fit through the gap – and if you could, I couldn't hold the wheel. Jack, if she's going to survive this Brodie needs us both to do what we're best at. You're strong and I'm little. Neither of us could reach her alone. Together we have a chance."

"You could die!"

"Yes. But if we do nothing, Brodie will die. I couldn't bear that. Knowing I might have saved her and didn't try. I have to try. You have to help me."

All Deacon's instincts told him Daniel was right, they had to try. But it wasn't his life at risk. It wasn't him that could be halfway through the stones when the brake slipped. "Help can't be more than a few minutes away. We can wait that long."

But Daniel shook his yellow head again, stubborn and insistent. In his own mind he was ready for this and would brook no hindrance. "She may not have a few minutes. I don't know how long it'll take me to find her and free her. But the water's already pouring into the cellar, and it may not be minutes that count so much as seconds. We have to do this, and we have to do it now. She can't wait. And I'm scared enough without having to twiddle my thumbs while you think about it!"

There was a raised flag in the stone floor under the axle. Deacon lodged the end of the beam against it and braced it on the turning shaft. Wood growled on wood but the axle barely slowed. In desperation Daniel put his hands to the trundle-wheel, adding his strength to that of the big man.

And the water-wheel turned, and the trundle-wheel turned, and the gap between the stones opened and closed, opened and closed. Sweat burst from Jack Deacon's face as he pitted his strength against the weight of water in the leat. The wood protested and then screamed as the makeshift brake battled the machinery's whole purpose in life which was to turn and turn.

And as the two men fought it, muscles and sinews strained and cracking against the unthinking force of gravity, the trundle-wheel began to slow. The gap in the stones yawned a little longer with each turn. Two seconds – three – five.

The wheel stopped.

Daniel looked at Deacon. He meant to ask if the big man could hold it but one glance at his face changed his mind. The only possible answer was no. It would defeat him and he'd let it go, and the grindstone would start to move again. Deacon couldn't say how long he could hold it. Stopping it had taken everything he had: wasting time discussing it would squander the effort before anything was gained. Deacon would hold on as long as he could: what Daniel did with that time was his decision.

He waited no longer but levered himself up onto the stone and went for the gap headfirst.

Gravity took over. With his shoulders through there was nothing to stop him. He felt the broken edges of the stones grip his hips but not enough to detain him. His legs, notable in most company for their brevity, had never seemed so long. Then his feet rattled over the edge and he free-fell through two metres of dusty darkness and landed in a heap.

He could have broken his neck. But the discarded furniture piled through the nearby hatch broke his fall. He rolled down the pyramid of domestic refuse, collecting bruises but no injuries, until he reached the floor where he picked himself up and looked back the way he'd come.

Deacon's torch was blinking at him. When he realised what that meant his knees went to string. The grindstone was moving again.

"Are you all right?" Deacon gasped through the occulting stones. It took him two breaths to get it out.

"Fine," said Daniel, coughing his voice down from an hysterical giggle to a manly gruff.

"Catch." At the next opportunity the big torch came sailing through the dark. "And this." It was the kit-bag Deacon had brought from his car, minus the wrench. "To cut her free."

"I'll find her," Daniel shouted back. "You find the sluice."

Hefting the bag over his shoulder he shone the torch around, trying to get his bearings. He'd visited mills before but every one is different, custom-built to the preferences of the owner and the idiosyncrasies of the location. Solitude used the level where the wheel was hung as the stone-floor, rather than the one above as was more usual. It had the advantage of simplifying the construction and while the mill remained water-tight there were no disadvantages. Now, though, Daniel was acutely aware that he was already at or below water-level and was about to descend further.

He located the cellar steps by logic alone. Everything in a mill is designed to one end: milling. Everything else is located about the stones. Immediately beneath them, on the spot where he'd landed, a hessian chute had directed milled flour into a waiting sack. No further from there than a man could swing a full sack was the hoist, and against the wall on the other side were the cellar steps. There was no point a busy miller walking further than he had to.

The steps were clear of any obstacle. The torch showed recent footprints on the dirty damp stone, at least at the top. At the bottom they were under water.

Daniel plunged on, up to his knees in brine, wading through floating garbage. The cellars stretched endlessly ahead of him, divided by brick walls into bays. If he had to search them all he'd run out of time. The water level was rising perceptibly. If he couldn't find her soon he'd have to turn back.

He wasn't turning back. He held Brodie's life in his hands, and it mattered to him more than his own. He hadn't known that before. He'd treasured her friendship, missed it those cold weeks it was withdrawn, but this was something else. There's only one word for caring more about someone else than yourself, and it's love.

He didn't think he was in love, though it was hard to be sure because he didn't think he'd ever been in love. Anyway, she was with Deacon so it hardly mattered what name he put to his feelings. But their power startled him. He wasted valuable seconds just standing there, stupid with surprise, when he should have been looking for her.

Then he pulled himself together, putting the thought to the back of his mind. If they got out of this damn sewer alive he might have to give it some more consideration, but unless he found her soon it would be immaterial. He took a deep breath and shouted her name. It echoed back at him off the damp brick-work and the oil-slick surface of the water.

But one of the echoes didn't say "Brodie". It said, "Daniel?"

Chapter Twenty-Seven

When she heard his voice, for a moment Brodie thought she was hallucinating. She was kneeling in water above her waist, she'd been blind since French left her hours ago, and she believed that sheer desperate need had conjured the memory of a familiar voice. It was odd to imagine Daniel's when actually Jack Deacon would be a lot more use to her right now, but there's no accounting for dreams. And in dreams a small friend may be as much comfort as a big one, and also as much use.

But the echoes repeated around her, twining like ribbons on a maypole, which seemed unnecessarily detailed for a fantasy. Not believing it still, but on the basis that being wrong meant there was no one to hear her make a fool of herself, she raised her own voice in reply.

Immediately he shouted back, his tone soaring with excitement, and then she could hear splashing as he waded towards her.

After the darkness the light of his torch was like a blow. She gasped and turned her head away, and full of apologies and laughing with relief Daniel was there, bending over her, asking if she was all right, asking could she stand.

She was wet through, and dirty, and bitterly cold, and her hair was a sodden mass where she hadn't been able to keep it clear of the water. Her eyes were rimmed with red and tears were streaming down her face, and her smile kept cracking and she couldn't speak.

He knelt in the water beside her and held her – not for

long, there wasn't much time to spare even for this. "Thank Christ," he kept saying, entirely forgetting he was an atheist. "Thank Christ."

But the water was rising too quickly for much hugging. Daniel pulled the bag off his shoulder. Searching with the torch he found a sharp knife. "Where are you tied?"

"By my right wrist, to the wall. But it's not a rope."

Already the ring-bolt to which Brodie's arm was shackled was below the oily turgid water. Snatching a quick breath Daniel ducked beneath the surface, taking the torch with him.

When he saw what Michael French had fashioned on his workbench, surrounded by his complex delicate models, Daniel gave an involuntary gasp that rose as bubbles. Brodie didn't know what it meant; but when he reappeared, dripping, before he could get his expression under control she'd read everything in it. She sucked in a breath and held it till she could speak without screaming. "You can't free me."

"Of course I can," he stammered, hunting through the bag again in mounting desperation. "There's a hacksaw. You can cut anything with a hacksaw." But he went on looking, because these manacles came from the same stable as the padlock upstairs, and if Deacon didn't reckon he could saw through the one, Daniel knew he'd never get through the other, not in the time available. Perhaps a well-judged thump with a hammer might spring the lock? But he suspected that if it was as easy as that to open manacles there would be no great point.

Still, you don't know what you can do till you try. They might be less strong than they looked – French may have figured that making them look unbreakable would be as effective as making them unbreakable in fact. Brodie held the torch while Daniel, armed with hammer and cold chisel, took another breath and ducked under the water. He stayed down as long as he could, hammering as hard as water-resistance would allow, and came up whooping for air. As quickly as he could he crammed his lungs and returned to the task. But even with the light squarely on the iron he couldn't find the scratch he'd made.

The water was still rising, a hand's span in the time he'd been down here. Restrained as she was, unable to straighten, it was up to Brodie's breasts. In ten minutes it would be swilling round her face. In fifteen, if Daniel couldn't free her, she would be dead.

He had to free her. He tried the saw. He laboured frantically for thirty seconds before he had to breathe again. Twice more he grabbed air, ducked and sawed until the pain in his chest made him stop, and only after that did he take the torch back to check his progress. It was insignificant. The iron was as thick as his thumb, the mark of the hacksaw no deeper than a fuse-wire. The task was impossible. But he couldn't abandon it.

The light wheeled dizzily as Brodie fastened her free hand in his collar and yanked him clear of the water – choking and gasping, uncomprehending – like landing a fish. "Go on like this," she said with more calm than she felt, "and you're going to drown. And if you die, I die. There has to be a better way."

"There isn't." He gulped down more air, ready to return.

She held him fast. "Yes," she said tersely, "there is."

When he understood what she wanted he shook his head, his refusal absolute. "No! I can't."

"You can. You have to."

"Brodie – I can't cut your hand off!"

"Yes," she said again, steely in her resolve, "you can. It'll take a fraction of the time of sawing through iron. A couple of minutes max. I'll tell you what to do. With luck they'll be able to sew it back afterwards."

She was utterly serious: of that Daniel had no doubt. Horror twisted his face into a gargoyle. "I can't! You don't know what you're asking. I can't."

"Daniel, you have to. This is the only way I'm getting out of here. Of course I don't want to lose my hand, but my life matters more. Not just to me. I have a daughter, Daniel. I have a five-year-old daughter, and if you can't do this she's going to lose her mother. I know it's hard. But if you care about me you'll grit your teeth and do it. I don't want to die here."

Her hand loosed his collar and slipped across his chest, and for a moment she just held him to her, for all the world as if he was the one in need. His slight frame shook and he could not look at her. She couldn't stand upright, only crouch with the water lapping her chin. The sound of the turning wheel rumbled in the stones.

"Oh Daniel," she murmured into his shoulder, "don't think I'm not scared too. If there was any alternative I'd take it. But there isn't.

"We can do this. Together. I'll scream and I'll pass out, and you'll have to control the bleeding, but I'll wake up in Dimmock General and next week I'll be home and the week after that I'll have an appointment at the Prosthetic Limbs Department. I'll get through this. I'll be glad to be alive, and I'll get through."

Finally Daniel made himself face her. His heart wrung within him. His voice was a whisper. "Brodie, do you trust me?"

From somewhere she found a smile. The radiance of it knocked him sideways. "Absolutely."

"Then believe me when I say I will keep you alive. I will. I won't let you die. And I don't have to mutilate you to do it."

The smile faded. She knew he meant it. She knew he meant every word of it, would die trying to keep his promise. But by then it would be too late. Fine words wouldn't save her: a few minutes' work with the hacksaw would. "Oh Daniel," she whispered brokenly. "Please. Please?"

He shook his head, water flying from the yellow hair, and twisted out of her embrace. "I'll find another way. Any minute now Jack'll find the sluice-gate and the water will start to drop. I'm not going to butcher you only to have the water drop before it gets high enough to drown you.

"Trust me, Brodie. Trust me to get you through this. I will keep you alive." He took her wet face in his hands, staring into her soul at point-blank range. "Do you believe me?"

She'd have given worlds to be able to say yes, for herself and for him. But it would have been a lie. "No," she whispered desolately.

"You will," said Daniel.

Daniel's need was the greater, but parting with his torch left Deacon at a disadvantage. He returned to his car for the one he kept in his glove-compartment, which, while it lacked the bells and whistles of the police-issue equivalent, at least stopped him walking into things. He quickly updated Mr Turnbull and left instructions for the back-up he was expecting at any moment.

In fact, as he headed for the lagoon he heard the growl of engines beyond the trees. He didn't wait. He didn't know that seconds counted but he didn't know that they didn't. And the instructions he'd left with the estate agent were plain enough: half the party to work on the grille over the steps, half to follow him to the sluice.

A man could wander round a factory all day trying to make sense of the machinery. But a water-mill is technology at its simplest: water runs everything. The water in the leat led him to the lagoon and the powerful cataract where it gathered itself to a point to race through a metre-wide sluice. Deacon heard it first, then he saw it: a torrent of water, oily black and brilliant white in the moonlight, crashing from the height of the lagoon into the depths of the leat.

When he saw the open sluice, and the force of the water piling through, he didn't see how human strength could stop it. But common sense told him this whole system was geared to the strength of a man's arm. He shone the torch up and down the sluice looking for how.

Daniel had said, a ratchet. Deacon had no idea how he knew that. Daniel knew all sorts of useless things, though he could be stumped by what most people considered common knowledge. But if Daniel thought sluices operated on a ratchet, Deacon was looking for a ratchet.

And he found it, a toothed metal track running up the side of the installation to a hand-crank at the top. For a second, perhaps two, he thought that shutting off the flow would be as easy as turning that wheel.

But French had anticipated him getting this far and done something about it. With a sledgehammer by the looks of it – the crank and the top of the track were bent so far out of true that the mechanism could no longer operate. The sluices were jammed open.

Deacon let out a roar of frustration. There may have been an obscenity in there somewhere, but mostly it was just the sound of fury.

Heavy breathing and the hiss of people running through grass, then he was no longer alone but at the centre of a knot of men and women he knew, all anxious to help. "What can we do?" panted PC Batty.

For reply Deacon shone the torch on the twisted metalwork.

"That's buggered," said Batty frankly.

Brodie held the torch and Daniel searched for something he could use to buy her more time. Two metres of garden hose was the preferred option but he was willing to compromise. Time was running out. The water was still rising steadily so that Brodie, tethered in her crouch, was already getting it in her mouth.

While he plunged down to finger-search the floor in increasing desperation, in mounting fury she continued to berate him every time he burst to the surface.

"If you can't do it," she raged, "give me the hacksaw and I'll do it myself. You think I can't? I can do anything that my life depends on. Are you going to make me do it? Would you rather watch than help? And if I pass out, what will you do then? Watch me bleed to death? Or drown, whichever comes first? Daniel, this is the last ditch. There's nowhere left to fall back to. Either you do this, or you help me do it, or I die here. God damn you, Daniel, I do not want to die here!"

Her words lacerated him, making him flinch. There wasn't time to argue with her. He kept searching, skinning his knuckles in his haste.

In a split second everything changed. Even before he knew what he'd found, he recognised it as what he needed. He surfaced, spluttering. "Shine the torch this way!"

The light picked up the colour of what he had felt poking from a pile of anonymous rubbish. Not many things found in an abandoned mill are blue, but one is the polypropylene pipe used in plumbing. He snatched another breath, fastened both hands on it and pulled. It came out just before his lungs did.

It was four feet of water-pipe left over from when the mill was converted for residential use. Not enough to be worth using elsewhere, a thing of no value – except that in these precise circumstances it might save a life.

Daniel rinsed it out as best he could, and blew through it until a steady stream of bubbles was emerging at the other end. "All right," he said shakily, "this will work."

It was clear to Brodie what he intended. He thought it would make a snorkel: when the water closed over her head she could breathe through it. It was dirty and heaven knew what diseases she could contract from putting it in her mouth, but she'd live long enough to get them treated. And she'd still have her hand.

If it worked. If it didn't clog. If she could go on breathing steadily through it as the water kept rising, up her face and over her head and on up the pipe, and she didn't panic and thrash about and lose it. If the water stopped rising before it reached the top of the pipe.

So Brodie knew, and she guessed that Daniel knew too, there were no guarantees. It might save her. It might only come close to saving her. But it was a chance. She nodded. "All right. Now we wait for Jack."

Chapter Twenty-Eight

Deacon wouldn't believe it till he'd tried. He knotted both hands on the drunken hand-crank and wrenched at it. It moved half a turn before seizing solid. No human endeavour would have shifted it. It needed removing with an angle-grinder and a new piece welding on.

It wasn't rocket-science, Deacon could have done it himself given an hour. If he'd had an angle-grinder with him. If he'd had his welder. If he'd had a suitable bit of iron for the graft, and if he'd had an hour. What he in fact had was a wrench and no time at all. Even with willing hands to help he saw no way to close the sluice.

With a JCB and five minutes he'd have dammed it. A few bucket-loads of earth dumped in the channel would have held back the lagoon as effectively as thirty years' worth of silt. But he didn't have a JCB either, and fetching one would take time he also didn't have. He toyed briefly with the idea of driving his car over the edge, and would have done if he'd thought it would help. But he didn't.

With this many people around him, all of them strong and fit (except Sergeant Cobbitt), stout of heart and used to doing what he told them (except Constable Huxley), he couldn't believe there was no way to stop the water flowing. But French had been a step ahead of him all the way. What he needed was a bit of unconventional engineering to do what the twisted gear could not. A bit of lateral thinking.

He studied the problem. The sluice was accessible

from downstream but the force of the water would carry away anything he tried to cover it with. Conversely, if he could manoeuvre a cover over the sluice from upstream, the pressure would hold it in place – but it would be all but impossible to do in ten feet of water. Because that was what he was dealing with. From the leat side he could see that the sluice-gate, little more than a metre wide, was three metres high, with slats ranged one above another like a heavy-duty Venetian blind.

As he wrestled with the problem, his clarity of thought in no way aided by the pressure of time or the cost of failure, an image behind his eyes kept getting in the way. Himself and Daniel forcing their way into the mill, stumbling over the accumulated rubbish. He dashed it away with an impatient flick of his head that puzzled the onlookers. He supposed he was having regrets – he didn't have many so it was hard to be sure – about letting Daniel go into the bowels of the drowning mill. If he hadn't, Hood would be here now and might have seen how the damaged sluice could be shut. But if he'd been up here he wouldn't have been down there, and if Brodie was still alive Daniel might be the only reason.

The mental merry-go-round left him dizzy. He tried to disengage from it, to concentrate on the problem at hand and not on something he no longer had the power to influence. Daniel was where he was, doing the best he could; so was Deacon. Both of them had known that if it wasn't good enough lives would be lost. He doubted if Daniel was cursing him for the fact that the water was still rising, so why was he flaying himself?

Suddenly he understood. It wasn't Daniel his mind was trying to draw his attention to but something else in the picture. But what? – there was only him and Daniel. And the rubbish Daniel was falling over...

Then he was running, back the way he'd come, back to the mill, trailing the startled looks of his colleagues like a cloak. "Don't look at me like that," he yelled over his shoulder, "come and help me!"

Alone he'd have wasted vital time digging it free. But Huxley took one corner, Deacon gripped the other, and when they pulled together four metres of galvanised metal roofing slid screeching out of the pile.

"Yes!" exclaimed Jill Meadows; and then everybody had a hand on it and they were belting back down the water-meadow like a crew of world-class optimists entering a raft-race.

Deacon climbed onto the sluice-gate, his legs chilled and bludgeoned by the pouring water, to manoeuvre it into place. In fact it wasn't difficult. They slid the corrugated sheet down the upstream face of the sluice and the water fixed it there. The jets pouring out of the lagoon fell in an instant to a trickle.

It wasn't a perfect fit. Water could still get through gaps on either side. But not enough to fill the leat: the water level dropped in seconds. In a few more seconds, Deacon knew, it would drop at the mill, and then what had found its way into the cellars would start finding its way out.

"Stay here," he ordered Huxley. "If it shifts, put it back. If you can't put it back, damn well get in there and block it yourself. Everyone else, with me."

By the time they reached the mill the great wheel had stopped turning.

There was cutting equipment in the area car. Even so, getting the padlock off the grille took ten minutes. When it finally parted Deacon threw the iron grid out of his way as if it had been chicken-wire and hurried down the stone stairway, pausing momentarily on the meal-floor to locate the steps down to the cellar.

By now only the top three were dry. But the water-level had dropped to about a metre now and he was able to wade thigh-deep through the floating refuse in the pit of the mill. He shone his torch around, looking for signs of life, and found brick walls.

Other feet splashed, other torches joined his. At his elbow Jill Meadows said quietly, "Shout, sir. Call their names."

Deacon was afraid to – afraid of hearing no reply.

The young woman seemed to understand. She raised her own voice in a clear hail. "Mr Hood? Mrs Farrell! Can you hear me?"

Deacon stopped breathing. As the silent seconds piled up his heart turned to stone and sank.

Meadows tried again. "Where are you? We're right here – just tell us where you are."

Everyone stood still so no sound of splashing would drown a reply. If any reply came. If there was anyone still alive down here.

Finally a reed of a voice reached them along the surface of the water. "Here. We're here." It was so thin and frail that neither Deacon nor those with him could be sure if it was a man's voice or a woman's.

They were in the last bay, against the far wall of the mill. Deacon broke into a run, pushing a bow-wave ahead of him. He turned the brick wall and the beam of his torch found them in the corner. Daniel was on his feet, just about, dragged down by the sodden weight of the woman clamped against him. The only way he could keep Brodie's face out of the water was with his arms under hers and his hands knotted across her chest. Her eyes were blank, the pupils rolled back, and her face was fish-belly white.

"Take her," whispered Daniel. "Take her." When Deacon did, hauling her as far clear of the water as her shackled wrist would allow, Daniel slipped exhausted to his hands and knees.

When the buffalo ruled the plains of North America, the men who lived there too could feel the herd coming before they could hear it, and hear it before they could see it. Deacon's progress through Battle Alley Police Station was somewhat similar. The towering fury of his stride shook the floors and set the glass rattling in the windows.

None of those with him thought it was a good idea for him to resume interviewing Michael French right now. Some had suggested as much: they were the ones now trailing at the back of the group with glazed expressions, waiting for the other half of the sky to fall.

Only WPC Meadows stayed with him, matching his driven stride with two of her own, ignoring his savage dismissals and repeating as calmly as she could that she had a duty to protect the suspect from abuse, although she was actually more concerned about protecting Deacon from himself.

Afterwards, strong and sturdy men who had scuttled from Deacon's rage like schoolgirls told one another that it was all right for Meadows, she knew Deacon wouldn't deck her. In fact, in the heat of the moment, Meadows had no such confidence. All she knew was that, if he'd been here, Charlie Voss wouldn't have let his chief run riot and suffer the consequences, and since he wasn't he needed someone else to do the job for him. If she was doomed to fail, at least she'd have a black eye as evidence that she tried.

French was back in Interview Room 1 with Superintendent Fuller. He wasn't talking, but Fuller couldn't let events take their course without trying to get some sense out of the man.

There's a formal procedure for entering an interview room while an interview is in progress. Deacon ignored it. He flung the door wide and stormed inside without a word for Fuller or the tape; and French, though this was the moment he'd been waiting for, the nexus to which all his planning had brought him, couldn't watch him come with equanimity, making no move. He was on his feet and backed up against the far wall before the order to hold their ground got through to his limbs.

Fuller was on his feet too, ready to intervene but hoping like hell he wouldn't have to. One blow and Deacon's career would be over. "Jack..."

Like a charging buffalo, like a rising tide, Deacon was unstoppable. He may not even have heard Fuller's warning. He crossed the room in three giant strides, and by then his powerful body was between Michael French and any help he could look to, from Superintendent Fuller or WPC Meadows or anyone else.

By now French had his reactions under control. He didn't care if Deacon hit him; he didn't actually care if Deacon killed him. That look on Deacon's face made everything he'd done worthwhile. Now he knew what pain was, what loss was. The emptiness. The crushing hopelessness. The raging futility. Now he too had suffered the crucifying helplessness of having the most important thing in his life taken away, wantonly, not for a cause but carelessly, almost by default, because it would have put someone to a bit of trouble to prevent it. Michael French believed in poetic justice. The only currency capable of paying for his agony was Deacon's.

"Yes?" he asked softly. "Now do you know? Do you understand now what I was talking about? Do you understand what you did?"

Deacon's voice was thick. His hands were fisted at his sides as if he was afraid what they might do. "I know what you did. You terrorised a woman who never did you any harm, and you left her to die in the dark because you were angry with someone else. An honourable man would have come after me."

French looked him up and down. Something like a smile touched his lips. "What would that have proved? That you're big enough to knock me through doors without opening them first? Like I needed to risk my neck and liberty to establish that!

"Superintendent, this isn't about who's the stronger man. It isn't even about who's the better man. It's about the fact that my wife died because she came to you for help and you treated her like trash. Like nothing. As if she had no rights and no feelings. Her death was your responsibility. Her blood is on your hands.

"And even that didn't mean anything to you, did it? The only way you were going to know what it meant was for you to live it. To see someone you cared about hurt the way you hurt Millie. To stand by helplessly and watch someone you loved destroyed, and to know who was doing it and how it was going to end and yet be powerless to stop it. I wanted to see you walk a mile in my shoes, Superintendent Deacon. I thought it might do you good – teach you a little about people, a little about power. But even if it didn't" – he looked away, dismissively – "I knew it would do me good."

Deacon might have hit him then. Fuller was a policeman too: he'd heard what Deacon had heard, and he knew what Deacon had been through, and the big man might have gambled that Fuller wouldn't even try to move fast enough to stop him getting in one good thump. He wouldn't ask, and Fuller wouldn't offer, but Deacon thought there was a chance. He might have taken it, and whatever consequences arose, if he could have been sure of stopping at just one thump. He couldn't be sure. He thought, if he hit French at all he'd go on hitting him until he was a bloody pulp on the lino.

He sucked in a deep unsteady breath. His fists, twitching slightly, stayed at his sides. "There are two things you need to know, Mr French. One is that I am deeply sorry about what happened to your wife. I know you blame me. I hope – I believe – you're wrong, but I know I could have done better by the pair of you. I could have made a difficult period of your lives a little easier, and I'm sorry I didn't make the time to do so. Maybe Millie would be alive today if I had. Maybe she wouldn't, but at least my failure wouldn't have tormented you for the last five years. I owe you an apology.

"And the other is: Michael French, I am arresting you for the attempted murder of Elspeth Brodie Farrell. You do not have to say anything. But it may harm your defence if you do not mention when questioned something which you later rely on in court. Anything you do say will be taken down."

The silence in the room was palpable. As an understanding of what he was hearing grew in French the last vestiges of colour drained from his face and all the strength from his muscles, so that his body slumped against the wall. His chin dropped on his chest and his eyes closed. He'd known loss – God knew he'd known loss. He had not, before this, known defeat.

Peter Fuller, on the other hand, was strung like a bow with hope stretched to breaking point. He knew what Deacon had said, could only read one meaning into it, but didn't dare believe it until he could get it in words of one syllable. "She's alive?"

Deacon nodded, his head suddenly heavy. "She's alive. They're keeping her in hospital for a couple of days but she'll be fine. Thanks to Daniel."

Now French wanted a solicitor. While they waited Superintendent Fuller took Deacon to his office, sat him down with a cup of tea in a strong mug and got the details from him.

"Thanks to Daniel," he agreed when the story was told, "and to you. She's a lucky woman. She has some good friends."

Deacon scowled into his tea. "Her friendship with me damn near cost her her life."

Like a housewife in a crisis, Fuller pressed him to another biscuit. "You can't legislate for people like French. All you can do is deal with them when you meet them. None of this was your fault. Not what happened to Mrs Farrell, and not what happened to Millie French."

Deacon's heart swelled with gratitude in a most unexpected way. There was possibly no one else he would have believed. But Fuller was an experienced police officer, and wouldn't have lied about that even to make him feel better. "Thank you."

Deacon finished his tea and headed for the door. With his hand on it, however, he paused and turned back. "I need to borrow some kit out of stores. I left most of mine scattered round the mill and I'm not going back hunting for it tonight."

"What do you need?"

"A torch. And a nice big wrench."

There was something in the way he said it that piqued Superintendent Fuller's curiosity and made one eyebrow climb. "What do you need a wrench for? At this time of night?"

Deacon considered. "You know that motorbike that Charlie Voss fell off?"

Fuller nodded, uncomprehending.

Deacon smiled nastily. "I'm going to take it apart."